
★

I sat back down at  took another look
with the poem, wip
jelly from my doug
alphabet, numberi
theory that the num
ed to a letter of the
words, which would
the alphabet. The second line of the poem had one
word, which translated to an A.

When I came up with the word "BACK," I cheered
and clapped and clapped. When I got the second
word, "OFF," I was still enthusiastic, but when I got
the whole message my stomach knotted. It read:
"BACK OFF BITCH."

★

Also available from Worldwide Mystery by
SALLY CHAPMAN

RAW DATA

SALLY CHAPMAN

LOVE BYTES

WORLDWIDE®

TORONTO • NEW YORK • LONDON
AMSTERDAM • PARIS • SYDNEY • HAMBURG
STOCKHOLM • ATHENS • TOKYO • MILAN
MADRID • WARSAW • BUDAPEST • AUCKLAND

For my sister, Carol Lundmark

LOVE BYTES

A Worldwide Mystery/April 1996

First published by St. Martin's Press, Incorporated.

ISBN 0-373-26197-7

Special thanks to Brant Carter, Jim Nichols,
Kevin Gibbons, Eric Rollins and Greg Hansen of ESL,
Mark Grandcolas and Ruben Pereida of
Sun Microsystems, Joe Valentino of SSTG, Peter Ling
of Morling and Company, and Rick Reese and
Gregg Adams for their help in researching
the material for this book.

ONE

WHEN I FIRST SAW Lorna Donatello she reminded me of a small-caliber bullet—tiny, fast-moving, and hard enough to crack your teeth on. Vic Paoli, my business partner/*mi amore*, and I were in our office bickering through our latest pile of past-due bills when Lorna burst in, pushing the front door open so hard it hit the wall with a teeth-grinding whack that jolted me out of my chair.

"Are you Julie Blake?"

"Yes," I said with a laugh, embarrassed that her entrance had so startled me. We weren't used to visitors. "And your name?"

"I'm here to see you," she said, not responding to my query. Her voice was high-pitched and gravelly at the same time, like Minnie Mouse after thirty years of chain-smoking. She stayed in the doorway and I watched her eyes, bright blue, round as nickels and sharp as radar, as they scanned our office, which was small enough to be viewed in its entirety from the door. "If you're busy, I can come back later," she said, "but I've gotta be at the courthouse in an hour, and I'd like to get this over with."

Paoli had been frozen in his normal work posture, which was leaning back in his chair with his hands clasped behind his head, but when she spoke he swung his tennis-shoed feet off his desk, sat up, and straightened his collar.

Since Paoli and I had quit lucrative high-tech jobs six months earlier and started a computer fraud investigation business we hadn't seen many prospective clients. In fact, we hadn't seen much of anybody, and it didn't take a degree from MIT to know this was no computer person standing in front of us. She just didn't have The Look. Intense computer types usually have sallow complexions, glasses held together at the bridge with Scotch tape, and a look on their face like they're receiving telepathic transmissions.

Could the utility company have sent someone in person to turn off the electricity? She didn't look like the utility type either. Anything but. Dressed in a black sweater adorned with sporadic tufts of ruby-dyed rabbit hair, a shiny red skirt pulled taut over childishly narrow hips, and purple Joan Crawford hurt-me pumps, she seemed more like a streetwalker than a representative from Pacific Gas and Electric. Her frizzy bleached hair looked as though it had been set with a waffle iron. She gave it an insolent toss, but the hair didn't move.

"Well?" she said with a raised penciled eyebrow after Paoli and I stared at her speechless for a minute.

"Please, sit down," I replied, remembering my manners, even though my stomach was in a knot. I rose from my chair and walked around the desk toward her, gesturing to a black upholstered chair. "What can we do for you?"

Paoli's eyes grazed anxiously across our rented Deluxe Package office furniture. We were behind on a couple of payments. I was determined to be polite and professional and was glad that I was wearing my best librarian-with-attitude look—serious navy blue suit, tortoiseshell glasses, and light brown hair pulled into a no-nonsense ponytail.

The smell of gardenias wafted toward me as our visitor moved across the floor with staccato steps, a bundle of raw nerves and contained energy. Her petite body was as tight and muscular as that of a girl in her early twenties, but her face revealed a woman who had been around the dance floor a few times. She walked to the chair but remained standing.

"I have a job for you. I know I should have called ahead of time, but I was in the neighborhood and thought, hell, take a chance."

At the word "job," Paoli jerked out of his chair to an atypical standing position, and I straightened my shoulders as my face burst into a welcoming smile.

"We happen to have some time right now," I said.

"We encourage spontaneity," Paoli chimed in as he walked to my side, his step jaunty.

"Then I think I'll take a load off." She plopped down into the chair. Smiles were exchanged, and we were all starting to feel pretty chummy when a voice like a bassoon sounded outside the doorway.

"Lornie!"

When she heard it her eyes rolled upward and she exhaled with exasperation. "Shit," she muttered as she settled into her chair. "Can they come in? They get edgy having to wait."

"The more the merrier," said Paoli.

"Come on in!" she yelled, and a few seconds later a dog sauntered into the room with a confident gait. He was medium-sized and looked like some sort of Labrador/terrier mix, but his curly black coat indicated somewhere along the line a standard poodle had joined the party.

"Nice dog," said Paoli, as he walked over and reached down to pet him. The dog responded with a low growl, and Paoli jerked his hand back. "And friendly, too."

"Aw, he's just protective. Bronco's really a sweetie pie." She leaned down to the dog. "Aren't you a sweetie pie?" she said in a baby voice. "Here; give him this." She reached into her handbag and handed Paoli a dog biscuit. Paoli looked at the biscuit, then at the dog. "It's okay. He won't bite you," she assured him. Paoli offered the biscuit gingerly and Bronco grabbed it, then strolled away, careful not to communicate any gratitude. "See, he's not so bad," she said, although I wasn't sure if she was talking to Bronco or Paoli. I was still looking down at the dog when I noticed a shadow spread across the floor. I glanced up and saw a man as big as a condo standing in the doorway.

"Sit," our prospective client commanded. The man lumbered over to a chair near the wall and carefully lowered his bulk into it while the dog remained standing. "This is Bronco." She pointed to the dog, giving him a loving look. "And this is Ox." The loving look evaporated as she tilted her head toward her companion.

"Vernon," he said, his tone apologetic. "My name's Vernon." He gave me a bashful smile, then turned his gaze to the floor. He was thirty-fiveish and had the neck and build of someone who slipped steroids into his orange juice—the kind of guy who gets his money's worth at all-you-can-eat buffets.

Bronco checked out Paoli's shoes, sniffed my crotch, then lay down at his mistress's feet. After giving the dog's head a few affectionate scratches, she settled back in her chair, ready to do business.

"So, I'm Lorna Donatello. Like I told you, I have a job for you."

The word "job" resounded in my ears with the loveliness of a Bach concerto. I'm a classic Type A workaholic who at this point hadn't seen any projects in six months. I thirsted for work like a boozer thirsts for a martini. "Well, that's very interesting," I said, trying not to sound too eager. "Let me introduce myself."

Lorna raised a hand to stop me. I noticed there were little stars glued to her purple fingernails.

"That's okay. I know who you are. I read about you in the paper last year when you solved the murders at that big computer company. You see, I always like to read about smart people, you know, people who think a lot. I don't go in for *People* magazine or the *Enquirer*. I go for the business section of the newspaper. That way I can read about people with some brains. Anyway, I remembered reading about you in the *San Jose Mercury,* so when this little situation happened I decided to look you up." Her brow furrowed. "Although I expected you to be older."

"I'm old enough." I know I'm supposed to like the fact that I look younger than my thirty-four years, but it can be a hindrance in business.

"Your skin must retain a lotta moisture."

I reached instinctively for my cheek. "I guess so. I've never really thought about it."

She wiggled a finger at me. "You should think about it. Your skin won't last forever. In my family we've got skin like rawhide. Yours, it's like a baby's butt."

"Thanks," I said, assuming the "baby's butt" part was a compliment. "This is my associate, Vic Paoli. He helped me with the ICI situation."

Paoli reached out and vigorously shook Lorna's purple-nailed hand. "So, what can we do for you, Ms. Donatello?" he asked in his best sales pitch voice.

She struck a match, lit a cigarette, and inhaled deeply; then she patted her lap. Bronco jumped up onto her legs, and Ox looked on wistfully as she kissed the dog's nose. When she returned her attention to Paoli and me she said, "I want you to find somebody."

My heart, which had been soaring at the prospect of a client, took a swan dive. For a brief, glorious moment I had actually believed someone had walked into our office with a computer fraud problem. I tried not to show my disappointment, but I have one of those faces that doesn't hide much. I took a deep breath and attempted to put a smile back on my face.

"I'm sorry, Ms. Donatello, but you've come to the wrong place. Data9000 Investigations works on cases of computer fraud." I noticed the blank expression on Lorna's face and wondered if my words were registering. "You know, somebody plants a computer virus in a mainframe or breaks into a computer's software."

"I want you to find somebody," Lorna repeated, this time a little louder, like maybe I just wasn't hearing her.

We weren't communicating. I took another pass over the target. "We don't do that kind of work. If you'd like, I can pull out the phone book, and we can see if there's some sort of investigative agency in this area that could help you."

She waved her hand at me again. "You don't get it. This is special. It's gonna take somebody like you guys to handle it. My card." She reached into her purse and handed me a card that read:

Donatello Bail Bonds.
No Personal Checks. No Credit.
Fast Bail. No Jail.
CALL 1-800-924-B-A-I-L

I read it, then passed the card on to Paoli. "I'm in the bail bonds business," she said proudly.

"You don't look like a bail bondsman," said Paoli with a smile.

"Bondsperson. And yeah, I hear that a lot. I inherited the business from my dad. It's not bad. You'd be surprised at how few people actually skip on you. But that's why I need you guys. Somebody skipped on me and I need you to find him."

"I thought people skipped parole," I said.

Paoli pointed his cocked thumb in my direction. "You have to excuse her. She's led a sheltered life."

"That's okay," said Lorna. "It's like this. People get arrested, they come to me, and I put up the cash to get 'em out of jail. They pay me 10 percent; then I get my money back from the court when they show up for trial. It's kind of a public service with a profit."

"Sounds admirable," I said. "But I still don't see how we could help you."

As I watched Lorna, I saw the crustiness suddenly drain right out of her, and in an instant the previous steeliness on her face had softened into a wounded expression. "You can help me with . . . Arnie Lufkin.'' Her voice had temporarily deepened, and she swirled the name Arnie Lufkin breathily, like it was an incantation. ''You may have heard about him. He stole some money from a big company in San Francisco.''

Paoli thought a moment, then snapped his fingers. ''Hey, I read about that guy. He was a computer hacker. Didn't he steal a million bucks from Anco?'' My partner leaned forward, his interest heightened.

''Only half a million,'' Lorna said in Arnie's defense. ''But he's the one. A computer guy. And I put up his bond. It cost me fifty grand.''

''And the bum skipped,'' said Ox, breaking his silence.

''Shut up, beefhead,'' Lorna snarled, then primly straightened her posture and recrossed her legs. ''Arnie has sort of disappeared. No note, no nothing. He had a court date set for two weeks from now, and I haven't heard from him in a month.'' She paused to prepare herself for something painful. ''I don't think I'm gonna hear from him.''

Lorna's eyes got all fuzzy around the edges as they filled with tears. But then, I'd cry like a baby if I were about to lose fifty grand. She took a shuddering breath.

''I've gotta pull myself together,'' she said, pushing Bronco from her lap and rising from her chair. Ox got up and moved toward her, but Lorna waved him away. ''Is there a ladies' room?''

''Down the hall on your left,'' I told her. Lorna left the room, and Ox stood staring at the door after her looking sad, like some big, dumb animal. Bronco, on the other hand, maintained a demeanor of perky intelligence. Confident that his mistress would be returning for him, the dog jumped up into her chair to keep it warm. I opened my mouth to object to his being on my rented furniture, but Bronco anticipated this reaction and gave me a narrow-eyed look of determination. I make a point to never let myself be intimidated by humans, but there was something about this dog. He had a distinct human quality, like an old soul who had been through many incarnations.

"She was crazy about him," Ox said after a moment. He looked forlorn as he stood there, staring at the door Lorna had walked through. "He don't deserve her. I tried to tell her, but she never listens. She thought 'cause he gave her a ring they were engaged, but I knew he'd skip. He's just that type. Thinks he's smarter than everybody."

The situation had suddenly gained new dimension. It was more than the fifty grand Lorna was after. Lorna wanted her man back, and Ox wanted Lorna—your average heart-breaking, gut-wrenching love triangle. My sympathy went out to them, since my own heart had been broken a few times, but that didn't mean I was interested in chasing down Arnie Lufkin. In the first place, I wouldn't know how. In the second place, it wasn't my line of work.

I was trying to think of some other way I could help Lorna when she walked back into the room blowing her nose into a wad of toilet paper. Bronco jumped off her chair.

"Are you all right? Can I get you anything?" I asked.

"I'm okay now. Sorry about that. I've gotta case of pre-mens that would choke a horse. Anyway, I want you two to find Arnie. Usually if someone leaves me holding the bag like this I send Ox after 'em, but Arnie, he's different. He's smart, super-smart."

"I could find him," said Ox.

Lorna crossed her eyes. "Oh, yeah, sure. You couldn't find your tush with both hands." Her cockiness now returned, Lorna looked at me with bright, intense eyes. "Arnie's got a mind like a machine. He did some stuff where the computer makes 3-D pictures and you think you're some-place you're not, but it seems like you're there."

"Virtual reality," I said.

"Yeah," she said, her voice suddenly happy, her palms upturned. "See? That's why I need you guys. You're computer people. You think like Arnie. You could figure out where he went. I'm willing to pay.'' She took a scrap of paper and a pen out of her purse, scribbled something, and held it out to us. Paoli took it from her. He looked at the paper, then at Lorna. ''Half now, half when you find him,'' she said.

''I'm sorry, truly sorry, Ms. Donatello, but as I told you, we're not in that type of business.''

I felt a tug on my arm. ''Would you excuse us just a moment? We need to conference,'' said Paoli, pulling me toward the door.

''Fine with me. Conference all you want,'' said Lorna.

Paoli and I stepped into the hallway that separated our office from the other small businesses in the building. I leaned against the wall and steeled myself for the confrontation I knew was coming. Placing his hands firmly on my shoulders, Paoli gave me the kind of penetrating look I found hard to resist. On his very worst days, when he's hung over, cranky, and has forgotten to brush his teeth, I'm still more attracted to him than to any other man on earth. Husky, broad-shouldered, and baby-faced, with the kind of well-developed muscles that make shirts too tight in the chest, Paoli had this sexiness about him I call ''eau de testosterone.'' He smiled and his blue eyes crinkled up at the corners. I gathered up all of my self-control.

''Julie, let's be open-minded here. I remember reading about Lufkin. He was one of the best virtual reality whizzes in the country. A brilliant guy. He also figured out some way to hack into Anco's accounting system and peel off a ton of money. If we find him, our names will be in every paper in California.''

''It's not our kind of work.''

''For the right kind of cash we could make it our kind of work.''

''It will distract us from going after the type of clients we really need.''

"It won't take long enough to be distracting. How tough could it be? We know people like him. We think like him. We can get inside his brain and figure out where he went. It'll be easy."

"We're not in the missing persons business. We are highly skilled computer professionals and are supposed to be investigating computer fraud. Our clients are supposed to be large corporations like General Motors, AT&T, not female bail bondsmen. I mean bondspersons."

"But, Julie, it's five thousand dollars."

My eyes widened as my resolve weakened. "Five thousand?"

Paoli nodded. "Twenty-five hundred now, another twenty-five hundred when we find him."

"But what do we know about finding people? Our chances of actually locating this Lufkin person are minuscule. We wouldn't find him, and then she would want her first payment back." I pushed Paoli's hands off my shoulders to minimize emotion- and mind-altering body contact, but he grabbed my hand to maintain the physical connection. The man knew my weaknesses.

"I realize this is a little off our game plan, but we can find this guy in a couple of days. A quick slam dunk and we walk away with an easy five grand. Five grand and we pay our back bills, Julie. Think about it." He gave my hand a meaningful squeeze.

"But this isn't the kind of work we intended to get into. It's . . . sleazy."

Paoli smiled at me. "If anything sleazy comes up, I'll handle it. In fact, I'll do all the work, sleazy and nonsleazy. It'll be fun."

I pulled my hand away from his to make a point. "But we're not supposed to be having fun. We're supposed to be running a business. We'll be wasting precious time that we could use going after real clients. And what about your programming job? How will you find the time to work on both projects?"

To help out with the bills, Paoli had taken a consulting job writing a billing program for a company called Dayton Electronics. Although programming was outside our desired niche, it was closer than finding missing persons.

His face turned serious. "Listen, Julie, in our financial condition, anything that makes money is not wasting time. We've been in business now approximately four months—"

"Six months and thirteen days."

"Six months and thirteen days, and we've only made about five hundred dollars."

"Four hundred and twenty-five dollars if we're talking gross receipts."

"I stand corrected. So right now we have an opportunity to grow our current revenues ten times over. How can we pass it up? And to address your second point, who says we're not supposed to have fun? That's why we dumped our old jobs, so we could get a little more zest out of life, feel some thrills."

As I gazed at my partner's handsome face, I realized that his last statement illustrated perfectly the basic problem between us. I did not quit my corporate job at ICI to get more thrills. Finding a corpse in my ICI data center was plenty of excitement as far as I was concerned. I quit my job so I could have more control over my career and my life, so I could pursue my own goals rather than those of some huge corporation, and it bothered me more than a little that Paoli had taken the entrepreneurial route so he could experience the professional equivalent of a bungee jump. Why did I adore him so?

"I'll find time to do the work, I promise. You can stay in the office and make goal-directed calls. I'll find Arnie Lufkin and bring home the big bucks. What do you say?"

I wanted to say no. I wanted to show Lorna Donatello, her dog, and her henchman the door, but the reality was that I

needed money badly. I hadn't told Paoli exactly how badly.
We had run through our initial start-up capital by our third
month in business, and I was now using my savings to pay
the bills. I didn't want to tell him, because if he knew he
probably would want to close the business down, and I
couldn't face that. Paoli wouldn't get any money from his
programming job until the end of the month, and I had to
come up with some funds to carry us. To stave off embar-
rassing questions I told him that the $425 recently put into
our business checking account had been a payment from a
quick security analysis job I had lucked into. The money had
actually come from some stock I had sold. I was only a few
thousand dollars away from having to dip into my IRA.

Without some quick cash, my dream of my own business
would vanish faster than Arnie Lufkin. It would mean I
would have to reenter the corporate world with my tail between my legs. All those people would smugly say, "I told
you so"; Paoli and I would have to admit that our vision of
working together had been foolhardy. Worst of all, it would
mean that I had failed. Lorna Donatello's five thousand
dollars would keep us afloat for another two months and
give us time to turn things around.

"Okay, we take the job."

Paoli raised his fist in the air and gave a silent victory
cheer; then he pulled me back into the office where Lorna,
Ox and Bronco awaited. When we stepped inside, Lorna
and Ox looked at us with expectant faces, but Bronco, who
was lying at Lorna's feet with his head between his paws,
stared at me with worried eyes. I had this weird feeling he
knew something we didn't.

TWO

THE THINGS you have to do these days to make a living. I couldn't help but feel that I'd cheapened myself professionally by accepting Lorna Donatello's job offer, like a thousand-dollar-a-night call girl forced by hard times to work a Shriners convention. But pride doesn't pay the bills.

Lorna relaxed a little after we told her we would accept her job—relaxed meaning she smoked one cigarette every five minutes instead of two. The look on Ox's face made it clear that he didn't share Lorna's joy at the prospect of retrieving Arnie Lufkin. Slumped in his chair, he pouted in silence, raising his head occasionally to look at Lorna with lost, lovesick eyes.

"So, Ms. Donatello," said Paoli, rubbing his hands together greedily as he sat on my desk. "Let's get started." I retreated to my swivel chair.

"Call me Lorna," she said with a sudden hint of silkiness to her burlap voice. "Everybody does."

"Sure, Lorna. And you call me Vic. Hardly anybody does." He shot me a look of mock disparagement. He couldn't get used to the fact that I still called him by his last name. He just didn't look like a "Vic" to me.

"Aren't the police looking for Lufkin?" I asked.

She swept the air with her hand, waving away the idea like a fly.

"Hell, the friggin' FBI's after him. But they'll never find him. They're used to dealing with your everyday common criminal. Arnie's not a criminal. He's a genius. I need you two to find him, and I'm willing to pay."

"Well, that settles it," Paoli said. "So let's get started. Can you describe Arnie Lufkin for us? If we're going to look for him, we'll need to know what he looks like."

"He was a shrimp!" shouted Ox, coming to fresh attention. He bellowed the words, stiffening and pressing on the chair's arms with his meaty hands so hard I thought the chair would fly into pieces. Upon hearing the offensive tone in Ox's voice, Bronco rose to his haunches, his eyes alert and hopeful that, at last, this man was going to show some bravado. "I could snap him in two." Ox released the poor chair and made a fist with one hand, twisting it at the wrist to demonstrate how easily body snapping could be accomplished. I smiled and nodded, making a mental note to stay on Ox's good side.

Lorna's blond head rotated in Ox's direction, her saucer eyes now narrowed in disgust. "Mind your own beeswax or I'll make you wait in the car."

The woman was fearless. In a nanosecond that single disparaging remark deflated Ox's brief moment of confidence. Bronco lay back down, his eyes closing in disappointment.

"Vernon. Why can't she call me Vernon?" Ox asked, his shoulders hunched in defeat. For some reason he looked at me for the answer. I gave him a smile of encouragement, although I doubt it helped him any.

"Because you're big like an ox and dumb like an ox," Lorna said, salting his wound.

Ox sat up in his chair and I could see the wheels in his head spinning frantically as he attempted to come up with a clever retort, or any retort for that matter, but those wheels spun helplessly, unable to get traction. For Ox's sake, I jumped in and changed the subject.

"Do you have a photograph?" I asked Lorna. Ox shrank back into his chair.

"Yeah, I've got one somewhere in here." Lorna opened her handbag and dug through it, taking out a hairbrush, a small squirt bottle of hair spray, two compacts, a Swiss army knife, and a black gun no larger than my hand, placing them casually on my desk while she scavenged. She saw my eyes fixed on the gun. "Hey, I've got a license for it. I deal with some pretty unsavory types, you know." She returned to her search. "Got it." She held up a bent Polaroid with a bright red lipstick smudge on the corner. Had Lorna actually kissed Arnie's picture or had it merely been a convenient lipstick blotter? Inquiring minds wanted to know.

Paoli took the photograph from her. I got up from my chair and walked around the desk so I could see the man who had gotten under Lorna Donatello's thick skin.

"Isn't he dynamite cute?" she asked, the question, at least in her mind, rhetorical. "And hung like a Brahma bull."

Paoli and I looked at Lorna, then at the photo. It was hard to tell much. The photo was blurred and obviously had been taken from a distance. I saw a man of medium build, maybe in his thirties, his brown hair worn in a long antiestablishment ponytail. His features were even, just shy of handsome, and his clothes looked rumpled and haphazard, the typical uniform of a Silicon Valley engineer. But, I had to admit, there was a sexy strength about him that shone through the Polaroid haze. He was neither "dynamite cute" nor the shrimp that Ox had described. And as for the Brahma bull part—I'd have to take Lorna's word on that one.

Looking more closely at the picture, I could tell by the scene in the background that Lufkin was standing at Vista Point, a paved area at the north end of the Golden Gate Bridge where tourists stop to take the customary sweeping San Francisco photo. Arnie's arms were crossed, and he looked at the camera with bored confidence.

"Do you think you can find him?" Lorna asked, as if we could figure it all out by looking at one fuzzy picture. Apparently still stewing over Lorna's rebuff, Ox leaped out of his chair with gazellelike agility.

"Lornie, you just make me crazy sometimes! He dumped you, Lornie. Tossed you aside like some old beer bottle, slammed you around, and now you're out fifty grand and talkin' like you're still nuts about the guy!'' Ox paced around the room, his eyes fixed on Lorna while his huge arms flapped, and the wretched expression on his face reminded me of the way King Kong had looked at Fay Wray for the last time. Bronco sprang to all fours, pacing along with Ox in sporting encouragement.

In a fit, Lorna popped up from her chair and used the heavy gloss on her lower lip for a cigarette holder while she pointed a purple fake finger-nailed finger first at Ox, then at the door.

"Out! And I mean now!"

Ox looked at her for a moment, then hung his head and slowly walked out the door. Bronco watched Ox leave with sad, empathetic eyes, then returned to Lorna's feet.

The outburst cast a brief pall on the business meeting.

"You're kind of hard on the guy, aren't you?'' asked Paoli once Ox was out of earshot. Paoli always saw things from a man's point of view. Still, in this case, I had to agree with him.

Lorna flicked ash on the carpet. "Maybe, but I gotta keep him under control. To me, he's just employee number 2056."

The number stunned me. "How many employees do you have?"

"Just him. But the number helps me keep things impersonal. I couldn't call him 'number 1.' It would sound stupid. Anyway, he has nothing to do with me and Arnie. I never should have brought him here, but he was with me and this was on my way and all." She settled back in her chair again and smacked her lips in readiness to move onto more pleasant subjects. "So let's take another look at that picture."

I wasn't going to let her off that easy.

"What did Ox mean when he said Lufkin slammed you around?"

Her face turned hard for a second; then it settled into resignation.

"He hit me once. No biggie. I had a tiny little bruise, right here," she said, pointing to her cheekbone. "Ox saw it and jumped around like he had sat on a cattle prod. But I could handle Arnie. I can handle Ox, too."

The idea of anyone using Lorna's petite body for a punching bag turned my stomach. I picked up Arnie's photograph and took a harder look. He didn't look like a woman basher, but I guess that sort of tendency doesn't show up in photographs. Yet I had a bad feeling about him.

"Lorna, if Lufkin is hiding from the police he could be anywhere, even out of the country," I told her.

"Nah, I don't think so. Getting out the country would be too tough with the cops after him." Lorna looked wistful a moment; then her hand slipped again into the horn of plenty she called a purse and she pulled out two CDs in plastic cases. She slapped them on my desk.

"I thought you might want these."

"What are they?" I asked.

"I don't know. They belonged to Arnie. I thought they were CDs like you play on your stereo, but I tried to play them last night. They don't work."

I opened one and examined it. "CD ROM," I said, handing them off to Paoli. Lorna gave me a blank look, but she was right: Arnie's CDs did look just like the kind you play on the stereo, only they held data for a computer.

"I figured they might be computer stuff. That's why I brought 'em to you."

"It seems odd that he would leave them," said Paoli.

"I don't think he knows. Arnie took every scrap of his stuff with him when he cleared out, but I had done some straightening up the week before. I took the CDs out of this leather case he had and put 'em in the stereo cabinet. I mean I thought they were music and the stereo cabinet was where they belonged. I was always trying to put his stuff away so he'd feel like my place was permanent. Do you think they could be important?'' She looked hopeful.

"I don't know. I'll have to find out what's on them first," I said.

"So what else do you need from me to get started?"

"A check for the first twenty-five hundred would get things rolling, right, Julie?" said Paoli. I have to admit when I saw Lorna get out her checkbook I felt pretty damn good.

VIRTUAL REALITY is a curious term. The word *virtual* in the dictionary is defined as "existing in essence or effect, though not in actual fact." In the computer world it describes a machine-made simulation, in this case a computer simulation of some environment in which the participant, with the aid of 3-D goggles and tactile stimulation, actually feels like he's somewhere else.

Think of a video game, but stretch your mind and imagine you're inside the game itself, that you're popped into the bright, surreal colors of a video world, that you can touch and move objects, walk the video landscape. That's virtual reality.

The VR concept isn't new. The air force has been using a low-tech form of VR for years with what they call "flight simulation." The pilot sits in a mock cockpit of an airplane, and through the use of a video landscape he looks out the windshield, sees a moving horizon, and gets the experience of flying. The mock plane actually responds to the use of the controls. If he pulls the joystick up, he feels the plane move upward; if he points the plane down, he may experience a nosedive, complete with warning sirens and red lights flashing, although without the final nasty crash.

Life is a lot like virtual reality, only we're not saved from the nasty crash at the end. We experience what our minds and emotions perceive as real, but our perceptions are rarely based on actual fact. Similar to everyone else, I view my life through a gauze of self-delusion, which is why I've always loved computers. Computers tell the truth.

AT SIX the next morning I opened my eyes and faced my reality with a dull headache and a mouth that tasted as if I'd been licking ashtrays. I could feel the bedspread bunched up into a big lump on top of me, Paoli's arm and leg wrapped around my waist. With a groan I untangled myself, sat up on the side of the bed, and, with difficulty, opened my eyes a little wider. The morning light was still dim, but I could see my bra on the nightstand, my skirt and blouse lying crumpled on the floor. I didn't remember my clothes flying off like Scud missiles, but at that groggy moment I couldn't remember anything further back than the previous ten seconds.

As I made an aborted attempt to stand, my foot hit a Moët bottle that lay empty on the floor. Inhaling the aroma of stale champagne, I fell back on the bed and mouthed an "ouch." Memories of the previous night came floating back to me. The check. After receiving it from Lorna, Paoli and I had celebrated our new almost-solvency with champagne, and now my head suffered the aftereffects. I've always been a lousy drinker. My body ached and my brain felt swollen, but I was religious about getting to the office by seven. Old habits die hard, and today I actually had work to do. I allowed myself a lingering look at Paoli's bare, well-muscled torso. He was sound asleep and, knowing him, probably wouldn't wake for hours.

I showered and before I dressed summoned the nerve to stand on the bathroom scale. A hundred and twenty. That may not sound like much, but I'm short and small boned and never weighed more than 110 in my life. That is, until recently.

All my life I'd been working too fast and too hard to have much time for eating, but since starting my own business I had begun to fill my empty hours with snacking. Someone told me it's called "stress eating." I call it packing my face with foodstuffs. My special weakness is doughnuts. I can resist a lot of things, but lately doughnuts seemed to fill the void that had been left by leaving my old job, and as a result I had gained ten pounds in the past six months. My clothes were getting tight and a few days before I thought I felt my thighs touching when I walked. Paoli claimed he didn't notice my extra pounds, but how could I be sure he was telling the truth? Each day I vowed to diet, and each day I failed. I wondered if they made business suits with elastic waistbands.

I decided to skip breakfast, and an hour later I was in the office starting the day's toil, which up until today had consisted primarily of worrying. There was only one activity I knew of that took more nerve than getting on a scale, and that was looking at our accounts payable. When I finally gathered up the courage, I flipped on my computer and brought up the accounting software. I stared at the numbers, and the numbers stared back, giving me the usual bad news. With Lorna's twenty-five hundred I would be able to pay the back rent, plus have some left over for PG&E, but that left overdue bills for office equipment, stationery, and the cost of a logo. The logo was a sore point with me. Paoli had insisted on having it professionally designed by an expensive graphics firm where all the employees wore trendy outfits and had hair colors not found in the human gene pool.

Even with Lorna's check I was still short twenty-three hundred and some odd cents. I only had enough to cover the odd cents, unless I wanted to cash in my IRA or my ICI stock. I didn't want to do either, especially since my stock was at a nine-year low and I feel about IRAs the way folks in Bombay feel about cows. Deep down I have fears of becoming a bag lady in my old age. I thought longingly about the twenty-five hundred awaiting me if we found Arnie Lufkin. I checked my watch. Almost eight-thirty and Paoli still wasn't in the office. His casual attitude about working hours really annoyed me. Every once in a while I would bring the subject up to him, but he would just laugh and call me "tense."

I was about to start printing off a few checks when my computer made an urgent and unexpected beeping sound. I thought the beeping was a little strange, but not as strange as what happened next. As I looked at my check ledger, all the words and numbers on the screen began melting into each other, the characters swirling toward the center like they were being flushed down some computerized toilet.

I blinked my eyes a few times just to make sure the previous night's champagne wasn't having more serious aftereffects, but the numbers in front of me continued to waltz and jiggle, finally melting into the center.

"What the hell . . ." I said out loud. At that moment the computer screen went black; then new words popped up in front of me.

"Hi, Julie. I have a poem for you. Pay attention," the screen said. Those letters disappeared, replaced with the following:

DOWN FROM
THE
MOUNTAIN, SWOOP THROUGH
THE SKY. PEEK THROUGH THE KEYHOLE, SPYDER IN YOUR EYE. IF
YOU SEE ONE NEAR YOU TRY TO GET AWAY. IF HE DOES COME CLOSER, YOU
WON'T FORGET THE DAY. LOOKING IN
A MIRROR YOU MAY JUST SEE
A FOE,
BUT WHAT IS REAL AND WHAT IS NOT AND
WHAT IS JUST FOR SHOW? WHEN LIFE AND DEATH TURN LIKE A
   WHEEL THEY BRING ITS VICTIMS WOE. BE CAREFUL
FOR THE ONE
YOU FEAR MAY BE THE ONE YOU KNOW

I sat there stunned for a moment, my fingers frozen as they hovered over the keyboard. "Hit the print key," I told myself, getting enough of my senses back to use my hands. I wasn't a second too soon, because the letters on the screen started drifting, becoming fainter as they twirled. Once the poem had evaporated, the words, "BYE BYE, JULIE!" flashed; then my check ledger popped back up on the screen, as if it had never left.

The snapping sound of the printer pulled me back to reality. I got up from my chair, took the page out of the tray, and studied every word. The poem was senseless, like some grammar school rhyme. Ordinarily I would have assumed I have been the victim of some bored computer hacker pumping a virus through the network, but this one had actually used my name. It had been directed solely at me, and there had to be some reason for it.

I put the poem in my desk drawer and tried to forget about it, to get my mind back on the paying of bills, but my thoughts remained fixed. Most people think of computers as only machines, a complex mass of wires and electricity but nothing more. To me they were more than that. Although I normally don't broadcast this, deep down I suspect that computers have personalities. I think they know things the rest of us don't know and my personal computer knew who had planted the virus in it. I retrieved the poem from the drawer and looked at the words again, but I still couldn't fathom the poem's meaning.

I was about to put the poem away when I noticed an odd thing. Each line of the poem had a different length that didn't jibe with the poem's phrasing. I considered the variables. Fact one: It had to be a computer geek who had hacked into my software. Fact two: Computer geeks love mind games. It would be typical of a geek to play some sort of game with the poem, like a message within a message. The line lengths had to mean something. The morning was getting interesting.

I decided to take a stab at it. At first I wrote down the last letter of each line of the poem to see if they spelled something, but they didn't, at least not in the sequence in which they were written. Next I tried rearranging the letters in some of the words, then the words in each sentence, but again came up with nothing.

Frustrated, I took a break and walked next door to the Hard Drive Cafe for my usual double cappuccino. When I had my nice secure job at ICI, I only drank decaf, but times had changed.

When I reached the Hard Drive, I found the door wide open, welcoming me inside. It was nothing more than a glorified deli, but it was close by and I liked Lydia, the owner. That day she was wearing a running suit with an apron over it that said: "Kiss the Cook."

"The usual," I said.

She took one look at me and frowned. "You look 100 percent stressed, and it's barely nine-thirty. You should try decaf sometime. The way I make it, you can hardly tell the difference."

I laughed. "One of these days. So how's Meg? Is she doing okay with her PC?"

"Since you helped her, she is," Lydia said as she negotiated with her cappuccino machine. "She did a geography paper last night. It was as good as something out of college."

Lydia's daughter was eleven. A few weeks before, I had given her my old PC, and I had spent the previous Saturday showing her how to use it. Meg had caught on fast, and Lydia had shown her gratitude with a pan of lasagna, which I was now wearing on my hips. I saw Lydia grab a napkin and reach into a pastry box.

"Have a jelly doughnut. It's on the house." The woman knew me. The doughnut in her hand oozed red jelly and looked scrumptious.

"I shouldn't. What's the occasion?"

"Don't play coy with me. The new client. Congratulations. Vic told me yesterday. See, I told you things would pick up."

I thanked her and accepted her congratulatory free doughnut. Lydia, shaped like a jelly doughnut herself, loved to see the office building's occupants thriving, because it meant she would sell more cappuccinos, a drink that enjoyed a nice profit margin. When she had learned through the grapevine that Data9000 was on the ropes she offered marketing suggestions whenever Paoli and I came in for coffee. She even suggested we change the company's name, but I wouldn't hear of it. "Data9000" had sentimental value for me. Paoli and I had met because of a hack into an ICI 9000 mainframe.

I sipped my coffee as I headed back to the office. The caffeine stimulated my gray matter, so I sat back down at my desk and took another tack with the poem. I counted the words in each line and wrote that number in the left-hand margin, wiping away numerous drips of red jelly from my doughnut as I worked. Next I wrote out the alphabet, numbering each letter, operating on the theory that the number of words in each line pointed to a letter of the alphabet. The first line had two words, which would signify a B, the second letter in the alphabet. The second line of the poem had one word, which translated to A. A consonant and a vowel. So far, so good.

When I came up with the word "BACK," I cheered and clapped. When I got the second word, "OFF," I was still enthusiastic, but when I got the whole message my stomach knotted. It read: "BACK OFF BITCH."

I shivered. The only job I was working on was the Lufkin case, but who would want me to back off it? No one even knew I had the case, except Lorna and Ox, and neither of them had the motive or knowledge to break into my computer. The image of Lufkin formed in my head. He had the knowledge and the motive as well, but how could he know I was working for Lorna?

I opened my desk drawer and got out my Maalox, unscrewed the top, and took a gulp straight from the bottle, the chalky taste mixing unfavorably with the doughnut residue.

"Having your usual Breakfast of Champions, I see," said Paoli, breezing in the front door wearing the goofy grin of an eternal optimist. He was wearing a suit—an ill-fitting suit, but a suit. I wondered who had died. I put down my Maalox but remained mute.

"Julie, what's wrong?"

"This," I said, and handed him the poem. He looked at it for a moment.

"Okay, it's not Robert Frost, but I wouldn't upset myself over it."

"Paoli, it came to me on my computer. Someone broke in and planted it in my system."

"Did you lose any data?"

"No."

He shrugged. "So you got hit with a virus. What's the big deal?"

"It's more than that. My name showed up on the screen. This wasn't random. It was directed at me. And look at this." I showed him my scribblings with the alphabet. "I thought that the different line lengths meant there was a code. I was right." Paoli's face went pale when he read the message. "I'm not sure what it means yet."

He threw the paper on the floor. "I know exactly what it means. It means we're dropping the Lufkin case." He walked over to his desk while I scooped up the poem.

"How did you reach that conclusion?"

"Don't pretend you haven't figured it out. Let's sift through our list of active cases. Okay, we have only one case. And it just happens to focus on a technical genius who just happens to be wanted for breaking into a computer system. And it just happens that your computer gets broken into. Give me a break, Julie. You and I both know it's Lufkin. I'm calling Lorna right now. We'll have to return the money."

He lifted the phone receiver and began punching numbers, but I jumped up from my desk and grabbed the receiver. We both held onto it.

"Give me the phone, Julie."

He tugged, but I held tight.

"You're not calling Lorna."

"Wrong. I am calling Lorna. You might as well hand me the phone."

I still didn't let go. Paoli's expression grew churlish. "This town's full of phones, toots."

I let go of the receiver. "The poem's an empty threat. When I first figured it out it bothered me, but now I realize Lufkin's just trying to scare me. It's no big deal."

"It is a big deal, Julie. The guy's violent. We know ' knocked Lorna around, so what's to keep him from fo'-lowing you into some dark alley? What's come over you, anyway? Yesterday you weren't sure we should even take this case. Now you're willing to risk your neck for it."

"I'm not risking my neck. I don't think Lufkin would hurt me. For the first time I think we're going to find him."

"Why?"

"Because yesterday I thought he could have been anywhere in the country. Now we know he's in the immediate area."

Paoli put the receiver back. "We do? Julie, isn't your computer hooked into one of those public data networks where you can get stock updates? That's how he did it. He broke into your computer through the network. He could have done that from anywhere."

"I agree, but how did he know Lorna hired me to try and find him?"

"Somebody could have told him."

"Who? It wasn't Lorna. I doubt it was Ox."

Paoli threw his hands into the air. "Okay, a friend maybe. A mutual friend."

"I doubt he and Lorna had a lot of mutual friends. They didn't exactly meet at a dinner party. I think he was following her."

"Your imagination is in overdrive. It's that Greek food from last night. I warned you to ease up on the retsina."

But I didn't hear him, because my circuits were humming. Unable to sit still, I paced the floor while I talked.

"He saw her come in here. He checked out who we were, figured out why she was here, and now he's getting worried. He went home last night, sat down at his computer, and started writing poetry. A guy like Lufkin could easily break into a public network. He may be a subscriber himself. Then all he has to do is tinker with the network's electronic mail system. For him it's child's play."

Paoli held his fist to his mouth. "Earth to Julie. Earth to Julie. Listen to me. There's a possibility that he didn't follow Lorna at all. That he had someone else follow her."

"Okay, maybe, but remember that Lufkin's on the run. He wouldn't trust anyone unless he absolutely had to. I'm placing my bets on him following Lorna himself, and that means he's right here in Silicon Valley."

"Fine. You place your bets wherever you want to. What I don't get is why he would want to threaten you in the first place. Data9000 Investigations doesn't have a list of successes that would strike fear into someone's heart."

"It doesn't matter. He knows me. He thinks I might be able to find him."

"And what am I? Chopped liver?"

"You're from Washington, D.C. You just moved here six months ago, but I've been around Silicon Valley for years. I've been fairly well known, and during the investigation at ICI my name was in the newspapers. Lufkin's bound to know me."

Paoli grimaced. "I can't let you get involved in something where there's any chance of you getting hurt."

"When did I ever ask you for permission?"

He hit the top of his desk with his fist. "Fine. Risk your neck. What time is it?"

I checked my Seiko. "Almost ten."

Paoli picked up his briefcase and headed for the door.

"Where are you going?"

He stopped. "I called Anco from your place this morning. I have an eleven o'clock appointment with Lufkin's former boss."

"I'm going with you."

He glared at me, then headed out the door. I grabbed my briefcase and purse and followed him.

The Lufkin poem had unnerved Paoli, because either he was afraid for my safety or he was ticked off that Lufkin obviously thought that of the two of us, I was more of a threat. I preferred to think he just feared for my safety.

When we reached Paoli's Porsche, he suddenly stopped and grabbed me by the arm.

"I'll be watching your backside the whole time."

I grabbed his tie, pulled his faced toward me, and kissed him. "Then I'll make sure my skirts are tight," I whispered with a laugh, but he didn't return my smile.

Although I would never let Paoli know it, the poem's threat frightened me as much as it did him. But although it was a threat, it was a dare as well. Whoever had written it had presented me with a challenge, and after six months of sitting on my behind and doing nothing, a challenge was one thing I couldn't resist.

THREE

I WON THE TOSS and drove us in my car to San Francisco. Paoli jumps at any chance to get his car on the highway, but that's a mode of transportation I do my best to avoid. Paoli describes his weathered orange 1969 Porsche as "vintage." To my way of thinking, *vintage* is a term you use when discussing cabernet sauvignon, furniture circa 1920, and shabby chic clothing found in tiny shops on Fillmore Street. It's not a term I use for a car that looks like someone dropped a truckload of golf balls on it, then shoved it headfirst into a ravine. And I've sat in folding chairs with better shock absorption.

We didn't talk much during the ride. Paoli was still miffed over our little argument, and my mind was fixed on the poem. The "Back off bitch" part was clear enough, but I wondered if the poem itself had some meaning as well.

If Lufkin had found out that Lorna had hired me, and if he had quickly checked out my background, then the first few lines of the poem made some sense. Six months earlier I had left my vice presidency at ICI, the largest computer manufacturer in the world. ICI could be seen as a "mountain" that I swooped down from. "Peek through the keyhole" referred to the fact that I was looking for Lufkin. The "spyder in your eye" part could be viewed as a mild threat, but why the strange spelling of *spyder?*

The meaning of the rest of the poem was more elusive. At this point I didn't have much to go on, and we arrived in San Francisco before I had time to come up with a theory I trusted.

The previous night, before the champagne kicked in, Paoli and I had decided that the best way to initiate our search for Lufkin was to interview the people he had worked with. After we asked Lorna who his friends had been, she told us that as far as she knew he didn't have any. He wasn't the type to go bowling with the guys, she said, and for the past two months he had spent almost every evening with her. He was gone during the day and some evenings, but where she didn't know. When she asked him about it, he turned cold, then angry, and finally she stopped asking. Our only option was to start with Lufkin's coworkers, and Paoli figured Lufkin's boss should be first.

As we introduced ourselves to Alan Chambers, director of development services at Anco International, a peeved look etched itself onto his face. We were sitting in Chambers's office, the type of smallish, gray-walled, windowless cube assigned to middle managers out of favor. The poor guy didn't even rate a potted plant. Chambers slouched behind his dull metal desk looking as if he were being pinched where it hurt. He was a diminutive man in his fifties with a cheap sandy-colored toupee and lightless eyes the color of sludge.

"Ten minutes and that's it. It's the end of the month and I have to consolidate activity reports. I'm very busy."

I glanced around the room. Chamber's office didn't look like that of a very busy person. It was too clean, too orderly, his desk clear except for a small stack of papers. Busy people created clutter, but I chose not to argue the point with him.

"We won't take up much of your time. We're looking for information about Arnold Lufkin," Paoli said.

If Chambers's lips had pursed any tighter they would have turned inside out.

"My administrator told me you mentioned Lufkin on the phone. Very bad business, that was. Are you his attorneys?"

I eagerly awaited Paoli's answer. What were we? I was dying to know myself. Paoli avoided a verbal response by handing Chambers one of our fancy, top-of-the-line business cards, complete with expensive logo. Chambers studied it so long I wondered about his reading abilities; then he raised his eyes, looking at us as if we had just arrived via alien spacecraft.

"Computer investigations?" he said, his voice high-pitched and belligerent, the aggressive bark of a man anxious to protect his turf. "Who hired you? No one at Anco did. That general ledger program was taken out and archived as soon as the fraud was uncovered." He tossed our card on his desk, and I noticed his hands shaking. "What do you want?"

Now I know how IRS auditors feel. I was offended and intrigued by Chambers's negative reaction. In the few moments it had taken him to read our business card he had gone from vague irritability to focused nastiness. I wondered what he was afraid of.

"We're looking for Lufkin. He's disappeared, and we're being paid to find him," said Paoli.

Chambers let out a metallic laugh. He crossed his arms, placing his hands in his armpits so we couldn't see their continuous vibrations.

"Well, I certainly can't help you there. I haven't talked to Lufkin since they took him out of here in handcuffs, and that was six months ago. Good luck finding him. I don't envy you."

"Why do you say that?" I asked.

"Because Arnold is a crook, plain and simple, but he's also very cunning. If he wants to hide, I would imagine he'll stay hidden." Chambers paused, his face turning thoughtfully. "What a mind that man possessed. Sometimes I wish we had him back. My job would certainly be a lot easier."

"What is your job?" Chambers was starting to get chatty, so I thought I might as well keep him going.

"I'm responsible for a virtual reality project. You're familiar with VR?"

"No direct experience, but we're familiar with the concept," said Paoli. "How did Anco figure out Lufkin was stealing?"

A self-satisfied smile crept over Chambers's face as he relaxed into the moment. "I got suspicious," he said, with emphasis on the pronoun. "I thought he was up to something and ran some checks on the deposit accounts. After that it didn't take long to figure out what was going on."

"What made you think he was up to something?" I asked.

"Lufkin and I had some problems over the security software."

"What kind of problems?"

"It has nothing to do with Lufkin's disappearance."

"Was Lufkin working on the VR project?" Paoli asked, taking a new angle.

"Lufkin *was* the project. He was doing almost all the work himself. Anco got the chance to compete for a huge government bid from NASA last year. Among other things, it includes some virtual reality development to simulate in-flight repairs on space shuttles. We had eighteen months to complete the demo. With Lufkin on it we would have finished with time to spare. Now we'll probably end up dropping out."

"Surely there are other programmers in Silicon Valley who can do that kind of work," I said.

"You'd be surprised how few," answered Chambers. "Sure, there are companies playing around with VR, doing video games, demonstrations, things like that, but there aren't many developing the kind of intensive, full-body applications we are. It's very specialized."

"Who are you competing with for the NASA deal?" Paoli asked. *Nice,* I said silently. He was fishing for companies where Lufkin might make connections.

"There are several, but I'm not allowed to give their names. If we could show some results in the space shuttle segment I think it would push us in front of the pack. But now with Lufkin gone . . ." Chambers let it hang a second. "He worked night and day."

"And during coffee breaks he was hacking into the accounting system?" Paoli asked.

"Apparently," Chambers said with a scowl. He checked his watch. "Your ten minutes are up. Like I said, I'm very busy."

"Just one more thing," said Paoli. "We'd like to talk to a few of the other people who worked with Lufkin. They might be able to give us some information that would help us."

Chambers put both hands on his desk and leaned forward. "No," he said, slapping the desk for emphasis. "Absolutely not. The Lufkin business disrupted things around here enough. I won't have you bothering my people. We're under too much pressure."

Paoli got up to leave, but I stayed put.

"Lufkin's a criminal. If he's not found, he can hack into other computer systems the way he hacked into yours. If we find him, we stop him," I said.

Chambers eyed me haughtily. "That's a job for the FBI."

"You said yourself that Lufkin is highly intelligent. No slam on the FBI, but they may not be able to catch him."

"Oh, and you think you can?" Chambers raised a pale, scantily haired excuse for an eyebrow. I believe this was meant to intimidate me.

"Yes." Out of the corner of my eye I saw Paoli smile.

"Lufkin is no longer my problem. Please leave now."

"I get the impression you don't want him found," I said. That really irked him, and his face turned the color of my mother's living room drapes. I think she refers to the hue as "ripe pomegranate."

"I told you to leave."

"Be nice, Mr. Chambers," Paoli said in a warning voice.

Chambers got up from his chair. Paoli stepped toward him. I could see a case of testosterone poisoning coming and decided that if we didn't want to get into fisticuffs, we had better exit. I was ticked off at Chambers, but there was nothing I could do about it, at least for the moment. I grabbed Paoli's arm, thanked Chambers for his time, and pulled my partner out of the office. We walked through a maze of cubicles toward the bank of elevators.

"Were you really going to hit him?" I asked Paoli as we walked.

"Of course not. That sort of thing could muss my suit. The weasel isn't worth hitting, anyway. Although I thought maybe you were going to punch him out. You sounded awfully tough back there. I found it sexually stimulating," Paoli said, whispering the last part in my ear.

"You find road kill sexually stimulating. I thought Chambers was just a little too defensive. If we dug around a little and—"

I was interrupted by a voice before I could finish. "Excuse me."

We turned in unison, and I saw the young guy from the front desk who had escorted us to Chambers's office. He was magazine-cover handsome, with black hair pulled into a slick ponytail and the kind of cheekbones women pay thousands for. "Ms. Gallagher would like to see you," he said, his voice as dry as the Sahara.

"Gallagher?" I asked.

"Chief financial officer," he said in a tone indicating that we should have already known that. "I told her administrator that you were seeing Chambers. Apparently, Monique passed it on to Ms. Gallagher that you were here. Now she wants to see you." His voice had turned low and gossipy, and I was glad to know the corporate grapevine still worked the way it used to. Paoli tucked his chin to his chest and gave me a look I knew was supposed to silently communicate something to me, but I wasn't sure what. "She can see you right now. Fifth floor."

I thanked him. Paoli's hand rested on my behind during the elevator ride.

"I thought you were going to *watch* my backside," I said.

"This is the Braille method."

I let the hand linger a moment before pushing it away. The doors opened and Paoli whistled softly. The difference between the fifth floor and the second floor was approximately that between the Ritz and the local Motel 6. While the second floor was a model of Spartan efficiency, the fifth floor had the understated luxury of your basic executive lair—oak paneling, plush carpets, subdued lighting, and a churchlike hush that floated around your ears like a hymn sung by angels with their hands over their mouths.

"We're entering the land of the big bucks, Julie," Paoli said, keeping his voice appropriately low.

We approached a desk the size of a small barge. The gray-haired woman at the helm looked up from the letter she was reading.

"Yes?"

"We're here to see Ms. Gallagher," I said. "She's expecting us."

The receptionist gave us the once-over and apparently decided we weren't Jehovah Witnesses or hawking insurance.

"Your names?" I gave them to her; she punched a button on her phone and announced our arrival. "That way. Monique will meet you." She pointed down a hallway, and we obediently headed in that direction. A smartly dressed Asian woman met us halfway. Her black hair was pulled into an elegant French twist and her lips painted the color of poppies.

"Follow me," she said in a Brooklyn accent that didn't correlate with her Asian features. She bustled down the hall with short, quick steps and we trailed behind. "Arlene is busy-busy today, but she's squeezing you in. Here we are."

Monique stopped in front of an oak door so tall it reached the ceiling. After tapping lightly, she cracked it a few inches and peeked inside.

"They're here." Opening the door, she gestured for us to enter, and we stepped inside.

The office was simple yet spacious, with a wall of windows and a sweeping city view. There were nice personal touches—plants, a few pieces of art, a collection of framed photographs on the credenza behind the desk.

Ms. Gallagher's office was more impressive than Ms. Gallagher herself. She was plump and matronly, with badly applied coral lipstick and salt-and-pepper hair cut in a blunt chin-length bob. Unlike Alan Chambers's desk, Gallagher's was covered with papers. When we walked in, she was reading a thick report, and as soon as I saw her what struck me most was her glasses. She wore half-glasses perched on the end of her nose, but they were shiny red with rhinestones in the corners and hung from an elaborate pearl chain. Those rhinestones held the secret to her soul, I thought. We all have pieces of our hearts that get buried every day by the rigors of our jobs, but to maintain sanity we let our real selves peek out in small, subtle ways. For me, it was leopard print underwear beneath my serious suits. For Gallagher, it was the glasses. She looked more like someone's mother than the CFO of a mammoth corporation. I liked her immediately.

She put down the report, stood up, and walked around her desk to greet us. She looked harried and overworked, but her smile seemed sincere. We all introduced ourselves and executed the perfunctory pumping of hands.

"Thanks for stopping by. When I found out you were visiting Chambers, I wanted to see you myself. This Lufkin situation is such a disturbing business. Please sit down. Can

I have Monique bring you coffee?'' Gallagher spoke rapidly, her voice brusque yet at the same time friendly.

"No thanks,'' I said. Paoli also declined. I didn't approve of sending secretaries scurrying off for coffee. I'm not the typical militant feminist you see around the San Francisco area, but I believe in equality and in banishing certain stereotypes, including the one that had females fetching for their bosses like dogs—no offense to Bronco. Paoli and I settled in plush leather chairs.

"We'd like to know why you want to see us,'' Paoli said.

Gallagher sat down and gripped the desk in front of her. Tilting her head down, she peered at us over the top of her red glasses.

"I don't want to take any more of your time than necessary. I just have to know what your involvement is with Arnold Lufkin. Monique found out from Alan Chambers's administrator that you were meeting with Chambers, and that Lufkin was the subject to be discussed. She told me what she knew, including that you worked for some investigation firm. I want details.''

"What kind of details?'' I asked.

Gallagher stiffened. "Lufkin cost this company a great deal of money and even more embarrassment. I want to know what you're investigating and why.''

"It's not like we have anything to hide,'' said Paoli. He glanced at me, and I nodded my confirmation. "Ms. Blake and I own Data9000. We specialize in computer investigations. Normally we deal with computer fraud exclusively, but we were asked to assist in locating Arnold Lufkin. It sounded interesting, so we accepted the job. Apparently Lufkin has disappeared.''

"The FBI told us. He was scheduled for trial in a few weeks. Were you hired by the FBI?''

"No,'' I answered. "And we've been asked by our client to maintain confidentiality. We will, of course, respect those wishes.''

Paoli looked at me with questioning eyes. Okay, it was a lie, but the whole bail bonds thing embarrassed me. I thought my little misrepresentation sounded much classier.

"I'd like to clear one thing up," I added. "Mr. Paoli and I have very strong computer backgrounds. Our firm specializes in investigating computer fraud. Our search for Arnie Lufkin is very much out of our mainline business."

Gallagher gave me an appraising look. "What would it take to make it your mainline business, Ms. Blake?"

"I'm not sure what you mean."

"I mean I'd like to pay for your services in finding Lufkin."

Her statement threw me. Paoli and I exchanged glances.

"Someone is already paying for our services to find Lufkin," I said.

"So why not work for both of us? Anco is willing to pay."

"But we're already looking for Lufkin. Why should you pay us to do what we're already doing?"

"Because you said this isn't your mainline business, and I want your undivided attention in finding Lufkin. When I heard you were meeting with Chambers I wanted the opportunity to meet you, to size you up. If you two had turned out to be yellow pages private investigator types I would have politely tossed you out of here after the first sixty seconds. But you're not, and I want to be certain you find Arnie Lufkin."

"Why is Anco so interested in finding Lufkin? I would think it's a matter for the FBI," Paoli said.

Ms. Gallagher took off her glasses and let them dangle from their chain. "Have you ever talked to the FBI? They have a hundred cases on their plate. What I'm looking for is focus."

"Wasn't the money he stole covered by insurance?" I asked.

"We still don't like seeing anyone get away with stealing, especially that kind of money. If Lufkin disappears it looks as though he got away with it. It gives the wrong impression to our employees and our clients.''

"But that's not the main reason you want Lufkin found, is it?'' I asked, suddenly understanding her motivation for wanting to hire us, and in it I saw an opportunity for Data9000. ''If I were you, I'd want Lufkin back so he could explain in detail how he hacked into the accounting program.''

A faint smile crossed her lips. ''Exactly. That's why we need him. We've changed out all of that software, but it isn't enough. If it could happen once, it could happen again. It's not just the possibility of someone stealing money that we're concerned about. Our company competes for some very large projects, sometimes confidential government projects. The fact that our computer security was compromised has hurt our reputation. It's kept us out of several bids. We need to show our prospective clients where our system failed and how we fixed it so it won't happen again. We've had discussions with the federal attorney about using this as a negotiating tool for Lufkin's sentencing.''

"He gives the money back and tells you how he stole it in exchange for a lighter sentence?'' I asked.

"Something like that.''

I sat up with rapt attention. ''Ms. Gallagher, you've come to the right place, but not in the way you think. It's not ethical for us to perform the same job for two clients, but I think we can help you with a larger problem than Arnie Lufkin. Computer security investigation is what we do best. Give us access to your software and we can find out how Lufkin broke in.''

I was sitting on the edge of my chair. I didn't want to seem too eager, but I saw the chance for the kind of job I'd been after for the past six months. I knew we could figure out how Lufkin did it, and once we did, it would give us one hell of a reference. But I could tell by Gallagher's body language that she wasn't buying. She leaned back in her chair and looked solemn.

"I'm sorry, but we're talking about Anco's general ledger program. It's against corporate policy to let anyone from the outside work with our internal programs. We need Lufkin." My heart sank. "Who's paying you to find him?"

"We told you it's confidential," Paoli answered.

She was leaning forward again now, her voice and body more assertive. The gracious half-smile was still there, but now I saw the anxiety that lay behind it. There was a look in her eyes, a tension in her body, that didn't correlate to her circumstances, and I tried to understand it. Did the Lufkin situation put her job in jeopardy? I could see Lufkin's theft threatening Chambers's position. He had been Lufkin's manager and was close to the computer system Lufkin had broken into. But as CFO, Gallagher was above all that. Gallagher said she wanted Lufkin found, and she had stated all the right reasons, yet there had to be something else behind it.

"Maybe you can't give us money for finding Lufkin, but you can help us so we can find him a lot faster. Give us some cooperation, and you'll be getting what you want free of charge," Paoli said.

Gallagher's anxiety changed to interest. Chief financial officers like getting things for free. "How can I help?"

"We need the names of the Anco employees who worked closely with Lufkin. Chambers was reluctant to give out those names, but we need to talk to these people if we're going to make any progress."

"I'll have Chambers give you the names. If there's anything else you need, don't hesitate to ask me."

As I watched the intense expression in Gallagher's eyes, I couldn't help but wonder why Arnie Lufkin had such a strong effect on the people around him—Lorna, Ox, Alan Chambers, and now Arlene Gallagher. Mention Lufkin's name and these people acted as if they had just inhaled ammonia. What sort of power did Lufkin have over people to make them react so strongly?

We would soon find out.

FOUR

WHEN A FEW minutes later we told Chambers about our meeting with Gallagher, his body went rigid and I saw his hands clench into white-knuckled fists. He made a hasty phone call to Gallagher's office, but I could tell by the sour expression on his face that he didn't like what he heard. After slamming down the phone, he closed his eyes for a few seconds. Maybe he was saying his mantra, because when he opened his eyes again his body temperature appeared to have cooled off about five degrees, and he grudgingly wrote down four names on a yellow stick-it paper and handed it to Paoli. Paoli looked it over.

"So who do you recommend we start with?" he asked Chambers.

"Johnny Martinez. He was Lufkin's assistant on the VR project."

"Could you direct us to him?" I asked.

Chambers looked at me as if I had asked for a ride to Los Angeles. "Around the corner to your left. He's in a cubicle." Chambers paused; then he puckered his whole body into a prize-winning imitation of a human prune. "I'm going along with this because I have to, but I want the disruption to work here kept to a minimum. Do you understand what I'm saying?"

Paoli and I nodded obediently, although in our hearts we didn't give a damn. After we had gotten a few yards out of Chambers's office, I pulled Paoli into an empty cubicle and began untying his tie.

"Not now, Julie. Talk about hot and cold."

I chuckled. "Sorry, but that's not what I'm after." Having untied his tie, I pulled it off him, folded it, and put it in my briefcase. Next I ran my fingers through my hair to mess it up, wiped off my lipstick with a Kleenex, and put on my glasses. Paoli watched with interest. "Now take off your jacket," I told him. "And leave it here until we're ready to go back to the office."

"May I ask what we're doing?"

"We're going to be talking to heavy-duty programmers. I know these people because I used to be one of these people, and they don't trust outsiders. If we're going to get help from them, we're going to have to look less corporate. And we're going to have to remember to carry Birkenstocks with us from now on."

Paoli patted me on the back. "Good thinking, Julie. And next time lets bring Vaseline and rub it in our hair." He took off his jacket and tossed it on a chair.

I buttoned the top button of my blouse and gave my hair one last scrunch. "So how do I look?"

"Like my second-grade teacher, Mrs. Pesky. Luckily for you, I had the hots for her."

We walked down a short hallway and turned left into a bullpen of gray cubicles, stopping in front of a large one in the corner that had a name tag reading: "Martinez." A dark-haired man, very tall and very thin, sat hunched over a keyboard. By the length of body sticking up over the back of the chair I guessed him to be over six-foot-six. His hair was straight and long, pulled with a rubber band into a short ponytail. He stared at his computer, his face only a few inches from the screen, but he turned when he heard us approach. His face was hawkish, with a large hooked nose and small, closely set eyes. He looked like he was in his late twenties. A thick, oily smell wafted toward me, and I noticed a bag of packaged jalapeño-flavored popcorn on his lap.

"Excuse us. I'm Julie Blake, and this is Vic Paoli. We'd like to talk to you a few minutes."

Martinez looked at us with a wariness that made me wonder if Chambers had warned him of our arrival. My suspicion was soon confirmed.

"Alan called. You're investigators," he said in a voice less than friendly. "You want to know about Arnie."

"We just want to ask you a few questions," Paoli said. "Can we pull up two chairs?" Martinez didn't say anything. Paoli apparently took his silence to mean: "Sure, you guys sit down and take a load off," because he pulled two chairs over from an empty cubicle next to us. I took Martinez's silence to mean: "I don't want to talk to you, you scumbags," but then that's the difference between me and Paoli—he's the optimist; I'm the realist. Paoli and I sat down, and Martinez kept watching us with mistrust. It really made me wish I had remembered to bring my Birkenstocks.

"How do you like your workstation?" I asked, pointing to the ICI Series Ten sitting on his desk. "I worked at ICI as head of special development projects. The Series Ten is what we used for graphical interface development. I gave input to the Series Ten team on the graphics accelerator," I said, just to let Martinez know that I was a techno-dweeb.

Martinez tipped his head to one side and gave me a sidewise look. "I like it. The throughput on the SCSI disk could be faster."

He was testing me now. My eyes locked on his. "They're doubling the bandwidth in the next model. You'll see a forty-megabyte throughput, a new I/O optimizer, and an SCSI adapter for peripherals."

"Specmarks?" he asked, applying additional pressure.

"No audits yet, but my guess is you'll see 100 MIPS and 8 MFLOPS." Slam dunk. I had spoken his language, and part of the wall between us came tumbling down. Although

I wore a dress and heels, deep down I was as much a computer geek as any of them.

"So, how long did you work with Arnie?" Paoli asked.

Martinez weighed his options for a moment, then resigned himself to our being there. He rolled his chair to face us, keeping his popcorn possessively on his lap.

"Actual length of time or what it seemed like?" he said, his voice sardonic.

I smiled. "Actual length of time."

"About two years. Maybe a little less. Seemed like aeons, he was such a pain to work for." Martinez paused to put some popcorn in his mouth. "Why are you asking me these questions?" he said, exposing the soggy popcorn bits on his teeth. "I answered all these questions after they arrested him. I never knew what he was doing. I just worked for him. If somebody suspects me of something, I wish they would come out in the open with it. I don't appreciate these insinuations."

"Hold it," said Paoli. "We're not insinuating anything. Lufkin has bolted and we need to find him. Nobody suspects you of anything that I know of."

This placated Martinez. I could tell by the relaxed way he used his little finger to dig out some leftover popcorn from his molar. He flicked it across the cubicle but didn't aim it in our direction. I think that meant he was warming to us.

"I don't know anything about the money Arnie stole. I've never even accessed the accounting system. They can check the logs. I was working on the space-walk programming. That's all."

"Tell me about that," I said.

Martinez's face brightened. "We were working on a virtual reality program that simulated space walks. It simulated antigravity and weightlessness. You could float tethered around a space shuttle and practice fixing mechanical problems and other stuff. Very cutting-edge."

"So what happened to the project?" Paoli asked.

"It's slowed down to practically nothing without Arnie," Martinez answered with unconcealed bitterness.

"We want to know a little more about Lufkin," I said. "If you could give us your impressions of him it might help us."

Martinez just looked at me.

"What type of guy was he?" asked Paoli.

Now Martinez leaned forward. "Quiet. Intense. He could be charismatic when he wanted to be, when he thought it would get him something. And women liked him. But when you got to know the real Arnie, you found out he was sort of strange."

"How so?"

Martinez shrugged. "Well, like I said, he could be real charming when he wanted to. He liked to play with people, string them along. I think he did it so he could feel power over them. But he had a mean streak. If you crossed him, he didn't take it well." Martinez suddenly looked uncomfortable. "Maybe it wasn't all his fault. The guy worked too hard. He was heavily in troglodyte mode. It was a daily thing with him."

"Excuse me?" Paoli said.

"Troglodyte means heads-down, superintensive programming," I explained.

"Exactly," Martinez said. "I would get here in the morning sometimes and find Lufkin still in his office from the night before. He liked to turn off the lights, put on his wraparound sunglasses and his headphones, and program all night. Way too concentrated for way too long a period. That sort of thing burns brain cells."

Paoli and I nodded our agreement, and Martinez continued.

"Virtual reality projects had profit potential, but, jeezus, it wasn't like it was a cure for cancer or would bring peace to the free world. Not that Arnie was interested in making money for the company. All he cared about was the work and how much personal glory he could get from it. Our project costs were starting to go higher than our original budget. Way higher. The project was fun, a programmer's dream, but we should have cut back. But Arnie was obsessed. VR was like a religion with him.''

"And you didn't go along with that?''

"I mean, I have a life, you know. He wanted me to work on it all the time. Nights, weekends, the whole bit. He tried to get everyone else to do the same, and we did for a while, but it got to be too much.

"I also think Arnie wasn't logging the real amount of hours we were putting into the project. Once Chambers tried to give Arnie an extra project to work on and Arnie blew up. He yelled at Chambers in front of everybody, told him that the project was critical to the company and that he didn't have time to work on menial stuff.''

"From what little I know about Chambers, I don't think he would appreciate being called down in front of other people,'' Paoli said.

Martinez laughed out loud, obviously relishing the memory. "Arnie called Chambers mentally deficient in front of half the department; then he challenged him to an IQ test and offered to set up a betting pool. Chambers didn't do it, of course. He knew he wouldn't come close to winning, and no one would have bet a nickel on him.''

"Why didn't he fire Lufkin?'' asked Paoli.

"Because Chambers couldn't afford to lose him. He would just go work for a competitor.''

"But if Arnie was so busy working on the space-walk project, how did he find the time to hack into Anco's general ledger?''

"Maybe that's what he was doing at night. You see, it got to be a grudge thing,'' Martinez said, starting to sound friendlier as his discourse ran to gossip.

"Tell me about it,'' I said.

Martinez was on a roll now. He slid his chair closer to us so he could lower his voice. "Chambers was given the job to find a new security software program for the mainframe. Arnie said he could write the security software himself, but Chambers wouldn't let him. He said he could buy a better program than Arnie could write, since it wasn't Arnie's field of expertise. Arnie hated that. The idea of someone doubting his intelligence, well, it made him furious. I think at first he broke into Anco's security software just to show Chambers he could do it, to make Chambers look bad. But then other ideas came into his head."

"Other ideas?"

"Arnie had this dream of starting his own company, and he needed money for that. He had spent some time looking for start-up capital, but anybody willing to back him wanted some control. Arnie could never handle that. He had to do it on his own so he could control it completely. So by stealing from Anco he could get the money he needed and get back at Chambers. And believe me, it worked. Chambers looked like a fool. There was a rumor going around that he almost got fired. Obviously he's still here, but he got demoted." Martinez stopped to take a breath, then looked at his watch. "Look, I've gotta get back to work now."

"Just one more question," I said. "Is there anyone here who might have known Arnie better? Someone we could talk to?"

"Sure. Miranda. She was on his project team. She spent more time with him than anyone else. The girl followed him around like a dog. Some people thought they were dating, but I don't know that for sure. She's the one you should talk to."

Paoli checked the list of names Chambers had given him. "What's her last name?" he asked.

"Owens. She used to sit two cubicles over, but she moved to another project about a month ago. I don't know what building she's in now."

Paoli looked at me. "She's not on the list Chambers gave us. I wonder why."

"Let's go ask him," I said.

A smile crossed Martinez's face; he obviously enjoyed the idea of stirring up a little trouble for Chambers.

Paoli and I thanked Martinez, left him with his programming and his popcorn, and headed back to Chambers's office. Chambers looked up at us with the sort of welcoming expression people normally reserve for hemorrhoids.

"What is it now?"

"Why didn't you give us Miranda Owens's name? Martinez said she and Lufkin were tight. So why isn't she on the list?" asked Paoli.

Chambers looked irritated for a moment, then relaxed. "Because she's off balance, that's all. Don't go telling Arlene that I'm holding back on you, because I'm not. I didn't want you to waste your time with her. Miranda's a good worker, but she's reclusive. Too much rap music or something. You can talk to her if you want. She's over in M-Two."

"Where's that?" I asked.

"One building over. Go back to the lobby out the front doors, and turn right. It's across the parking lot. She's on the third floor on the east side. I'll call ahead and let security and her know you're coming. She wouldn't talk to you otherwise. She still probably won't talk to you."

"Thanks," I said as Paoli and I turned to leave. I heard Chambers chuckle.

"Good luck. You're gonna need it," he said as we walked out the door. I could feel his nasty little grin burning into my back.

We walked over to the M-Two building, got new badges from security, and took the elevator to the third floor, which was thick with cubicles. We negotiated our way through them and asked a few people where we could find Miranda Owens. The first two gave us blank looks and a shake of their heads, but the third person pointed to a doorway. We entered a large supply room and I saw a girl standing in front of a photocopy machine in one corner. She was busy feeding something into one of those copiers the size of a Pontiac that print in color, collate, staple, and shine your shoes for you.

"Miranda?" I said.

She turned. She looked about twenty-five, with melancholy brown eyes, a diamond stud pierced through one nostril, and straggly hair dyed an inky black, a color so flat and dull it seemed to soak up the light. As she turned, a strand of the stuff fell across one eye, but she didn't bother to brush it away. A shapeless gray smock hung on her thin frame, and she wore heavy black shoes and lacy white socks. She looked the way I had always imagined the orphans in Dickens novels. But in spite of her lack of fashion sense, there was a prettiness about her. Her features were delicate and her skin as luminous as a pearl.

"Yeah?" she answered.

I introduced Paoli and myself. She looked at us with disinterest until I told her why we were there. When I mouthed Lufkin's name she came to attention. She turned back toward the copier and thrust her finger at a button. "Leave me alone."

"We just want to ask you a few questions. It'll only take a minute," I said, and walked a few steps toward her. I could feel a white heat coming from her and I couldn't imagine its source. She raised her hand to her mouth and pressed her fingers hard against her lips. I saw she had lovely thin fingers and noticed a gold ring on her right hand. The ring had an Egyptian-looking symbol that looked like a sun etched in black. It took her a moment to regain her composure, and when she did her hand fell back at her side.

"Fuck you," she said. I didn't get offended, knowing from experience that computer types could be low on communication skills.

"Hey, wait a minute," said Paoli, injecting his manliness into the situation, but I silenced him with a look. I figured Miranda would require a different approach.

"Arnie's missing," I said. "There are people worried about him. We're just trying to find him, that's all. We thought you might be able to help us."

"I've said everything I'm gonna say to cops."

"We're not the cops. We're just private citizens looking for Arnie."

"Yeah, right. Who's paying you?"

"Both Alan Chambers and Arlene Gallagher know we're here and what we're doing. You can call one of them if you want. We'll wait."

Her face twisted into a smirk. "Arnie didn't have any friends except me."

"Why were the two of you such good friends?"

"Because we both had lousy childhoods," she said, her voice thick with contempt. "Get out of here. Get away from me. I'm not telling you anything. They can fire me if they want. I don't care."

"You don't care about finding Arnie?" asked Paoli.

Her lower lip quivered, but her eyes remained hard. She was in love with him. Head over heels, up to her eyeballs, in love with Arnie Lufkin. What kind of cologne did this guy wear that he could inspire such passion and loyalty from women as different as Lorna and Miranda?

Did she loathe the idea of talking with us about him because the conversation would diminish her romantic notions of the relationship, or did she have something to hide? If Arnie was as smart as everyone said, I doubted that he would have confided secret information to Miranda. Like me, she wore her emotions on the outside.

"Could you answer just one question for us?" I asked.

"Sure. Let me give the answer in advance." She turned to the copier and hit the copy button. When the machine spit out a sheet of paper, she held it up for us to see. It was the photocopied shadow of her hand with the middle finger sticking up.

I thanked her for her help, and Paoli and I made our exit. For lack of a better place to go, we ended up in a corner of the third-floor lobby outside the elevators.

"Not exactly Miss Congeniality, was she?" Paoli said when he was sure we were alone. "I think she knows more than she's telling, but she's not talking because she wants to protect Lufkin."

"Even if she doesn't know anything, she's so crazy about Lufkin that she would still fight like a tiger to protect him," I said.

Paoli shook his head. "I don't get what's so hot about Lufkin. Both Lorna and Miranda are wacko over the guy. What's he got going for him? He's not that great-looking."

"You mean you don't know?"

His face registered surprise. "You mean you do?"

"Let me explain it to you. Lufkin is a pretty good-looking guy, at least I think he is from the photo we saw. But that's not what attracts these women to him. It's something else."

"Lorna did say he was hung like a Brahma bull."

"That's not it, Paoli, but it's close. Lufkin is powerful to these women. He's self-confident, brilliant, and brutish, both emotionally and physically. Women with self-esteem problems go for that. He chooses women that he knows he can have power over, women with a gaping hole he can fill. Miranda seems like an emotional cripple, and Lorna's looking for someone to build up her self-image. Remember when Lorna said she liked to read about smart people? The woman has an inferiority complex the size of Nebraska. Believing that Lufkin loved her meant she could love herself."

Paoli looked at me a moment before responding. "I think you're complicating something that's nice and simple. I'm still thinking it's the Brahma bull thing."

So much for Deep Thought. "Let's forget it for now and take a look at Chambers's list. We have several other people to talk to, and I have things to do back at the office."

As far as I was concerned, things were going well. Our activity at Anco had banished the poem from my mind, and although we hadn't accomplished much, at least we were out in the working world, and I was getting more mental exercise than I'd had in months.

We managed to interview the other three names on Chambers's list that afternoon. Programmers normally just sit in their cubicles all day working at their computers, so they're not hard to catch. Two of the programmers Chambers had referred us to didn't have much to offer in terms of Lufkin info, but the third interview proved fruitful.

Reza Singhania was a man in miniature, about five-four, with small hands and feet, giving you the feeling he had been placed on a Xerox machine and reduced by 20 percent. His skin was dark, his face handsome, his black hair slicked back with something that looked like it belonged on a crankshaft. He wore a white cotton shirt, loose-fitting plaid pants, and sandals made of plastic you could see through.

"Lufkin had a problem with reality," Singhania said, his voice retaining some of its Indian accent.

Don't we all, I thought but asked him what he meant by the statement.

"Do you know the difference between objective and subjective realities?" he asked us.

"I guess so. I have a feeling you know more about it than I do."

He smiled, exposing the best teeth I've ever seen. "Objective reality is that reality which we all share. The sky looks blue, the grass appears the same green, to almost all of us. The three of us sit here and we agree that we are together at my desk here in the Anco building that is located in San Francisco. This is true?"

Paoli and I nodded. So far, so good, but I wondered where Singhania was taking us.

"But subjective reality is different. Our dreams are subjective reality. There are no rules, no boundaries, no laws that govern. Virtual reality combines the two, both the subjective and the objective. It creates a new reality where there are no rules. We make the reality whatever we want. We can see it, touch it, feel it, yet it can be experienced by others." Singhania could tell by our faces he had both of us hooked. He smiled again. "Lufkin used to brag that he could create a new reality in a matter of hours. After he became more involved in the VR work, when he began using the body glove—"

"A body glove?" Paoli asked.

"A nylon suit with cables and electrodes attached. It allows you to enter the virtual reality more completely. You move; you touch; your body feels. You truly experience the new reality. It's very powerful, and that's what I'm getting at. I think Lufkin, as he became more and more entrenched in these new realities he was creating, became confused in some way."

"How do you mean?" I asked.

"It's like this. When you're creating new subjective realities every day, with new rules and new paradigms, then objective reality begins to lose meaning for you. It shrinks in importance. There are people who have fears that VR could be as psychologically addicting as a drug, and comparisons have been made to LSD. Lufkin was always driven, arrogant, completely egocentric, and the virtual reality work deepened that. I think it made him feel he controlled things that no human is really capable of controlling. Do you understand what I'm saying?"

"Like he felt he was the master of the universe or something?" Paoli asked.

Singhania held up a finger. "Exactly. Lufkin believed he was the master of all realities."

FIVE

AT THREE-THIRTY Paoli and I pulled into our office parking lot back in Santa Clara. What had begun as a warm spring day had turned into a grey, rainy mess, complete with snarled traffic—an unusual state of weather for Northern California at that time of year.

Naturally, we didn't have an umbrella. Californians don't think about umbrellas in May. May is a month of constant sunshine, balmy afternoons, and a profusion of spring flowers. Or so says the chamber of commerce.

We did get the profusion of spring flowers. With that year's plentiful rain, Northern California erupted into bloom, with poppies, vinca, and rhododendrons growing out of every patch of ground. Nasturtiums seemed to sprout right out of the sidewalks. Still, Mother Nature has a mean sense of humor in this part of the country. As if earthquakes weren't enough, it refuses to rain more than a trickle for seven years, then it pours until even your armpits feel mildewed. You might even be able to get nasturtiums to grow there.

Late for a meeting at his consulting job, Paoli dropped me off in front of our building and promised to bring a pizza back with him when he returned. He pulled the car up to the curb, but I still got a drenching before I reached the front door.

Once inside, I shook myself off, checked my voice mail for messages then made a phone call to my best friend, Maxine LaCoste. When I told her I needed her help on a case, I could hear her perfectly formed nose turning up over the phone. Although Max had been in the computer business for years and was currently a manager at Comtech, she was strictly on the marketing side, and she assumed if Paoli and I were involved in a case it had to be some technical mishmash that would bore her. But when I told her we were looking for a missing person she perked up, even though she knew it was really Wayne Hansen's help I was after.

Hansen was a boy wonder and founder of Comtech, a biotechnology software firm I had worked with at ICI. Max had told me over lunch months earlier that Comtech was dabbling in virtual reality for a medical imaging application for surgeons. With the virtual reality program Hansen had conceived, surgeons could use VR to practice difficult operations using a diagnostic image of the patient. I thought Comtech would be a good place for me to begin some quick research into VR technology.

When it came to asking Wayne Hansen for favors, I didn't dare do the deed myself. I was not one of his favorite people, mainly because I refused to kowtow to him like everyone else in town, and when Hansen and I got together it was usually a contest to see who could be the most annoying. Hansen always won. But Max was my ace in the hole, especially since she and Hansen had gotten engaged two months earlier.

I told her I needed access to VR equipment, and she promised to get back to me soon. "Soon" turned out to be five minutes later, because Max had Hansen pulled out of a board meeting. I loved that part. She was the type of woman who could get men to do anything. I couldn't get them to change their socks.

"Jules, if you get over here in the next hour you can use the equipment today, and Wayne says it's okay if you want to talk to his people. He had three developers working on the VR project. It's not the full-body type of development you're after, not yet, but it'll give you a start."

"You're my hero, Max," I joked.

She laughed. "I know. It's such a burden. How soon can you get here?"

I glanced out the window. "It's still raining, so the traffic's going to be bad. I could be there in twenty minutes, but I don't want you to drop everything because of me."

"Don't worry about it. There's not much to drop. Ever since Wayne and I got engaged, everyone's afraid to ask me to do any work. They tiptoe around me like I was Princess Di. At first I thought it was funny, but now I'm getting bored with not enough to do all day."

"That's what you get for sleeping with the boss. I'll do my best to keep you entertained for a while. See you in twenty minutes."

After putting Lorna's CDs in my purse, I got in the Toyota and fought the traffic toward Comtech. Thirty minutes later I was in the Comtech lobby, and Max walked up looking her usual extravagant self.

"I haven't seen you in days. How's your sex life?" she joked, knowing I wouldn't tell her, even though Max could go on endlessly about hers. "I have to tell you that personally, I think virtual reality is the next step in mind-warping technology," she said as we walked down a hallway. For a person who had chosen a career in high technology, Max had surprisingly little patience with it.

"What's wrong with it?"

She gave me a look. "Why do you think these technical types devote so much of their time to machines?" She didn't give me time to answer. "Reality avoidance. They can't deal with day-to-day life, so they wrap themselves up in computers and software. Now with virtual reality, they not only get to avoid reality, they get to create their own. Why do you think Wayne is pouring so much money into it?"

"From what I've read, certain types of applications could be very profitable."

"Ha." She gave her long black hair a toss. "The money's secondary, tertiary even. Wayne's sinking millions into it because VR's the ultimate technoid toy, the final mind-bending extension of video games. Do you know they're developing virtual reality sex?''

"I hadn't heard that, although it sounds interesting."

"I'm all for a little safe sexual experimentation, but having sex with a machine is over the top in my book. Although a machine could come in handy sometimes, and computers don't require batteries. Did you know Wayne works twenty-hour days sometimes? And when he's not working he stays up till 2:00 a.m. in his video game room. I'm thinking of having a joystick attached to my panties. If they're successful with VR sex I'll never see him again. Here we are." Max paused at the doorway, and for a moment her expression turned grim. "I'm not joking anymore, Jules. This fascination with VR worries me, especially with Wayne. I promise you, VR is dope for geeks. It's like LSD, only LSD *kills* brain cells. VR makes them mutate." She sighed and the frown evaporated, suddenly replaced with a sly smile. "And speaking of mutations, I have a surprise for you." Max opened the door, letting me pass through first. "Look who's here," she said in a singsong voice.

The desk, chairs, and floor were all piled three feet high with printouts, computer parts, and precariously balanced piles of paper. On a file cabinet in a corner, on top of a stack of books, sat a mannequin's head wearing a beanie with a propeller, and on the window ledge I saw a plastic model of a human eye with half a pair of eyeglasses glued to it. Old movie posters of Tyrone Power, Rita Hayworth, and Joan Crawford hung haphazardly on the walls. With a silent groan, I recognized the perspiring, corpulent mass of flesh bobbing as heavy hands pounded a workstation keyboard. Long strings of greasy dark hair slapped his face as he labored.

"Hi, Eldon," I said. Fingers the size of fish sticks froze in midair as his body slumped over the keyboard like that of a concert pianist who had played the final, soul-draining notes of a Beethoven piano concerto. He twisted in his chair, and I saw the pale face of Eldon Gannoway, one of Wayne Hansen's favorite software developers. Hansen encouraged individuality in the workplace, and no one at Comtech embraced the concept more fully than Eldon. He was swathed in a brown floor-length caftan, with earrings in both ears. It was a different look than the dirty T-shirts and Bermuda shorts he had worn when I had last seen him, although his black plastic glasses were still held together with paper clips.

Max knew that Eldon Gannoway was a man I tried to avoid, although I couldn't fault her for setting up the meeting with him, since I had asked for it. It wasn't that I disliked Eldon. Not at all. It was simply that he was odd to the point where normal conversation proved difficult.

He eyed me up and down. "Julie Blake. So good to see you under more pleasant circumstances."

The last time Eldon and I had talked it had regarded a murder at ICI, and at the time he had been resentful because I had pushed hard on him for information. Now he reached for my hand and kissed it with full, wet lips. "How's the new business? Not going too well, I assume, because you haven't tried to hire me."

"Your kind of genius requires a delicate environment."

His eyelids lowered. "So intuitive of you to recognize it. Max says you're doing some research on virtual reality. I suppose she's already informed you that I've moved into the VR arena."

"Well, not exactly. She saved it as a surprise."

Max and I exchanged smiles.

"I think it was my interest in the time-space continuum that made them realize my ultimate potential. Besides, the mind stagnates without change."

At that point in our discourse, Eldon raised his hands, fanned his fingers, and took a long, deep breath. Holding in the air with his eyes closed, he stood there, not moving, while Max and I looked on. Eldon remained in this motionless state for what seemed a long time. I was getting worried and was at the point of shaking him back to his senses when he let the air out in short, staccato breaths. He opened his eyes and, apparently refreshed, smiled at me. "Now, how can I help you?"

"I just want to take a look at what you're doing with VR," I said, deciding to tell him later about the CDs in my purse. "I've never seen a real VR application. I've only read about them."

Eldon looked gleeful at the chance to impress a neophyte. "How about a little demonstration? The application we're working on isn't close enough to completion for viewing by outsiders, but we have a demo program that will give you an idea of what it's all about. Let me make a phone call and have the workstation set up."

He picked up the phone, had a brief conversation with someone, then led me out of his office into the hallway. When he rose from his chair I noticed he was wearing red hightop tennis shoes underneath his caftan.

Max and I followed him into another office, this one much larger and neater than Eldon's, housing two desks and half a dozen workstations as well as a mass of cables and boxes. A man in a wheelchair was working at a keyboard while another man—young, blond, and of slight build— looked over his shoulder. On top of a bookcase perched a cage holding a large snake, and next to it sat a smaller cage with a couple of what seemed to me anxious-looking mice. I tried not to think about it.

"Randall, Bobby, we have guests," Eldon said. The one standing turned and looked at us while the man in the wheelchair continued working as if we weren't there.

Max stepped forward and extended her hand. "I'm Maxine LaCoste." The younger man looked at her, then at her hand, and shook it with only his fingers. Comtech wasn't a large company, but being a marketing manager, Max made a point of staying away from its engineers. Of course I was sure that everyone in the company knew Max, at least by sight.

"This is Bobby. Bobby, this is Julie Blake. And this is Randall."

The guy in the wheelchair stopped typing and turned toward us. "I've got the demo ready," he said. "The goggles are over there."

Bobby picked up a pair of heavy plastic glasses with dark lenses and handed them to me.

"These will give you the 3-D effect. Sit here."

Randall pushed a button on the arm of his wheelchair and moved in reverse, then forward to the right so Bobby could push a chair up to the workstation.

I sat down. On the screen in front of me I could see some blurry shapes and colors, but when I put on the glasses they burst into sharp outlines and bright hues.

"Hold the wand," said Bobby. He stuck a pen-shaped object in my hand. It was black plastic and connected to the workstation by a thin cable. "What do you see in front of you?"

"A red ball. It looks like it's floating."

"Point the wand at the ball and turn it."

I tried it. Pointing the wand at the ball, I moved the wand to the right, and the ball revolved on its axis in the same direction.

"Interesting," I said with a laugh.

"Okay, now bounce the ball," Bobby said.

"How?"

"You'll figure it out."

I moved the wand up and down, and the ball bounced along with it.

"This is great," I said.

"It's hardly that," said Eldon, sounding offended. "This is just a silly little demo to show the effects of human interaction with the program. Once we finish our real application, lives will be saved."

"Okay, my turn," said Max, rather eagerly, I thought, for someone who had condemned VR so vehemently only moments before. I relinquished the goggles and the wand to Max and gave her the chair. I tried to keep my eyes on her and the screen, but I couldn't help looking at the snake. After wheeling his chair over to the cage, Randall reached up and poked his finger through the thin metal bars and cooed softly to the ugly creature.

Eldon saw me watching.

"That's Garbo. She's Randall's pet."

"Cuddly little thing, isn't she?" I whispered so Randall wouldn't hear.

"Beauty, as well as most things, is in the eye of the beholder. Randall's a part-timer and a little weird, I'll admit," Eldon said, his voice now low and gossipy.

I almost choked on that one. Eldon calling somebody weird was like Roseanne Arnold calling someone pudgy.

Eldon continued, "Still, he's gifted and we're trying to get this VR project off the ground. In his spare time Randall's developing a VR program that will simulate walking for paraplegics. He thinks we'll get rich off it."

I think that was the moment that I realized what power this new technology held. The demo they had shown me was very basic. It was interesting but simplistic. Yet the idea that Randall could sit there in his wheelchair unable to use his legs and through VR technology create a world in which he could walk—that was intriguing. I wanted to know more.

"How? You would need equipment much more sophisticated than what you're using here."

Eldon gave me a patronizing look. "We have access to other equipment, but we don't need it yet. Real VR work takes a couple of large workstations and much more complicated goggles and even gloves. This is only a demo. Randall's just getting started anyway. It'll be a couple of months before he's beyond the design stage. He's doing it in the evenings."

"How did he lose the use of his legs?" I asked.

"Car accident. It happened when he was twenty. Both his parents were killed by a drunk driver, and Randall was left in a wheelchair. He told me that's why he started programming. You don't have to move around much."

I looked at Randall with new interest. His hair was red, cut so short the scalp showed through, and he wore the type of round wire-rimmed glasses that John Lennon had once made fashionable.

The sound of Eldon's voice brought back my attention.

"So, Julie, why don't we shorten this little charade and you tell me what you're really after? You were never the type to diddle around, and I doubt that seeing our little VR demo is the real reason you came here."

I smiled, reached into my handbag and pulled out the CDs that Lorna had given me.

"I want you to take a look at these on your workstation and tell me what they are. I think they're VR programs, but I'm not sure."

Eldon took the CDs from me and examined them.

"Why are you so interested?"

"They relate to a case I'm working on, that's all. It's confidential."

Eldon eyed me suspiciously, then smiled. "All right. I'll have a look."

"But keep them to yourself, okay? If you need help with them, you can show them to Hansen, but no one else."

"Why the secrecy?"

"I don't want anyone else to know about them yet. That's why I came to you. I knew I could trust you."

"I thought you didn't know I was working on virtual reality until you saw me today."

I had to think quick. "I just said that to throw the others off."

Eldon's face beamed with pride. He put a finger to his lips. "I'm the soul of discretion."

A high-pitched laugh filled the room, taking Eldon's attention away from me. Max was being very vocal about her enjoyment of the VR program, and I wondered if she had suddenly changed her mind about its evils.

At that moment I noticed the snake loosening the coil of its thick body. I watched as it lifted its head. The mice and I were trying hard not to look at it, but in spite of my efforts I glanced over. I would have sworn the snake was looking at me.

Randall made a few kissing noises at it; then he reached into the mice cage, took one out by its tail, and dropped it in with the snake.

Max, Eldon, and Bobby were too busy bouncing the ball to notice the snake drama being played out, but my blood ran cold. Only Randall knew I was watching, and from the expression on his face, I felt he was enjoying it.

The mouse scurried back and forth, while the snake raised its head, arching the front portion of its body in readiness for attack. I didn't want to watch it, but my eyes were locked on the gruesome sight. The snake's body was motionless now, except for the slightest swaying of its head, its eyes fixed on those of its victim. The mouse froze, dazzled by the snake's stare and by the rhythmic swaying of its head.

The snake lunged forward. I closed my eyes in revulsion and immediately felt a hand on my arm. I opened my eyes. It was Randall.

"It's okay. It happens so fast, the mouse doesn't even feel it."

Something inside me didn't believe him.

I ARRIVED back at the office around six, settling into my comfortable, beloved swivel chair, trying to get the image of the snake and the mouse out of my mind, and before long I felt the old familiar burning in my gut. A few gulps of Maalox eased the fire, and I immersed myself in Deep

Thought about Arnie Lufkin. Around six-thirty the door opened.

"You've got that intense look in your eyes, Julie. Thinking about me?"

I could smell a delicious pizza aroma coming from the box Paoli cradled in his arms. He saw the Maalox on my desk and frowned.

"No, about Arnie Lufkin. I have a theory that proves he's somewhere around Silicon Valley."

"So who needs a theory?" my partner said, tossing the pizza on my desk. "I thought you had already decided Lufkin has been following Lorna. That means he's local."

"Like you said before, he could have had someone else follow her."

"Sure, he could have, but you talked me into agreeing with you. So what's the new theory?"

"I'm trying to think the way Arnie Lufkin thinks, to get inside his head. And I realized that Lufkin and I are a lot alike."

Paoli raised his eyebrows. "Your bust is larger; I'm sure of it." He opened the pizza box and inhaled its lovely aromas.

I ignored the comment. "Lufkin was devoted to virtual reality programming the way I was devoted to Project 6 back at ICI. Project 6 took all my energy. I ate and slept it."

"Agreed, but what's the point?"

"What I'm saying is that Lufkin feels the same way about his VR work. While you were out, I went over to Comtech and saw a virtual reality demo."

"Without me?"

"It wasn't much," I said, purposely downplaying it. "The real reason I went was to talk them into checking out the CDs Lorna gave us. But seeing the demo made me start thinking. I bet anything that Lufkin misses his VR work. He needs to get back to it, to continue his project. But he also needs more. From what I've read, virtual reality work re-

quires sophisticated equipment—two heavy-duty workstations, special goggles, a glove.''

"Couldn't he get that type of equipment himself? He's
got half a million bucks hidden somewhere," Paoli asked as
he took a bit of drippy cheese.

"I don't think he would buy the equipment himself. It
could easily add up to a few hundred thousand dollars. It
would eat up a lot of his money, if he could even get at his
money without risking being traced, which he probably
can't. Buying the equipment is too much exposure from too
many angles. And Lufkin has too big an ego to hole up in a
lonely apartment where the world can't see his work and tell
him how smart he is.''

"But what are his alternatives? He's too well known in
VR circles to get back into a company.''

"We can't be sure. Maybe he has someone covering for
him somehow. Or he's changed his name and works as a
consultant out of his house. The company would provide
equipment for him.''

I felt Paoli's hand on my arm, bringing me to a stop. He
looked at me with affection and held up what was left of his
pizza. "Here; take a bite. You need to eat something.''

"I can't right now. My stomach's on fire.''

"I can run to the Hard Drive and get you some milk.''

I shook my head. "It closes at five. I don't need anything. I'm fine.''

"I know you're fine, but . . .''

"But what?''

He put down his pizza and gave me a hard look. "Just
don't get too worked up over this Lufkin thing. It's not
worth wrecking yourself over.''

"I'm not wrecking myself.''

"Sure, except we're going to have to start buying Maalox
by the industrial drum, right? I thought when you quit ICI
your ulcer days were over.''

"They are. My ulcer's 100 percent better. I just felt funny today, that's all."

"You've gone through a whole bottle in the past week."

"You make me feel like an alcoholic. Should I start hiding my Maalox from you?"

He sighed and put his arms around me. "No, I just don't want you to ruin your health over this stupid business, that's all. If it's too stressful we should quit and move to North Dakota or Boise or anywhere and be programmers. Or maybe we'd be happier moving to Mexico and being bartenders in some beach town."

"I don't want to move to North Dakota or Mexico."

"One of the reasons we started this business was so we could be together. Now all of a sudden I don't feel like we're together anymore, not really. We're in the same room, but you're always wrapped up in worrying about our finances or how we're going to get new business. You're not really here half the time. And now you're worrying about finding Lufkin. Just remember, we don't need this business." He pulled me closer to him.

"We don't need this business? Sometimes your attitudes about life and work amaze me, Paoli." Just then I felt his tongue against my ear and my irritation began to melt.

"Let me show you something that will really amaze you," he said, placing my hand beneath his waist and kissing me, running his mouth against my ear, along my neck and shoulder. Next he unbuttoned my blouse, and in a few moments I had lost, at least temporarily, all concern about Arnie Lufkin, about business, and about the pizza that Paoli was about to sit on. There was no time for etiquette or ceremony. We made urgent love against the desk, removing a minimum of clothes. When we finished we laughed at the tomato sauce on the back of Paoli's shirt, then sat on the floor and ate the remains of the now-mangled pizza.

I brushed a tiny piece of crust off his lip. "Okay, you've relaxed me and gotten me to eat. So now tell me about you day."

"You'll be proud of me. After my meeting I used their li brary and did some research on companies doing VR. Ther are a couple of companies doing intensive virtual reality work that compares with what Anco is doing, and they're all competing for the NASA bid."

"How did you know they're competing for the bid?"

"I still have a few connections. I used to go drinking with a NASA programmer, and I called him. Virtual reality work is sexy, and everyone at NASA knew about it. My friend called one of his friends who called me back and told me the names of the companies. One's in Utah, the other in Sun- nyvale. The Sunnyvale one is D-Quest, and they're only doing minimal VR work, although lately they've been making some advances. D-Quest has been hurting from the defense department cutbacks, and right now they only have one person working on the project."

"And with one person they're making advances?"

"Apparently. It's a woman. Annette Parker. I've already called her, and we have an appointment for tomorrow."

"What about the Utah company?"

"Geo Pro? They have a small team. One of us should fly out there and check it out."

I was cringing at the thought of having to pay the airfare when the phone rang. I picked it up, listened to the caller for about one minute, then hung up.

"We won't be looking for Arnie Lufkin anymore," I said. Paoli looked stunned. "Why not?"

"That was Lorna on the phone. Lufkin jumped off the Golden Gate Bridge."

Ten minutes later I stepped into the dank, smoke-filled environs of the Rainbow Lounge, a dingy bar in a strip mall a few miles away from our office. I paused in the entryway and saw strings of colored Christmas lights draped in an arc across one wall creating the alleged rainbow affect touted on the half-lit neon sign outside. A fish tank sitting on one end of the bar contained three naked-from-the-waist-up plastic mermaids but no visible fish. Little bubbles streamed from the mermaids' mouths in a manner that made them look like they were puking.

After Lorna told me about Lufkin's unscheduled trip off the bridge, she had given me the address of the Rainbow Lounge and asked me to meet her, her voice filled with the slurred and miserable neediness of someone who had grown tired of drinking alone. There were things we had to discuss, she insisted. I assumed the topic would be the twenty-five-hundred-dollar check she would be wanting back. I didn't feel that bad about the check. All I had lost was money. Lorna had lost the love of her life.

My eyes adjusted to the darkness, which didn't improve the looks of the place. I could see that the bar's patrons were a different crowd than the usual Silicon Valley professional types I was used to. The clientele were mostly men, and they all looked a little haggard and sweaty.

I found Lorna at the bar, her body hunched over a shot glass of amber liquid. I walked over to her, and when she turned her face toward me her expression took me by surprise. After the weeping fit she had over Arnie the previous day in my office I now expected to find her in tears, but instead she looked steely. She patted the seat next to her and I sat down.

"Tell me about Arnie. What happened?"

She looked at me and gave a "que sera sera" shrug. "Somebody called in a 911 around 3:00 a.m. They said they saw a jumper on the bridge. When the cops showed up, all they found was a note from Arnie saying that he was killing himself because he couldn't stand to go to jail."

"The note was hand-written?" I asked.

Lorna nodded.

The thought of someone taking his own life made my blood run cold. I thought about the poem. If Arnie had really hacked into my computer, he had to have done it Monday night before he killed himself. It didn't make sense to me. "Have they found the body yet?"

Lorna shook her head. "Still lookin'. The tide was going out, and they said they might not find the body at all. He could be halfway to Hawaii with a couple of shark bites in him by now."

The image made me shiver. Lorna picked up her drink and held it up to her left eye, using the liquid as a whiskey lens through which she could view the bar with new perspective.

"If this happened at three this morning, why did it take until this afternoon for you to find out?" I asked her.

She down her drink. "Because they waited around, hoping to find a body to make a positive ID. The cops like a visual ID if they can get it."

"How did you find all this out? Somebody call you?"

She gave me a patronizing smile. "In my line of work you make friends in the police department. You wanna drink?"

I ordered a white wine spritzer, and Lorna and I sat quietly a few minutes. After a few sips of wine, I felt a new warmth in my blood. Lorna ordered a fresh drink for herself, this time on the rocks, took a big swallow, and crunched the ice.

"Thanks for meeting me," she said, breaking our short silence. "I don't have any girlfriends. I don't get invited to many Mary Kay parties, if you get my drift." Her enunciation was starting to get sloppy, and her last phrase sounded like "if you get by dwift," but I got it. I could tell she wanted to talk her insides out, and I was prepared to let her.

"Listen, babe; you and me, we're a lot alike," she continued. "We're professional women at the top of our fields. We're tough, can-do girls," she said, then waved her index finger an inch from my nose. Her voice got low and whis-

pery. "Yet we haven't lost touch with our feminine side."
She then picked up her drink, tossed down the remains of it
in one swallow, and slammed the glass back down on the
bar. "I just wanted to talk to you, you know, alone. Get
your perspective on stuff. I guess it would have been polite
to ask Vic along, too, but I wanted to talk girl talk."

I chewed on that one. I wasn't sure what Lorna's idea of
girl talk entailed, but I envisioned discussions of hairy-
chested truck drivers, garter belts, and neon-colored con-
doms. Studying Lorna's face, I thought she looked younger
in the dim lighting. But then, who doesn't?

She waved over the bartender and ordered tequila shots.
I told her I didn't like tequila, but she was insistent.

"Just one little shot. It'll make me feel better if you do it.
Be a good sport. Pleez?"

I agreed, against my better judgment, but I wanted to
make Lorna happy. The bartender poured a liquid the color
of urine into two shot glasses; then he put two wedges of
lime on a paper napkin and handed Lorna a salt shaker. I
had seen people do this, but I never had myself. When I
picked up my shot glass to take a sip, Lorna stopped me.

"No, babe, like this." She made a fist with her left hand,
licked one end of it, then covered it with salt. I did the same.
"Now pick up your glass. I have a toast." I picked up my
glass as Lorna stood up and faced the bar patrons sitting at
tables. "Here's to the men that we love. Here's to the men
who love us. But the men that we love aren't the men who
love us, so to shit with the men, here's to us." She licked the
salt, tossed down the tequila, then sucked on the lime, and
I followed right behind, although I grabbed my throat and
made an "ugh" sound. The males in the room didn't seem
impressed with the toast, but a table of women in the corner hooted appreciatively.

A pleasant glow washed over me as the tequila entered my
bloodstream. The bartender asked us if we wanted another

round. Lorna ordered tequila for herself. I asked for another spritzer.

"Are you in love with Vic?" she asked when she sat back down beside me.

Her question threw me. "I don't know. I guess I am."

"You don't sound so sure."

"It's just that I don't trust my judgment about men anymore."

"How come? You're so smart, so educated and everything."

I laughed. "I'm not too smart. I was engaged not that long ago to a guy I worked with, and it didn't turn out very well."

"So what? I've been engaged three times, and they've all turned out like shit. I thought things would be different with Arnie. He made me feel different. All my life the only guys I attracted were lowlifes—big talkers, but no heart and no brains. But Arnie, he was so smart and everything, and still a real animal in the sack. I thought if a guy like that could love me, then I was a better person than I thought I was. Arnie said I had entered spaces inside him where no woman had ever been. It sort of raised my self-esteem. Do you get what I mean?"

I nodded. I could see tears in her eyes and she looked on the verge of a major crying jag. My heart went out to her, but no encouraging words bubbled out of me. Arnie had used her, beaten her, then abandoned her. He was also possibly dead—emphasis on the possibly.

I retrieved a clean Kleenex from my handbag and gave it to her, and she took it and smiled. When she blew her nose she made a honking sound. I took a check that I had written earlier out of my purse and pushed it across the bar to her. She stared down at it, not touching it.

"What's this?"

"It's your twenty-five hundred."

She pressed the check with her index finger and pushed it back to me. "Keep it."

"Why?"

She smiled. "Because you and I both know that Arnie's not dead."

I set my wine spritzer down on the bar and decided to play devil's advocate. "It's unlikely that Arnie survived that jump, Lorna."

"So who says he jumped?" she said casually.

"You did. The police did."

"Nope. The cops said they found a note. They never found an actual Arnie."

"But didn't the person who called 911 see him jump?"

"She only said she saw someone about to jump. She didn't say she saw Arnie jump. They played the tape of the call for me." Lorna put her hand over mine and looked hard into my eyes. "Just keep looking for him. Arnie's not the kill-himself type. Arnie's the type who thinks he can outsmart everybody. Just keep looking for him. I'll start paying by the hour if you want."

"If Arnie's declared dead, at least legally, wouldn't you get your bond money back?"

"I care about the money, but I care about Arnie more." Lorna stared pensively at her drink. "Arnie and I were engaged. I thought we were gonna get married and have a household of children." She looked up from her drink, and her expression grew wistful. "Maybe we still can."

"You never told me about that part."

"Yeah, he gave me a ring." Lorna held up her small hand and pointed to her ring finger. When I saw it I almost choked on my drink. It was gold with black etchings, just like the ring I had seen on Miranda's hand earlier. "It's real different, isn't it?" I nodded. "Arnie was a really different kind of guy." She held up what was left of her tequila. "Let's drink to that. To Arnie, a real different kind of guy."

I raised my glass and tapped it against hers. Her eyes narrowed and her expression hardened. Lorna's eyes turned steely. "Just keep looking for him," she said. "Just keep looking."

SIX

I HAD TROUBLE sleeping that night. Maybe it was because too many questions about Arnie Lufkin kept rolling around my brain like Lotto balls at the Big Spin, or maybe it was the tequila mixed with the cheap white wine. Lorna had insisted on buying me another spritzer after our maudlin toast to Arnie, and this time I watched the bartender pour the yellow liquid from a large jug. A rare vintage it was not. Wine usually gave me a headache, and now I knew that cheap wine mixed with tequila gave me a headache that made my head feel like it was going to fall right off my neck.

After her third whiskey, Lorna underwent a transformation. She stopped grieving and starting singing old Supremes songs, doing several renditions of "Stop in the Name of Love." Loudly and with hand motions, I might add. After that the jokes began, all of them raunchy, about penises and hunting dogs and sexual encounters gone awry. If only I could remember them. She was still going strong at ten o'clock, when I put her in a cab and sent her home. When my cab dropped me at my house at ten-thirty I found Paoli lying in my bed in his underwear watching an old horror movie and eating pretzels. I had given him a key a few months before, and, although I loved having him around, sometimes I longed for solitude. This was one of those times. When he saw me he put down his pretzels, pointed the remote control at the TV, and turned it off just before the Mummy finished up a one-handed strangulation of an unwitting victim. But I already knew that the victim should never have disturbed the princess's tomb.

"Julie, I've been going nuts trying to find out what really happened with Lufkin. I called the police and the Golden Gate Bridge Authority, but no one would tell me anything. What did Lorna tell you?"

Paoli was standing now, and his underwear caught my attention because he normally wears boxer shorts, but tonight he was wearing the kind of briefs that in college we used to call "tightie whities." The man knows how to keep a relationship fresh.

I threw my purse and jacket on a chair. "She says Lufkin didn't jump. She wants us to keep looking for him."

"Does she know for sure? Has she heard from him since last night?"

"No, she's going on instinct, but I agree with her. From the little I know about him, Lufkin's not the type for suicide."

"Have you been drinking?"

"A little. I was being a good sport."

"So we've still got a job?"

I nodded. He grinned and raised a fist in the air. The man looked really good in his underwear, but I was too tired to do anything about it.

After filling him in on the rest of my conversation with Lorna, excluding the part where we had talked about whether or not I loved him, I exchanged my suit for one of Paoli's T-shirts and crawled into the warm bed beside him.

When I finally drifted off to sleep I dreamed about Lufkin. He was standing on the Golden Gate Bridge, his thin body balanced precariously on the railing. I was there with him, but on the walkway below, begging him not to jump, but he just looked at me, smiling. And then he leaped off the bridge, his body sailing through the air until, in midflight, he broke into a hundred bloody pieces.

By seven-thirty the next morning I was back in the office, dressed in a gray suit and new control-top panty hose that made my thighs feel like they were in a vise. And in spite of the tequila and white wine I had consumed the night before, I was feeling pretty good. Sitting at my desk and sipping coffee, I kept thinking about how Lufkin could have faked a suicide. Even if the person who had called 911 never actually saw Lufkin jump, surely someone would have spotted him walking away. And although all of this had happened at three in the morning, there would still be cars on the Golden Gate Bridge. Someone would have seen him. Or would they? A person dressed in dark clothes could have been missed in the bridge's amber lighting, especially if that person didn't want to be seen. There were posts to hide behind, dark corners where one could be concealed.

And then an even more unpleasant thought crossed my mind. Lorna had said that Arnie wasn't the type to kill himself. But he could have been pushed. That was an option we hadn't considered. As for the note he had left, it could easily have been left by the killer. But then what about the woman who had dialed 911? My mind negotiated the possibilities. Maybe it was the killer she had seen standing on the railing. Or maybe she had been the killer. Would a woman have the strength to push someone off a bridge? It was possible. And a guy who passed around engagement rings the way Lufkin did was bound to make a few female enemies. The image of Miranda surfaced.

I decided to call the police later that morning and ask them about the mystery woman who had dialed 911 and about Arnie's suicide note. Maybe they wouldn't talk to me, but it was worth a try. Since the note had been hand-written, I wondered if the police had checked it against other samples of Lufkin's handwriting.

While I concentrated, I realized that I enjoyed sifting through the fragments of Lufkin's disappearance. It was like a computer program that doesn't work right, and it was my nature to sort it out, to analyze the program line by line until I identified the glitch. This analytical temperament of mine had been developed in spite of my upbringing. My mother had wanted me to be a ballerina. I had danced on tiptoe dressed in pink tutus from the age of five, but the problem was that I was a rotten dancer. After years of my stumbling, my mother finally gave up and left me to my own desires, which, to her dismay, focused mainly on mathematics.

My body cried out for caffeine and I was getting ready to head out for the Hard Drive when the phone rang. I answered it, and a woman told me that a Mr. McCracken wanted to see me.

"Who is Mr. McCracken?"

There were a few seconds of silence on the line. "President of Anco," she replied icily.

"Is this about Arnie Lufkin?"

I could hear her sigh with administrative exasperation. "Mr. McCracken asked me to get you into his office as early this morning as possible. He did not tell me why."

I checked my watch. Eight-thirty. This was starting to get my interest. "I'll be there in an hour."

As soon as I hung up I called Arlene Gallagher to find out what was going on. Her secretary, Monique, was in, but Gallagher wasn't. Next I called my house, but Paoli didn't answer, probably too sound asleep. I scribbled a note for him saying where I was going, and after a quick stop at the Hard Drive for a cappuccino and turning down Lydia's offer of a doughnut, I was on Highway 101 headed toward San Francisco. It couldn't hurt to network with a company president. I would impress him with my knowledge and my impeccable credentials, maybe get some referrals from him. A guy like that had to be well connected.

An hour later I was sitting in the reception area outside Andrew McCracken's office. I waited over fifteen minutes, and I made sure I looked at my watch frequently to make the receptionist think I had many pressing appointments. She finally told me I could go in.

The office was expensively contemporary with thick tan carpeting, soft leather furniture the color of a dove, and a massive table that served as McCracken's desk. Through the glass wall I could see San Francisco Bay stretching its glistening blue toward Oakland. We're talking top-dollar square footage here. I admit I was impressed.

McCracken was almost as attractive as his surroundings. Sitting at his desk, a fan of papers in front of him, he looked like he was in his midforties, not pretty-boy handsome, but with a clean, athletic strength to him, even though his eyes looked tired. He was starting to go bald, but it didn't look bad on him. His jacket was off, his shirt sleeves rolled up. He looked intelligent, successful, and industrious, the kind of man with whom I had always pictured myself. I wondered if Paoli was out of bed yet.

McCracken looked up but didn't smile. "Ms. Blake, thanks for coming on such short notice. Have a seat."

I sat and immediately felt the pinch of my control tops, and I was glad I had passed up that doughnut.

"I'm sure you're wondering why I asked you here like this," he said, sounding weary, like a man with troubles.

"I'm assuming it has to do with Arnie Lufkin."

McCracken pressed his palms together in front of him. Nice hands—tan, the fingers long and thick, reminding me of certain bodily correlations we used to discuss in high school gym class. The idea made me want to laugh, but I stifled the urge.

"Let me explain," he said. "Arlene Gallagher told me someone had hired you to find Lufkin and that she was providing you with whatever assistance she could. We don't normally do things like that. Help investigators, I mean." He smiled, and I could tell this part of the conversation made him feel awkward. He picked up a pencil and twisted it in his fingers. "To protect Anco's interests I had someone look into your background."

It shouldn't have surprised me, yet it did. I narrowed my eyes and studied McCracken. "You looked into my background? You investigated the investigator?"

He didn't blink. With me now on the defensive, his confidence had returned. "Yes. I felt it was necessary, but don't concern yourself with it. I learned some things about your years with ICI. Also about your partner. The two of you have impressive résumés."

"Thank you." Aw, shucks, Mr. McCracken. I wondered where all this was leading.

"The bottom line is, I want to hire you to investigate our general ledger and security software."

My pulse quickened. "The software that Lufkin broke into?" I asked. "Alan Chambers told us it had been archived."

"It was, but we're having problems again, this time with the new software. Someone is getting our payment authorization codes."

I did my best to freeze my face so McCracken couldn't see my excitement. *This could be it, Julie. This could be the opportunity you've been looking for. But don't get overanxious. Stay calm. Get the facts first.*

"Arlene Gallagher told me it was against Anco policy for someone outside the company to tinker with general ledger files."

His mouth tightened, and he tossed the pencil across his desk. "I'm the one who makes company policy, and right now I'm making a new one. I want someone to investigate our security software and our general ledger software, past and present. The data processing staff here had looked into it, but they can't figure it out. We need outside help. We need you."

I wanted to jump up and shout hallelujah, do a tap dance on his desk, then maybe plant a kiss on his cheek. Maybe even kiss his secretary. But I managed to sit quietly a moment so he would think I was considering his proposition. I figured three seconds was long enough.

"I'm hired," I told him, and he looked relieved. "We'll need to discuss the fee, of course. We charge a five-thousand retainer up front, then charge a hundred an hour. That's for each of us. We invoice the balance once the job is completed." I held my breath.

"Sounds reasonable," McCracken said, much too easily. I could have kicked myself for not asking for more, but I was still thrilled. "Then you can jump right on it?"

Like a fat lady on a milk shake, I thought. "Let's start now," I said to let him know that I was, as Lorna put it, a can-do kind of girl. "When did you first find out that someone broke into your software? This time, I mean."

"Yesterday morning. A purchase order for ten thousand dollars with the correct authorization code went to accounts payable. Fortunately, it didn't get paid."

"How did you catch it?"

"Someone in accounting saw the transaction in the ledger and checked on the paperwork before the check went out. There was no paperwork. Someone had gotten into the general ledger software and simply authorized a check payment."

"Is this the same way Lufkin stole money? By authorizing check payments?"

"No. Lufkin was much more thorough, but at the time he had access to all the necessary documentation. He would make up fake purchase orders. As a level-two manager he had authorization to sign for purchases up to five thousand. Normally after someone has requested a purchase order it has to go through accounting to get an authorization code. Those codes are confidential and get changed daily. But Lufkin got inside our security software and stole the codes, so the purchase orders had signatures and authorization codes. Accounts payable automatically printed the checks. The checks went to about ten fake consulting firms, somewhere between three and five thousand a month to each firm.''

"Wouldn't somebody notice that kind of money going out?"

McCracken laughed without smiling. "No. Anco is a 20 billion dollar corporation. We work on very large contracts, both industrial and federal, and we've always used a lot of outside consultants. In the past two years we've been using them even more, trying to cut down on overhead. The money Lufkin stole wasn't that noticeable compared to Anco's monthly budget.''

"So how did you catch him?"

"Ordinarily we wouldn't have, but it was a fluke. We had hired an accounting temp to fill in for someone who had the flu, and the temp misfiled some purchase orders. When the regular person came back to work he couldn't find the POs and had to call some of the vendors to get tax IDs. In the process he found out that one of the companies didn't exist and Lufkin had signed for the purchase.''

So Alan Chambers had lied when he said he had figured out that Lufkin had been stealing. It made me feel sorry for Chambers that he would have to lie about something like that just to boost his ego.

McCracken continued. "After that we discreetly started checking all the purchase orders signed by Lufkin. There was a six-month period in which Lufkin stole over four hundred thousand. For some reason he had stopped about eight months before we caught on to him. I guess his conscience got the better of him." Something inside me said that was unlikely, but I didn't press it.

"Can you trace the money and get it back?"

"No. We tried, but once the money left Anco, Lufkin transferred it through a series of different accounts in the Antilles and Switzerland. By the time we located it, it was deposited into a nominee corporation in Bermuda.''

"A nominee corporation? I'm not familiar with the term."

"It means a corporation that's held by a representative, or in this case we call them a 'nominee.' Only, quite conveniently, the nominee of this corporation can't be found. Lufkin could have used a dead person's name or the name of someone who's currently unreachable. Maybe someone on an island somewhere or on a sailboat on its way to Tahiti. All we know is that they're untraceable."

"Then how does Lufkin get the money out?"

"That's tricky, but there are ways to do it. He could use an attorney to get the money out, or he could have his name on the company's bank accounts."

"This money that you traced, were you able to locate the entire amount?"

"That's the strange part. We traced close to 1 million dollars. But I'm sure only four hundred thousand came from Anco, because we tracked every single transaction Lufkin made since he began working here. He must have been stealing from some other company. I guess with his computer knowledge he could do it."

Our conversation paused while I thought over McCracken's last statement. I could see how you could embezzle from a company if you worked for that company. You could sign purchase orders. But embezzling money from a company you don't work for would be much tougher. You couldn't create the paperwork, which is exactly how Anco caught on to this latest attempt to steal ten thousand dollars.

"Let's get back to this recent transaction. Do you know exactly when the fake purchase authorization entered your general ledger?"

"Yes. Early yesterday."

"Do you have any suspicions of who did it?"

"I assume it was Lufkin."

"Someone claims to have seen Lufkin jump off the Golden Gate Bridge night before last."

McCracken suddenly looked rattled. "Are you sure?"

"Someone on the Golden Gate Bridge called 911 and said they saw a jumper. The police found a suicide note signed by Lufkin."

McCracken's eyes cast downward as he absorbed the news. "That's terrible. We were all angry as hell about him stealing, but nobody wanted him dead."

"Maybe he isn't."

He looked up again. "I'm not getting you."

"I mean I don't think Lufkin is really dead."

"But you just said someone saw him jump off the Golden Gate Bridge."

"That's not quite the way I heard it. Someone saw someone looking like he was going to jump. They haven't found a body."

"So if Lufkin's alive..." McCracken let the sentence hang.

"The way I see it, I'm sure he knows that the FBI has traced his money, so he can't risk touching it. But he still needs cash, maybe so he can bribe his way out of the U.S. So why not take another shot at embezzling from Anco? Sure, it's going to be tougher since he's not here to physically sign purchase orders, but if I were him I'd consider it worth a shot."

"But doesn't it increase his chances of getting caught?"

"Not really. Lufkin's a game player. He figures the worst-case scenario is that you catch the transaction, but I don't see it increasing your chances of catching him, especially if he confuses things by making everyone think he's dead, even if the confusion's temporary. I'm sure the purchase order you found in your general ledger system was for a dummy corporation with a post office box." McCracken nodded. I stopped a moment and thought. "Of course, there's another possible scenario."

"Which is?"

"That although Lufkin stole the original four hundred thousand, maybe someone else is trying their hand at embezzling, assuming we'll blame it on Lufkin."

"Someone here at Anco?"

"That would seem most likely. Knowing the corporate grapevine, I bet it's gotten around the company that Lufkin got caught because of a fluke. Someone here with some programming knowledge sees that Lufkin almost got away with it, and this person thinks he or she can do a better job. Maybe learn from Lufkin's mistakes."

McCracken was starting to look really worried. I think he saw his corporate bonus growing wings. "Do you think you can help us?" he asked.

"No problem," I said with a smile.

As soon as I left McCracken's office I found a phone and called Paoli.

"How much money did you ask for?" was the first thing out of his mouth when I told him about our new job. He shouted with glee when I told him the amount. To tell you the truth, for the first time in months money didn't matter to me that much. Although the money was wonderful, I was more excited about having our first real job, and potentially a great reference.

"As soon as we hang up I'll call Dayton Electronics and back out of the consulting job."

"Why do that?"

"Because you're going to need me full-time on the Anco case. Beside, we don't need the extra money anymore."

"Hold on, Paoli. We do need the extra money. The payment Lorna gave us only covered our back bills, and Anco's retainer will only cover us for this month and next. We may not see any more money from her or Anco for weeks, maybe months. We've still got to pay the rent." Silence on the line. "You can knock out that program in a week if you

put in two or three hours a day. Come on; you still have
plenty of time to work with me. And I want us to keep
looking for Arnie Lufkin. I still don't think he's dead," I
told my partner, and it seemed to have the effect I wanted.

"Neither do the police. I called Lorna this morning, got
the name of one of her police contacts, and heard the latest
scoop. They're feeling funny about the fact that no body has
turned up. They think he should have washed up somewhere when the tide came in. Lufkin's fair game."

"Great. We need to set up some appointments with people outside Anco who may be a lead on him."

"We can start today with Annette Parker."

"Who's that?"

"Don't you remember? The VR developer for D-Quest.
We have a two-thirty with her."

I checked my watch. Ten-fifteen. We arranged to meet
back at the office at two. I needed time to get set up with a
security ID and password so I could access Anco's software, and if I could get Chambers to put a rush on it I could
have a few hours with the software that day.

When I spoke to Chambers he sighed and pushed a
homegrown form at me to fill out. McCracken had called
Chambers personally and asked that I be given access to the
general ledger software, and as a result Chambers was
treating me with at least a grudging respect. I filled out the
form. Chambers made a phone call to an administrator in
operations, then wrote my ID, password, and access commands on a slip of paper and handed it to me.

"The ID is temporary. You'll have to renew it weekly
through me. When you do your initial log-on you'll be
prompted for a new password," Chambers said, his voice
taking on a dullness when talking about matters less titillat-
ing than the disappearance of Arnie Lufkin.

"I'll take care of it," I said, wondering if I should tell
Chambers I had personally designed the security software

for ICI. I decided against it. I didn't want to impress him too much in one day.

Just to make sure I still knew my place, Chambers led me to a computer terminal stuck in a dark, windowless hole of an office near the back of the building, a former closet suitable for wiggly albino creatures found on the undersides of rocks. Piles of discarded files lay stacked on the floors, and a film of old coffee roughly in the shape of the state of Florida spread across the desktop. The computer screen was covered with smudges as if former users had been trying to read it in Braille, and wads of paper sat crumpled on the chair seat and floor. Chambers smiled as I surveyed my new temporary digs.

"Enjoy," he said as he left.

"I will," I replied with a forced smile. As soon as he was gone I tossed the trash in a wastepaper basket, combined the files into one neat stack, then wetted paper towels in the ladies' room and cleaned off the desk and terminal screen. I was a woman who required some degree of cleanliness and organization, and once I had achieved it I sat down in front of the terminal and began my work. The next few hours passed without my realizing it.

I was doing what I loved best, tinkering with software, and my initial investigation yielded one thing—whoever broke into the software and authorized the ten-thousand-dollar payment had done it through remote access, meaning he or she had used a computer terminal at another site. It wasn't anyone on the Anco premises.

Lufkin was seeming more alive by the minute.

SEVEN

I TOOK A BREAK, walked over to Chambers's office, and asked him for a printout of the security code. For some reason Chambers looked at me the way you look at a dog who just made a mistake on a new carpet, but he promised to have it delivered within the hour.

I decided then that there wasn't any point to Chambers and me continuing our tug-of-war, especially since I was going to be on the premises awhile. Besides, it crossed my mind that maybe I had been too hard on him. My years at ICI had taught me how tough corporate politics could be, especially when you're on the losing end. Something about Chambers told me that he was the type who didn't play office politics well, and in that he had my sympathy. I was never much good at office politics either, only for me it was by choice. I think Chambers's problem was that he just didn't know how.

As a preface to peacemaking I asked him some questions about his work, made approving noises at his answers, and suggested we have coffee in the next few days so I could get his ideas on how Lufkin broke into Anco's software. The effort only took a few minutes and afterward he was all smiles.

After reinstalling myself in Hell Cube, I checked my voice-mail messages. Eldon had called saying he had news about the CDs. I wasted no time in calling him back.

"They're virtual reality, all right. Hyperintensive, full-body, computer-mind symbiosis. There did you get them? I want to know," Eldon said, his voice sounding urgent and annoyed, but then, he sounded urgent and annoyed a lot.

"Are they that special?"

He groaned. "Are the pyramids special? Are they pointed at the top? Whoever masterminded these programs has made some breakthroughs in intellectual amplification that make what we're doing at Comtech look strictly larval. I want a name. I want to meet the person behind the name. I want to press my fingers against his cranium and soak up his thoughts. I want to—"

I stopped the oration. "Listen; we'll get into all that later. I can't give out the programmer's name now, but when I can, you'll be the first to know. When can I look at the programs?"

He sighed loudly. "All right, we'll play your little game, but only because we have history between us. I had to borrow equipment to look at the programs, because they were way beyond the workstations we're using here. These programs require full-body equipment. It took some doing to get it together on such short notice."

"I'm grateful, Eldon. Can I see them today?"

"Unfortunately, no. I have to return the equipment for a few days. I can get it back on Monday."

"Then can I come Monday?"

"Be here at nine. Bring pastry." Eldon hung up.

Eldon had high standards when it came to technology. If he thought the VR programs were high-quality, that was enough for me. Monday seemed a long way away, but I would have to wait.

At twenty until two I glanced at my watch, hastily logged off the Anco computer system, and raced to Chambers's office to see if my printout was ready. Luckily it was. I thanked him and hurried out of the building with a new bounce in my step. For the first time in months I felt like things were going my way.

I reached the office ten minutes late, but Paoli wasn't the type to notice. I pulled into the parking lot close to our office window and honked. Paoli came out wearing a suspiciously large grin.

"I've got a new toy," he said as he fastened his seat belt.

I leaned over and gave him a kiss before pulling out of the parking lot. "Let me guess. A cap pistol? GI Joe doll? No, you'd rather have a Barbie so you can undress her."

"Cute. Take a look at this."

I stole a glance at him while I made a left turn and headed for the freeway. He had pulled a small, black, square something out of his pocket and held it in front of my face.

"A beeper?"

"That's what you're supposed to think, but it's really a camera. See here?" He tapped one end with his finger. "This little hole is a wide-angle lens. The lens is installed so you can wear it on your belt, and when you press this little button here it takes a picture of whatever's in front of you, and nobody's the wiser. It uses special film. You can't have a flash, but it works great in daylight or under fluorescent lighting."

I took the camera from him and gave it a quick once-over. "When I'm doing the bookkeeping, should I categorize this under 'office equipment' or 'recreation'?" I asked, handing it back to him.

"Don't worry; it didn't cost anything. I borrowed it from one of my old NSA buddies. I called him yesterday and had him send it UPS. I promised to get it back to him in a couple of weeks. Guess what, Julie?"

"What?"

"I just took your picture, and you didn't even know it. I just held it in my lap and pointed it at you. There are a hundred uses for this thing."

"Name two," I said with a laugh.

"Well, number one, I can take pictures of you naked and you'll never know."

"I should definitely categorize this under 'recreation,'" I told him. I had concerns about the camera, but there was no time to discuss invasion-of-privacy issues. I pulled the Toyota into the D-Quest parking lot. Paoli clipped the beeper/camera to his belt before we walked inside.

Like most Silicon Valley companies, D-Quest had chosen for its reception area an interior design I think of as neo-dull Danish Modern, with the furniture, walls, and nondescript art blending together in a blandly contemporary pale blue. Of course, compared to our linoleum-lined office I thought D-Quest looked regal.

We approached a curved white reception desk that wrapped around a languid brunette with long hair that was teased in the front. A small nameplate bore the name "Dawn." Dawn was leaning back in her chair thumbing through *People* magazine. The cover displayed a member of Hollywood royalty and promised lurid details of marital difficulties. I knew Dawn would not want to be disturbed, but I decided to let her earn a little of her salary.

"We're here to see Annette Parker," I told Dawn as gently as possible so I wouldn't startle her. She looked at me dull-eyed for a few seconds until my request finally registered; then, frowning, she lifted a phone receiver and, with the eraser end of a pencil, stabbed a few buttons.

"Names?" she asked like it was going to be a tough question. I told her. She announced us to the person on the other end of the phone, then hung up. "She'll meet you here in the lobby," Dawn said, then, official duties minimally administered, returned to her magazine.

Paoli and I parked ourselves on a couple of chairs and reinstated budget talks until I saw a tall redheaded woman taking long strides toward us.

"Mr. Paoli?" she said, her voice unexpectedly deep and throaty, like Marlene Dietrich's. We both stood up, and Paoli smiled and held out his hand. She took it; then he introduced me. Her handshake was firm, and she didn't smile.

Annette Parker wasn't what I had expected. Although she was dressed in black jeans, white cotton turtleneck, navy blazer, and loafers, her general look came off as formal. She wore heavy rimmed glasses with pink tinted lenses and had a boyish haircut dyed an inhuman shade of red and narrow lips painted a vivid crimson. The lipstick looked freshly applied. Most software developers looked diffident and spacey, like they didn't fit in the world unless they were sitting in front of a keyboard. Annette wasn't like that. She was composed and direct and had gray eyes that bored holes through you.

"I don't understand what you want with me. You're looking for Arnie Lufkin, but like I told you over the phone, I don't know him."

"We don't know him either. That's what makes it so tough looking for him," Paoli said with a big smile, laying on his best boyish charm.

I could tell by her face she wasn't going for it. She didn't notice as his hand casually moved to his beeper and pressed the button. "Who are you?" she asked.

Paoli grabbed a card from his inside coat pocket and handed it to her with a grander gesture than I thought necessary. She took the card, studied it a moment, then looked at us with a disturbed expression.

"Computer fraud investigations?" Her lean frame stiffened. She looked like she was on the verge of bolting, but I figured any programmer would tense up at the mention of computer fraud.

"That's right," Paoli said. "We've been hired to find Arnie Lufkin. We thought you might know something that could help us. It won't take long. Just a couple of questions. Can we sit down?"

Annette considered things for a few seconds; then she nodded. We all sat, Annette stiffly perching herself on the edge of her chair to let us know she wouldn't be staying long.

"You know who Arnie Lufkin is?" Paoli asked.

She shrugged. "I know a little about him."

"Like what?"

"Just what I read in the paper. He hacked into a computer system, didn't he?" Paoli nodded. "But that's all I know." Annette shifted in her chair and looked off into space. "I read some papers by him in computer journals. He was a brilliant developer."

"Maybe," said Paoli. He made the remark offhandedly and I don't think he meant anything by it, but when Annette heard it she gave him a sudden harsh look.

Paoli reached again into the inside pocket of his jacket and pulled out the photo Lorna had given us. He handed it to Annette. "Here's his picture. Does he look familiar?"

Annette glanced at the photo, then handed it back. "No, never met him." She paused, took a breath, then spoke. "Why do you care?"

"Because we need to find him. There's a limited number of people working on full-body virtual reality. He was one of them. We think maybe he's working somewhere under a different name. Are you the only person working with VR here at D-Quest?"

"For now. They talk about hiring someone else, but it's hard finding a programmer with the qualifications, plus the fact that money's so tight. Look; if you think this guy is working here, I can tell you he's not."

"Have you ever used any contract programmers who worked at home?" Paoli asked.

This question must have amused her, because she smiled slightly. She had one of those faces that's more attractive in repose.

"No, never. I don't know any programmers who work on this kind of project part-time. I've got to get back to work, but if I see this Arnie guy I'll call you," she said quickly, eager to get away from us.

We all politely shook hands and said our good-byes. I doubted Paoli and I would be hearing from Annette again.

We drove back to the office, where I made a phone call to Alan Shapiro, the purchasing manager at ICI and a personal friend. Paoli decided to stay at the office and work with the security code printout while I met with Shapiro.

It felt strange to pull into the ICI parking lot and take one of the spaces marked "Visitor." I had worked there for eight years. I always told Paoli that it felt like I had been gone from ICI for years instead of only months, but now, looking at the huge building in front of me, it seemed like I had never left. It was hard to admit, but I missed more of ICI than just the regular paychecks. I missed the people, the sense of importance of my work there. I had felt like I belonged at ICI, like I was part of a big family. Things had gotten tough there just before I left, but I now found myself remembering mostly the good things about my old job.

Alfonso, the guard at the front desk, grinned when he saw me.

"Long time no see. You get transferred?" At ICI most people get hired right out of college and work there until they retire. If people don't see you around for a while, they assume you got transferred. People just didn't quit ICI that often. The retirement package was too good, and jobs too hard to come by.

"I started my own company," I told him, and it felt good to say the words. "I'm here to see Alan Shapiro. He's expecting me."

Alfonso called Shapiro to let him know I was there. When he hung up the phone he gave me an embarrassed look. "Julie, I'm going to have to ask you to sign in. Gotta give you a guest badge." He said it sheepishly, as if he thought it might make me mad.

I laughed. "It's okay, Al."

Al gave me my badge about the time Alan Shapiro came out to retrieve me. Shapiro was a big, broad teddy bear of a man who was interminably good-natured. When he saw me he gave me a bear hug, lifting me high off the ground.

"Where have you been? You promised to call me for lunch three months ago and I'm still waiting," he said when he set me back down on the floor.

"I've been busy, you know, with the new business and all."

"Entrepreneurs. Well, you were always a workaholic. Let's go to my office."

I followed him out of the lobby, up the elevator to the fourth floor, and to the purchasing area. A few people I knew saw me and waved. Shapiro ushered me into his plant-and-photo-filled office and gestured to a chair.

"Have you seen my new grandkid?" he asked, handing me a small photo album filled with pictures of a pink-skinned newborn, and I took a quick look and made admiring noises.

Looking at baby pictures usually ends up making me feel nervous, like I'm suppressing basic maternal needs. Of course I still have time to have babies, but right now I'm not ready for it, and I can't imagine myself being ready for it any time soon. And that arouses another one of my fears—that one of these days I'll be having my annual pelvic exam and the doctor will find an expiration date stamped on my womb, like on a carton of milk.

"This makes three," Shapiro said proudly. I returned his smile. He was the kind of man who keeps his grandchildren's kindergarten art pinned to his office wall.

Shapiro settled down into his chair and gave me a fatherly look. "We miss you around here, Julie."

"I miss you, too."

"Are you still dating the NSA guy?" he asked, always interested in my love life. I wasn't sure how to answer. Dating? I wouldn't call what was going on between Paoli and me dating, but the dictionary didn't have a term to define it. I decided to simplify things by responding with a simple, "Yes."

"I can see you shifting in your chair, tapping your foot, still fidgety like always. You want to get down to business, right? So what can I do for you?"

"I want to talk about embezzling."

"The business not going so well, Julie?"

We both laughed. I told him about my case with Anco and about Lufkin's theft of four hundred thousand. I also told Shapiro about the extra six hundred thousand they had found when tracing Lufkin's bank accounts and about McCracken's theory that Lufkin was stealing from another company.

Shapiro's face fell into an atypical frown.

"Maybe he would like to think that, but I don't think so. It would be very hard to steal that much money from another company. Stealing from your own company, that's easier."

"How come?"

"Because when you steal from your own company you can create the paperwork—purchase requests, purchase orders, check requests. You said this person who stole the money wrote his own purchase orders and stole the authorization codes from the computer. Were the POs for hard goods or for services?"

"Services, I think. Consultation work."

"Clever. Services are very hard to trace. If you make out a PO for something like furniture or office equipment, then the receiving department gets a copy of the paperwork, and when the piece of furniture doesn't show up they get suspicious. But a PO for consultants? It's hard to catch that."

"But companies bring in outside auditors every year. Wouldn't they figure it out?"

"Maybe, maybe not. Auditors look for paper trails. If a transaction has the right paperwork, then to them it looks okay. And they don't go through every transaction anyway. They go through the POs over a certain amount, or they look at random sampling."

"So you're saying it's impossible that our thief could have stolen the rest of the money from an outside company."

"I didn't say impossible, but it's unlikely."

"But Anco can't find where the additional money came from."

"They're not looking hard enough. Let me tell you one more thing. When you have one person embezzling it's hard to catch them, but frequently they do get caught. But when you have collusion between two people, two people in the right departments, that's almost impossible to catch."

I MET PAOLI back at the office. We worked a couple of hours, had a quick dinner at Fung Lo's, then headed home. Paoli wore his beeper camera the whole time, and I had this uncomfortable feeling he was photographing me while I ate. Twice I started to say something to him about it, but I stopped myself. Paoli is like a kid sometimes, and if I complained about the camera it would only encourage him.

The last six months had brought out some childlike qualities in Paoli that I hadn't recognized when I first fell in love with him. Not having to be in the office at a certain time every morning, not having management looking over his shoulder, had given him a feeling of freedom that had appreciably heightened his spirits. And Paoli's spirits were pretty high to start with.

I admit that Paoli's fun-loving personality was a needed complement to my own seriousness, demonstrated by the fact that I had laughed more in the past six months than I had laughed in my whole life and that for the first time I had a really great sex life. But I found myself reminding him to get to work early, to not leave his clothes in piles on the bedroom floor, to hang up wet towels in the bathroom so they'd dry. Would I eventually start nagging him to eat his peas?

High spirits or not, when it came to security software there was no one better than Paoli. And the good news was that he had spent several hours that afternoon digging through the printout of Anco's security code, and he said he had made progress. I knew if I could just keep him tied to a chair long enough we would work out Anco's security problems in no time. The problem was keeping his mind on business and off spy cameras and sex. Well, at least off spy cameras.

At ten-thirty I was lying in bed wearing one of Paoli's T-shirts and my hair piled on top of my head with a clip. With a tablet on my lap I was drawing out a flowchart of Anco's general ledger program when I became aware of Paoli standing in the bathroom doorway. I looked up and saw him leaning against the doorjamb wearing nothing but white boxer shorts with little green golf clubs all over them. I grabbed the beeper from the nightstand where he had left it, pointed it at him, and pushed the button.

"Let's make prints of that one and slip it inside your Christmas cards this year," he said, plopping down on the bed next me, sending my tablet to the floor.

"I was trying to work."

"Save it for morning," he mumbled as he kissed my ear.

"I'd like to, but I can't."

Paoli rolled over on his back and moaned, and I ran my fingers through his curls. He hates it when I call them curls, but that's what they are.

"Sorry, but I have work on my mind, and I'd like to talk some things over with you," I said.

He took my hand and kissed my fingers. "Sweetheart, sometimes you confuse things. We work in the office, and in the bedroom we fool around. Get it? Work, office. Fooling around, bedroom. I can write it down for you and pin it to your shirt if that would help."

I gave him a pleading look. "Just for a while?"

He propped himself up on his elbows. "Okay, so what is it?"

"Arnie Lufkin."

"Big surprise. What about him?"

"I'm sure that with a little time you and I will be able to find out how he broke into the security software."

"Undoubtedly," said Paoli. "By my estimations we'll have the problem knocked out in about four working days. And I'm accepting bets."

"What makes you so sure?"

"Because in my experience there are only six or seven ways to break into security software, and I already eliminated two this afternoon. So how long can it take? Now tell me what's on your mind."

I sat up, crossing my legs under me. "Here it is. Andrew McCracken told me today that they traced close to a million dollars through Lufkin's bank accounts. McCracken seemed certain that only four hundred thousand of it had come from Anco, but when I saw Alan Shapiro today he told me that Lufkin had to have stolen the whole amount from Anco. He said it's almost impossible to embezzle like this from a company you don't work for."

"But don't you think Anco would have missed that last six hundred grand?"

"McCracken says it was a fluke that they found out about the first four hundred, and afterward they checked every transaction Lufkin had authorized and they couldn't connect him to the rest of the money. That's why McCracken thinks Lufkin got the money somewhere else."

"So what are you getting at?"

"I think the money came from Anco, only I think someone else was involved in the theft along with Lufkin. That person started filling out the purchase requests, which is why Anco didn't find them. They were only looking for purchase orders authorized by Lufkin."

"So who's this other person? It would have to be a peer of Lufkin's, because anyone lower than him wouldn't be able to authorize purchase requests, would they?"

"I'm not sure. But I think I know a way to find out. When I was at ICI we had audits once a year where people came in from one of the big accounting firms and went through our records, including the computer files."

Paoli stopped caressing my thigh, and his face became serious. "That same thought hit me yesterday, but until today we were only looking for Lufkin, not how he hacked into the software, so I didn't waste any time on it."

"Shapiro said that auditors wouldn't be able to uncover fraud as long as the paperwork for a purchase order was in place, but if I could see the audit files, it might help us figure out who might have helped Lufkin embezzle."

"*If* anyone helped him. Let's not get carried away and start assuming there's another crook in Anco."

"That's what we have to figure out. I'm not sure about anything, not yet."

Paoli gently pressed me into a prone position. "If you would just kiss me, I'm sure things would clear up for you."

"I guess this means our business conversation is over," I said, snapping the waistband of his shorts. "You know you have an underwear fetish, don't you?"

"Yes. It's a perversion that takes years to master," he whispered in my ear, making my corpuscles do the limbo.

I laughed. "Can it be cured?"

"Give me about an hour and I'll show you."

EIGHT

SOMETIMES IN THE MIDDLE of the night when I'm edgy and can't sleep, I lie in the darkness and wish for an earthquake. Not a big one. No eight-point-sixer that sends the Financial District sinking to the fishes, but something in the five-point range—a nice, long, rumbling crescendo that freezes the blood and chills the soul, that slowly intensifies into one final, bowel-curdling jolt.

My reason? Earthquakes cleanse the soul. When the ground beneath you moves, all your petty troubles shrink into perspective and you start thinking about God and nature and all those things they write about on the back of herbal tea boxes. I wanted an earthquake that Thursday night. It would shake my mind out, give me a clear perspective on life, love, and the whereabouts of Arnie Lufkin. But the ground remained deadly still beneath me, and I spent another night tossing and turning in my bed and in my mind.

Paoli, on the other hand, slept like the dead. I'm usually up and off to the office two hours before him, but that morning, by hitting him in the face with a wet washcloth, I managed to get him out of bed before six-thirty.

While he was in the shower, I paced the bathroom floor and we summed up what we knew. One: Arnie Lufkin wasn't dead. Even the police had big doubts, with no body and no witness actually seeing him jump. The whole suicide was faked, and Lufkin was merely goading us, toying with us to prove his mental superiority.

Two: somebody was still hacking into Anco's software, and I had learned from yesterday's scrutinizing of their security code that the hacker was coming in from the outside. Whoever was doing it wasn't using a computer terminal on the Anco premises, and Paoli said that after his previous day's work he felt certain that the current hack was the same type as Lufkin's, which pointed the finger at Lufkin once again. Within a few more days I knew Paoli and I could figure out how Lufkin or whoever was breaking in and how to put a stop to it, but now that wasn't enough for me. Lufkin thought he was smarter than everyone else. I was going to prove to him that he wasn't. I was going to find him.

With granola breakfast bars in hand, Paoli and I were out the front door when we both stopped on the walkway. There was Ox standing on the curb in front of my house, leaning against a beat-up green Camaro, his hands stuffed inside his pockets. From my five-foot-three vantage point Ox looked colossal—a whopping, jumbo-sized, family pack of a man, his massive body dwarfing the low car behind him.

Bronco lay on the ground, his head resting on Ox's scuffed brown cowboy boot. A low, protective growl squeezed out of Bronco's bared teeth as Paoli and I approached. Ox bent down and scratched behind one furry ear, and Bronco once again became docile.

"Hey, Ox," Paoli said with a friendly wave of his half-eaten granola bar.

"It's Vernon," I corrected him, and Ox gave me a grateful smile.

"Of course," said Paoli, embarrassed by his gaffe. "So, Vernon, what's cookin'?" Paoli's tone was good-old-boy casual, as if Ox in my front yard at seven-fifteen in the morning was a common occurrence.

"Gotta talk to ya." His face looked cautious.

"How long have you been waiting here? Why didn't you come to the office?" I asked.

"Don't want Lornie to know I'm here. She'll still be sleeping for a couple a hours." He looked at his feet.

I set my briefcase down on the sidewalk. "Are you okay, Vernon?" He looked so forlorn, I had this urge to hug him, but, of course, I didn't. Although there was a sweetness to Ox, my instincts told me that he was a volatile man—part puppy, part gorilla. My arms wouldn't fit around him anyway.

Ox took his beefy hands out of his pockets and gave Bronco a gentle shove off his shoe. He looked at us, his face a fusion of emotions. "It's Lornie. I think she could be in trouble."

"What do you mean by trouble?" Paoli asked.

"I mean Arnie Lufkin," Ox said, his voice gaining confidence and volume. "He ain't dead. Lornie knows it. Even the police don't think he's dead anymore."

"So?" I asked.

"He's a bad guy. A real bad guy. I think he could hurt her. Like, you know, physical. He did it once before."

"Why would he want to hurt Lorna now?" I asked Ox.

"Because I think he told her things, things he probably shouldn'ta told her."

"Like what?"

Ox shook his head. "I dunno. Maybe about the money. I just got this feelin'. It's something about the way Lornie acts. Lornie thinks I don't know nothin', and maybe I don't know much, but I know crooks and cheats. It's my business to know 'em," he said with a fleeting look of pride. "Lufkin may talk smarter than the rest of 'em, but that don't mean he ain't a crook and a cheat."

"Okay, he's a crook and a cheat," said Paoli with a shrug, "but why does that mean he would hurt Lorna?"

Ox's thick fingers curled into tight fists, but his brown eyes remained painfully vulnerable. "'Cause I seen it in his face, just like I seen it in other guys like him. He don't care about nothin' but himself. If he saw a bug on the sidewalk he'd squash it just to see it go splat."

As Ox spoke the last sentence he ground the toe of his boot into the sidewalk to demonstrate the senseless crushing of an innocent insect. He stared down a moment at the insect ghost, then looked at me with pleading eyes. "You gotta help me protect Lornie."

Looking at Ox standing there, his body seeming as powerful as a steamroller, it was hard for me to imagine that he required help protecting anyone. But from the aching look on his face I knew it was something else he needed from us. He had a powerful physique and enough street smarts to chase down the crooks who bounced checks and robbed corner stores, but what Ox didn't trust about himself was his brain. He wanted us to figure things out, to look into this tangled situation and come up with answers, answers I wasn't sure we would be able to find. And Ox was not a man I cared to disappoint.

"She's paying us to find him so she can be with him. That's a far cry from protecting her from him," I said.

"Just look out for her. I can't be everywhere all the time, can I? Lufkin don't think of nobody but himself. Cold as ice. Just look out for her. Lornie's smart about a lot of things, but she ain't no good with guys."

I nodded appreciatively, having made a few mistakes about guys myself.

"We'll do everything we can, I promise you," Paoli said, his hand on Ox's shoulder.

Ox mumbled his thanks and bent down to stroke Bronco's head. In spite of his lumbering body and rotten grammar, there was an elegance about Ox, a fineness to him that transcended his bulk. Without good-byes, Ox and Bronco got in the green Camaro and took off down the street with a loud rumble I'm sure woke up a few neighbors.

"He needs a new muffler," I said as I watched the Camaro turn the corner.

"He needs more than that. He's got woman troubles."

"That I'll agree with, but I'm not buying that Lorna needs protection from Lufkin. Besides, we can't watch her twenty-four hours a day."

"I know," said Paoli. "But we'd better keep our eyes open. Ox knows what he's talking about."

An hour later we were at Anco. After we checked in at the front desk I led Paoli to the tiny cavity Chambers had assigned to us. When Paoli saw it, he cursed under his breath, but I assured him it looked better than it had the day before.

The office had an L-shaped desk that filled most of the usable space. I sat on the side with the computer terminal, and Paoli sat opposite me. We were crammed in so close together our bodies touched, which wasn't necessarily a bad thing as long as our oxygen held out. I logged on to the Anco on-line system while Paoli worked with the printout of the security software and general ledger program. After about an hour we compared notes. We agreed on which code lines looked like security weaknesses and were engrossed in a mild argument over the methodology Lufkin could have used when we were interrupted.

"Julie?"

I looked up and saw Andrew McCracken standing outside our cubicle. Dressed in an expensive dark pin-striped suit, with blue-green silk tie and a matching silk handkerchief that peeked out of his breast pocket, McCracken looked out of place in the lackluster surroundings. His eyes surveyed me, and I wondered if he was looking at my suit. I was wearing an olive green skirt and jacket that I had bought at a consignment shop in San Jose. When I had been more flush financially, Ann Taylor had been my favorite store, even though my time constraints meant I had to do my shopping out of their catalog. Now I had plenty of time on weekends to browse the stores, I just couldn't afford to buy anything. The secondhand suit was the only clothing I had purchased in six months, and it embarrassed me that it wasn't new. I kept expecting someone to point at me and say, "She's wearing my old suit!"

"Good morning, Mr. McCracken," I said, wondering what he was doing there.

"You have to start calling me Andy." He flashed a smile.

"Yes, well, Andy, let me introduce my partner, Vic Paoli."

Paoli stood up, and the two shook hands quickly, each man sizing the other up like roosters in a barnyard.

I remained seated. "So what brings you down here?" I asked, wanting to add "among the little people," but refrained from doing so.

"I asked Chambers where you were. I wanted to see how you're doing, make sure you had everything you need. By the way, I like that outfit. Green's a good color on you," he said. After glancing at Paoli's face, I realized that my dress wasn't the only thing green in that cubicle. Paoli looked at McCracken with an expression I'd only seen on him once before, and that was when the Porsche got towed.

Was it possible that McCracken had come here to flirt with me? The idea filled me with guilty pleasure, but I shook off the thought. The man just wanted to keep an eye on us. We were, after all, tinkering with his company's most vital software. In spite of my rationalizations, I could feel myself blushing.

McCracken looked around our cubicle and frowned. "This is not the right environment. Much too cramped. I'll get you moved to an office."

"That would be fantastic," I said.

"It's nothing. Listen, Julie, I know you're busy here, but I would appreciate it if you could make time to have lunch with me in the next few days. I'd like to keep up on your progress," he said. "Could we arrange that?"

I started to respond, but Paoli beat me to the punch.

"Lunch sounds good. We'll be there," Paoli said with the slightest snarl, and I shot him a reproachful look. I couldn't blame him. It was obvious that the lunch invitation had been directed only at me, which was less than courteous. Still, the man was our client.

Paoli's lunch acceptance clouded McCracken's face only for a second.

"Good. Call my administrator and set it up. She knows my calendar. I've got to run. Nice meeting you, Vic." McCracken turned to exit, but I couldn't let him leave without making good use of him.

"Wait a minute."

McCracken stopped and turned back toward me. He looked hopeful.

"I have some questions. I'd like to know who works with the accounting firm that does your annual audits. Is it you?"

McCracken gave me a curious look. "No, Arlene Gallagher has always handled it. Why do you ask?"

"No big reason," I told him, which was the kind of big, fat lie my mother had always warned me about. "I'm just covering the bases. All part of the service."

I smiled. McCracken smiled. Paoli smiled while he turned the colors of the Italian flag.

"I have a meeting. Don't forget to call and schedule lunch."

After McCracken walked away, I felt Paoli's eyes on my back. A frigid silence enveloped the room.

"So, let's take up where we left off," I said too cheerfully.

"Yes, we want to have a good report card when Andy checks our progress." He didn't even try to hide his irritation. He sat down at his side of the desk. "Okay. Let's get back to work."

"Fine with me." I resumed my position in front of the terminal.

Paoli and I worked for another three hours, an unfriendly silence between us resounding like a boulder in a cement mixer. I wanted to say something to him that would make things all right between us, but I couldn't find the words. Although I resented his jealousy, I had to admit there was a part of me that felt happily smug about it. The man was obviously crazy about me.

Paoli offered to go find a phone and check our voice mail, since we didn't have a phone in the cubicle. Having little real business, we usually didn't have messages except from vendors, bill collectors, and weekly calls from our mothers, but there was the possibility that Lorna could have tried to reach us. Besides, I think Paoli just wanted to get away for a few minutes, and I didn't blame him.

Our hot exchange had left my own concentration in tatters. To be honest, my reaction to McCracken bothered me as much as it bothered Paoli. There was something about strong, clean-cut executive types that attracted me. I think it's because my father died when I was little and I remember him as being that type of man. He was a lieutenant colonel in the air force. I don't have many concrete images of him, but I remember him as very conventional and serious.

But I was supposed to be in love with Paoli, and it troubled me that I found McCracken appealing. You shouldn't be in love with one man and find other men attractive. It's not right, although I had been guilty of it before. That's how I ended up with Paoli.

I managed to make some progress in going through the software line by line, but I didn't come up with anything new. The places in the programming that had appeared weak the day before now seemed fine after taking a closer look. It had turned out to be a wretched morning.

"Guess what."

I heard Paoli's voice behind me. He sounded happy and I wondered if he had slugged McCracken.

"What?"

"I got a call I was expecting from a buddy of mine at NSA."

"The same one who gave you the camera?"

"Different one. His name's Jake. This guy works in data research. I asked him to run some checks and find out if there are any headhunters in the country who handle programmers with unusual specialties like VR. He couldn't find anything in the data base, but he called a friend of his who referred him to another friend. Jake found out that there's really only one headhunter who fits the description. Her name's Lorraine Sajak and she's in San Francisco. He gave me her phone number and address. Jake says this woman's more aggressive than the average, which means if we cross her we're in danger of losing limbs."

If we hadn't been in the middle of a squabble, I would have kissed Paoli. The headhunter angle could be an important lead. Headhunters are high-powered personnel agents who act as brokers between prospective employees and employers. Most high-tech companies used them. My guess was if Lufkin was going to find VR work anywhere in the country and remain anonymous, he wouldn't be able to do it on his own. That meant he would have to go through a headhunter, but probably under another name.

Paoli insisted we pop in on the woman without making an appointment, reasoning that way we had less of a chance of her refusing to see us. I didn't like the idea of cold-calling her, but I didn't want to make things worse between Paoli and me by debating it with him, and since we were downtown anyway it seemed worth the shot.

Before we left, I stopped by Gallagher's office to ask her for the files she had on Anco's last audit. Gallagher was in a meeting, so I asked Monique if she would get the files for me so I could pick them up later.

Sajak's office was down California Street about eight blocks, some of which ascended at ninety-degree angles. I was wearing high heels, inappropriate footwear for hill climbing, so Paoli and I grabbed a couple of hot dogs from a street vendor, tried not to think about cholesterol or nitrates, and looked for a cable car.

The air was cool and clear as Paoli and I caught a cable car at California and Sansome. It was already filled with camera-laden tourists, and Paoli and I had to stand on the side runner and hang onto the railing as the cable car chugged up Nob Hill, then down the other side. A perspiring, overweight man in his sixties wearing Bermuda shorts, a golf shirt, and a New York Yankees baseball cap noticed my knuckles turning white from my death grip on the handrail and gallantly offered me his seat, but I politely refused. I figured his chances of falling off were a lot greater than mine. As a Bay Area resident I felt personally responsible for protecting bewildered tourists.

"You like that guy, don't you?" Paoli said once the cable car began its struggle up a second hill.

My absorption in monitoring the cable car's every jolt and quiver left me ill-equipped to listen to Paoli, much less prepare an appropriate response. I've never trusted cable cars. The technology is too old, too backward, to inspire my faith, and a few years earlier the local television news had run a horror story about a cable car running out of control. I was a devout believer in the technological cutting edge and in the concept that everything improved with science and time. The crude cable-gripping theory behind cable cars made me suspicious that its designers weren't familiar with the more finely honed aspects of the laws of gravity. Paoli risked freeing one hand from the handrail to touch my arm.

"You like that McCracken guy. Admit it."

With a clunk the cable car stopped at the intersection to let off passengers. The man with the golf shirt got off, and I took his seat. Paoli remained standing, facing me, still hanging onto the handbar.

"I'm waiting for an answer."

We braced ourselves for another bump as the cable car began to rattle once more down California Street.

"I don't like him or dislike him. He's the president of Anco and our client. I'm nice to him because he's eventually going to be our reference."

"Right, Julie. He's just your type, isn't he? You love those boys with the big offices and big corporate titles with initials on their cuffs and sticks up their—"

"Stop it. You're being ridiculous. Half the people in the world are men. I can't be rude to all of them just so your fragile ego won't be damaged."

"My ego is not fragile."

"I've seen sturdier Venetian glass."

Paoli looked genuinely miffed by my last remark. I opened my mouth to apologize, but pride and stupidity wouldn't let me.

I wasn't good at this. In high school, when other girls were learning the basics of charming males and losing one's virginity, I had been doing science projects and studying for my SATs. In college, when my girlfriends were frantically dating, I was in the computer lab writing FORTRAN programs. Of course, after college there was graduate school and after that my career, and pretty soon I was thirty and hopelessly awkward around any male unless he was discussing computer chips. In the past couple of years I had made up for some of that lost time, but I was still a bumbling novice when it came to men.

We passed the remaining minutes of the ride in silence. At the corner of California and Van Ness we jumped off the cable car and looked for the headhunter's address. Her office was in a corner building built in the old San Francisco style—five stories with a white facade and bay windows on every floor. We walked into the small lobby, looked up Sajak's name on the directory, and took a small, rickety elevator to the fourth floor, turned left, then backtracked to office 46. The small brass plate on the door read: "Lor-

raine Sajak, Personnel Placement, Please ring." Paoli
pushed a small black button to the left of the door. We
waited about three seconds, heard the buzzer, and pushed
the door open.

Stepping inside, I immediately like the style of the office.
An Oriental rug lay on the floor, and colorful contemporary art hung on the old brick wall, illuminated by track
lighting. Everything looked tastefully expensive, including
the large metal sculpture and ornate gold-framed mirror
near the window. There's a lot of money to be made in corporate head-hunting if you can get the right clientele.

Behind a dark, carved antique desk sat Sajak, her tortoiseshell glasses perched on the end of her nose as she
scrutinized us.

"You're not Joe Valentino," she said, stating the fact as
if the news might surprise us. Sajak looked a well-
moisturized forty. Her smooth skin was expertly made up,
her streaked blond hair cascading straight, then curling under just above her collar. Her nose had the kind of chiseled
perfection that probably made six months of payments on
a plastic surgeon's Maui condo. "I was expecting Joe. Who
are you?" she asked, and I could hear the annoyed edge in
her voice.

"Vic Paoli and Julie Blake," Paoli said with a flourish,
and handed her our card. She accepted it, pushed her glasses
back up her nose, and gave it a hard read. During all this I
saw Paoli slyly push the button on the camera still attached
to his belt.

Sajak looked back up at Paoli. "So? Are you looking or
hiring? I don't handle this computer investigation type
thing, but I can refer you to someone," she said rapidly,
then began flipping through her Rolodex with manicured
rose-painted nails. Her voice held the slightest trace of a
New Jersey accent, but it was suppressed, like she had taken
diction lessons.

"Neither," he said.

Her fingers froze and her gaze turned steely. This was a woman who knew time was money.

"You work with high-level developer types?"

"Yes," she said flatly. "That's the only type I work with."

"We're looking for a virtual reality developer named Arnie Lufkin. We thought you might be able to help us," I said.

Her blue eyes shifted toward me. I watched the expression on her face, and it didn't change when she heard Lufkin's name, but she paused before answering.

"Don't know him. Why are you looking for him? You've got a job for him? Because I have connections in this business and can get you the best," she said, her voice softening as it moved into her sales pitch.

"As I said," said Paoli, "we're not looking to hire anyone. We just want to find him."

"Can't help you. You might try the people at Walker and Friedman. Look, I don't want to be rude, but I'm expecting an appointment, and I'm up to my neck. Good luck to you. If I hear anything about this guy, I'll call you."

Fat chance, I thought. We thanked her and made our exit.

"That was fruitless," said Paoli once we were alone in the elevator.

"I'm not so sure."

Paoli looked at me with interest. "What are you thinking?"

"I'm thinking that it's odd that Sajak had never even heard of Lufkin."

"So? I bet a lot of people haven't heard of Lufkin."

"But she said she worked in a niche of the business. That's what bugs me. Sajak works in a narrow field of high-level software developers. Silicon Valley is a small world. How could she not have heard of Lufkin, who was one of the best in the business? Wouldn't she have at least read about his arrest in the newspaper? That was blasted all over the Valley as well as San Francisco, wasn't it?''

"Lufkin had been at Anco a long time. She didn't know him because he hadn't been on the market." Paoli could tell by my face that I wasn't convinced. "I'm playing devil's advocate here, but to me your idea that she should know of Lufkin makes it absurd for her to lie about not knowing him. Sajak seemed like one shrewd cookie, too shrewd to tell a lie that stupid."

"Unless she was so unnerved that she wasn't thinking straight. We surprised her. I think when you mentioned Lufkin's name it staggered her."

"She didn't look staggered."

"But a poker face is the tool of her trade, and from the look of her office, she's a pro. She's taught herself not to react. It was second nature."

Paoli mulled this over as we exited the elevator and walked out onto Van Ness. I checked my watch. It was three-fifteen. "I think we should head back to Anco," I said.

"You go. I'm going back to the office. I've got the print-out in my briefcase. I can work on it there."

I tried not to act surprised. "But we came in the same car."

"You can keep it. I'll take the train to Redwood City, then catch a bus."

"Then I'll see you at home about eight? I'll grab some take-out."

He looked at me, his expression somber. "Not tonight. See you at the office tomorrow morning." He turned and walked down Van Ness. I opened my mouth to call out after him, but he disappeared around the corner.

NINE

IT AMUSES ME that people think computers are complicated. Computers are simply electricity and logic. They take
information, process it, and spit it back out again—all nice
and predictable. We humans are the truly complicated, un-
fathomable machines. We're a labyrinth of uncharitable
needs and passions that we don't understand in each other
or in ourselves. That's why I'm frequently more comfortable with computers.

Computers don't get jealous if you happen to access the
disk space on another computer. They don't get their feelings hurt if you get busy and don't pay much attention to
them for a couple of days. Only problem is they aren't that
cuddly in bed.

And speaking of what's cuddly in bed, Paoli's unexpected exit outside of Sajak's office left me confused. I can
understand a little honest jealousy, but what sin had I committed to deserve that kind of treatment? It wasn't as if I had
flirted with McCracken. He was our client. I was civil to him
and nothing more. Was I supposed to hiss and spit at him?

I admit that what really bothered me was that I *had* found
McCracken attractive. It was my guilty secret, and somehow Paoli had done a Vulcan mind meld and figured me
out. On the other hand, being in love with one man doesn't
mean your eyes get struck blind whenever you lay them on
other examples of the male gender. And why should I feel
guilty about noticing the simple fact that McCracken was
good-looking, when I've frequently seen Paoli cast appreciative glances when women walked by? And though I
couldn't swear to it, I'm sure that during one of those times

I heard him mumble, "Nice hooters," even though when I mentioned it he denied it and acted offended.

I rode the cable car back up California, hopped off at Powell, and walked the rest of the way back to the Anco offices, where I could focus on computer software and get my mind off my love life. I worked at Anco until eight-thirty, then got a pass from the security guard so I could come back the next morning, which was a Saturday. On my way down Highway 101 toward home I considered dropping by Paoli's place, then nixed the idea. Instead I went to Fung Lo's, had the Number Three Szechwan Special, and chatted with Nicky for half an hour about his sister's asthma. Apparently the woman, having moved here recently from Hong Kong, was having troubles adjusting to the high pollen content. I gave Nicky the name of my allergist, paid my check, and headed for home. By this time it was ten-thirty and I was dead tired, but when I got within two blocks of my house I turned the car around and drove the ten miles to Paoli's condo just to see if his Porsche was in the driveway. It wasn't.

In my entire life I had never lowered myself like that. Driving past a man's house to see if he's home is an insipid act suitable for schoolgirls, and I wondered if I should try again in another hour. Maybe he just went to grab a pizza. But at ten-thirty? Hardly. Then maybe he was at some nightclub dancing with a blond twenty-two-year-old with a behind so tight you could bounce a quarter off it. I chided myself for my insecurities, then hoped I had plenty of white wine left in the fridge. It was going to be a long one.

I pulled in the driveway, did my usual fumbling with my keys, and let myself in. My home is not an inviting place, being cursed with a decorating style I describe as neo-public rest room—everything a colorless, inoffensive beige, giving the unwitting visitor expectations of seeing a toilet paper dispenser in every room. I had always been too busy for interior decorating. The only colorful thing in my house had been Paoli.

I peeled off my clothes and put on one of Paoli's T-shirts and the pink satin mule slippers he had given me on our one-month anniversary. The T-shirt had his scent on it. I pulled the cotton fabric up to my nose and inhaled, drinking in the smell. It was his aroma that had first attracted me to him.

I still had my face buried in his T-shirt when it occurred to me that what I was doing was not emotionally healthy for a mature, independent woman with advanced degrees from major universities. I got a grip on myself, sat on the couch, drank white wine, listened to my favorite Frank Sinatra album, and read *Computerworld* while I waited for Paoli to call. By eleven-thirty I was morose and angry at myself for having been so cold toward Paoli. The man was the best thing that had ever happened to me. I adored him and intended to tell him about it in person as soon as possible.

I changed into my best lacy underwear and pulled on a denim skirt and a yellow V-neck cotton sweater that showed what little cleavage I had, as long as I bent way over and held my arms close to my sides. Yes, I, Julie Blake, president of her high school graduating class, honors graduate from MIT and Stanford, vocal proponent of women's rights in corporate America, have stood in front of my bedroom mirror and performed contortions to see if I could create the illusion of larger breasts, although I only did it once and was mad at myself afterward.

A quick comb through the hair, a few spritzes of the Opium perfume that Max had given me for Christmas, and I was en route to Paoli's on what would be an ill-fated mission of love. I turned onto his street, anxious to see if his car was there. It was. Problem was, there was another car parked in the driveway behind his.

For a good five minutes I just sat in the Toyota, my eyes boring a hole through that car. It was a sexy white convertible, a young woman's car, I told myself, a love machine built for wild nights and hot kisses and long blond hair blowing in a summer's breeze. I felt slightly ill as my mind conjured up hazy images of a young beauty in there with my loved one. Maybe there were several young beauties. I wondered how many girls you could fit into a Chrysler LeBaron.

I parked my car down the block, turned off the ignition and the headlights, and tried to clear my head. I told myself that I should just drive home, take some aspirin, and forget about the whole thing, but somehow, while I was telling myself all this, my body got out of the car and started walking to Paoli's window.

His place was on the first floor, and the living room window was located conveniently in front behind some shrubbery. I crawled through the bushes outside Paoli's window, being as quiet as I could, the whole time telling myself that what I was doing was stupid and wrong, but my heart wasn't listening. For that moment I was an animal of passion, a woman reduced by love to spying on her boyfriend like a jilted schoolgirl. Straddling a young shrub, I peered around the edge of a window that was covered with miniblinds. The blinds were slanted downward, making it difficult to see anything. I could make out figures, two of them in a sitting position, although not too close together.

Get out now, I told myself. *Go home before you make a complete fool of yourself,* but unlike a computer, my output did not follow my input. The lights were dim, making it hard to see faces, but I heard a woman's voice and my heart stopped. Moving to the center of the window, I tried to get a better look, but it necessitated stepping directly over a young oleander bush that must have been freshly planted, because it was only a couple of feet high and the ground around it was moist and loosely packed. It crossed my mind that stepping on it could damage its root system, but that bush was standing between me and looking into that window, which meant the oleander could kiss its ass good-bye.

I stepped on it with a crunch, and stooping as low as my skirt would allow, I tried to position myself so I could look up through the blinds, resulting in the oleander sticking inconveniently against some of my privates. I was in this position when I heard him.

"Julie, is that you?"

I jumped, startled, taking half the oleander with me. When my heart started pumping blood to my brain once more, I saw Paoli standing in the driveway looking at me. I was dumbstruck. What could I say, standing there in the dark in his flower bed with shrubbery hanging out of my underwear?

"You have raccoons," I muttered.

"Raccoons? I've never seen any."

"You have them. I saw a couple and chased them off."

He gave me a funny look. "Raccoons can be dangerous, Julie. You read stories in the newspaper about them being rabid all the time."

"I know. It was a stupid thing to do. I guess I just wasn't thinking."

He extended his hand, grabbed my arm, and pulled me out of the flower bed. I was perfectly willing to stay there, especially if I could have been buried on the spot.

"I heard someone out here, and then I saw a face in the window. I thought there was a prowler," he said, then paused. "You were looking in my window, weren't you?"

"Is everything okay?" a voice said from the driveway. I looked over and saw Joshua Lambert, a thin and nervous technical type who had worked for me in my old job. Since then he and Paoli had struck up a friendship. Under different circumstances I would have been very glad to see Joshua.

"Hi, Josh."

"Hi, Julie. This is cool. Long time no see."

I saw Paoli eyeing me. "I saw Josh in the video store, and we decided to watch *Chinatown* together." So it was Faye

Dunaway's voice I had heard. "Julie, were you checking up on me?"

My mouth opened and closed a few times before actual words spilled out. "No, I wasn't. Of course not. I was dropping by to see you, and as I walked up I thought I saw raccoons tearing up the bushes and I decided to chase them off, and this is the thanks I get." It was lame, but it was all I could come up with. What else could I say? That I was checking the water meter? I couldn't have felt any lower.

"You were dropping by? It's almost midnight. You were checking up on me to see if I had a woman here. Admit it."

I could see a grin on his face, and it irritated me.

"Listen, I've got to go. Nice seeing you, Josh."

"Yeah, nice to see you, Julie."

Paoli grabbed my hand and pulled me to him. "Don't go, Julie, and don't be embarrassed. I'm flattered you were worried about me, whether or not it was over raccoons. It's funny and now it's forgotten. Look, the movie's going to be over in another hour. Stay with me."

I wanted to, but shame wouldn't let me. "No, I have to go." I walked quickly down the driveway, hoping Paoli couldn't see the leaves and twigs dropping on the cement.

"Where's your car?" Paoli shouted after me.

"Down the street. There weren't any parking spots," I said, realizing of course that the street was empty in front of the condo complex.

"Drop by and coon hunt anytime, Julie." Paoli yelled after me, and I could hear the laughter in his voice.

I ended up falling asleep on the couch that night, and awakened the next morning feeling humiliated. Needing some female counseling, I called Max, woke her up, and told her what had happened, including the part about dragging off half the oleander in my underwear.

"You actually got in the flower bed and looked in his window?" she asked after she stopped laughing. "That's priceless. I wish I had a picture."

"You call that priceless? I call it degrading."

"It's not degrading. It's just a normal reaction, and that's what's so great about it. A year ago you were way too prim and proper to do anything like that. If you thought there was a woman at your lover's house you would have just stayed home and grown a tumor. Love is making you human, Jules. Every once in a while you need some leaves and twigs in your panties. Rejoice in it."

I didn't feel like rejoicing. I felt more like having plastic surgery and moving to Argentina.

I took a quick shower, skipped the makeup, and decided that drying my hair was too much trouble. After pulling on some jeans and a sweater and grabbing my briefcase, I got in the car, bought black coffee and a doughnut at 7-Eleven, and made the long drive to Anco. I needed to get the previous night's debacle off my mind, and the best way to do it was to work.

The Financial District was deserted at 8:00 a.m. on a Saturday, and that was fine by me. I was in no mood for company. After flashing my pass at the security guard, I took the elevator to the third floor. Compared to the constant staccato of business only one day before, the third floor was eerily silent. I did a quick, "Anybody here?" but got no response. The quiet gave me the creeps.

I took a deep breath to calm myself, then walked back to the Pit. I wondered when my pal Andy would come across with the office he had promised. Even Paoli would have to be grateful for that. The thought of Paoli stung me, and I pushed him out of my mind.

I threw my briefcase down on the desk and took out a yellow lined tablet in case I needed to make notes. After sitting down at the terminal, I entered my ID and password and was waiting for the system to acknowledge me when I saw it. At first it flashed so quickly I wasn't sure it had been there, but then it flashed a second time, hovering against the screen's blackness as my body went rigid. "Pay attention, Julie. Snooping Bitches Die," it said, then evaporated.

There was no poem cloaking the threat this time. It had been laid bare so there was no chance of missing the meaning. The words left a brief green shadow before disappearing completely. I felt my arms and hands tingle with panic.

The computer screen returned to normal and I tried to continue working, but I felt afraid and couldn't shake it. I threw my tablet in my briefcase and left. It crossed my mind to tell the security guard what had happened, but what could he do about it and would he even believe me? I walked straight past him and stopped at the first pay phone and dialed Paoli's number, panic diminishing my humiliation from the night before. It rang four times with no answer. My heart was lodging itself somewhere near my throat when he finally picked up with a sleepy hello.

"I'm coming over," I said without salutation.

"Julie?" His voice sounded drugged.

"We've got to talk. Something's happened. I'll be there as soon as I can."

I hung up the phone, then ran to the parking garage and got in the car. A half hour later I was ringing Paoli's doorbell and he yelled that the door was open.

Paoli is the only person I know whose living quarters look worse than mine. At least I have furniture. He has a mattress in the bedroom that functioned as sleeping unit and dirty clothes hamper. The living room was adorned with a pile of computer books that serve as a coffee table, a widescreen TV, and a battered futon, which is where he was parked when I walked in. Sprawled across it, eating a bowl of multicolored cereal while he watched pro wrestling, Paoli was wearing a T-shirt and a pair of very old gym shorts.

"Any coons out there?" he said with a grin. Another time I would have laughed, but at that moment I was too stressed to do anything but just stare at him. He sensed my anxiety.

"What's wrong?" He shot up and was at my side.

"Something happened."

"Here; sit down and we'll talk."

He led me to the futon, where we both sat down, and I told him about the message on the screen. Telling him the story relaxed me, at least a little.

"Lufkin?"

I nodded. "It said 'pay attention,' just like the last time."

"We need to go to the office today and take another look at that poem."

"Don't need to. I've run it through my mind so many times I've got it memorized." I took a moment to collect the poem in my head, then began to recite. "'Down from the mountain, swoop through the sky. Peek through the keyhole, spyder in your eye. If you see one near you try to get away. If he does come closer, you won't forget the day.'"

"Sounds simple enough. He's threatening you, trying to get you to back off, and today's little note from him was just a stronger message," Paoli said.

"By why 'spyder,' and why the odd spelling?"

"That's not hard. A spider can be poisonous. Again, a threatening symbol. As for the spelling, he just got it wrong. But there's more to the poem. Do you remember the rest?"

"'Looking in the mirror you may just see a foe, but what is real and what is not and what is just for show? When life and death turn like a wheel they bring its victims woe. Be careful for the one you fear may be the one you know.'"

Paoli looked puzzled. "If you look in a mirror you see yourself."

"And his reference to life and death, and 'the one you fear may be the one you know.' It all sounds kind of religious, almost Zen-like."

"Didn't Reza Singhania say that to Lufkin virtual reality was like a religion?"

I thought back on our conversation with Reza. "Yes, he did. This is great. We're supposed to decipher a religious message. It's impossible. But then, maybe he meant for it to be."

"Then let's work on what is possible. Maybe figuring out how Lufkin broke into Anco's software today will help lead us to him."

"That's easy. If Lufkin is stealing from the new general ledger system, then he's already broken into the security software. All he had to do was look for a temporary ID given out last week."

"He wouldn't even have to do that. Someone at Anco could have told him what your ID was and saved him the trouble."

I mulled it over a moment. Then I mouthed the name Miranda.

"What was that?"

"Miranda," I said out loud. "She knows Chambers, knows his habits. She used to work for him. All she had to do was rummage through his desk to find out what ID he gave me."

"But why her? Why not Martinez or the others?"

"Because she had the motivation to help him. She was engaged to him."

Paoli looked confused. "I thought his girlfriend was Lorna."

I explained about Lorna and Miranda wearing the same ring.

"We have to tell someone at Anco about the message you got today," he said.

I agreed. Paoli and I searched through the phone book, called information, and finally ended up calling three different guys named Alan Chambers before we found the right one. Chambers sounded ticked off at being bothered at home on a Saturday, especially when it meant he would have to work on a weekend, but he said he would alert the weekend operations staff about the security break and have computer system access frozen until Monday.

When I suggested to him that Miranda could have given my ID to Lufkin, he said he kept all his employees' home phone numbers and that he was sure he still had hers even though she no longer worked for him. The list was at the office, he said with real regret, but he said he would drive in and get it so he could call her and question her right away. I was starting to like him a little better, even though he refused to have me or Paoli in attendance when he had his chat with Miranda. As a former manager I have to admit I would have done the same.

When I hung up, Paoli leaned back on the futon and looked smug.

"It's a little after ten. I'd say we've put in a full day here. How shall we spend the rest of our Saturday?"

I was relieved that he was still automatically including me in his activities in spite of my stupid behavior the night before, but I had other plans for him.

"We have to work."

Paoli's smug expression turned into a frown. "Why?"

"Because things are escalating. The tone of the message I got today makes me think that Lufkin is getting desperate."

"But Anco is closed."

"Doesn't matter. Can I use your phone?"

Paoli grimaced as he handed it to me. Pulling my electronic address book out of my handbag, I pushed a couple of keys and came up with the number I was looking for. The phone rang once and was picked up by Steve Elkjer, a headhunter in Silicon Valley. I had used his services when I was at ICI; Elkjer always had tabs on the software developer market.

"Steve, it's Julie Blake.... Sure, the business is going great. Steve, I have a question for you. Have you ever heard of a software developer named Arnie Lufkin...? Yes, he's the one. That's what I needed to know.... Can't tell you now. No time. I'll call you next week and see if you can fit in lunch.... Thanks." I set the phone down. "Just what I thought," I said.

"And what is that?"

"That anybody in the computer headhunter business would know about Arnie Lufkin, even if it was just from the papers. Elkjer recognized his name immediately. Sajak was lying through her teeth."

"But Sajak is in San Francisco. Elkjer is in Silicon Valley, so he's probably more in touch with this stuff," said Paoli.

"Wrong for two reasons." I held up a thumb. "One, Lufkin worked in San Francisco, which is also where Sajak works. For that reason it's more likely that Sajak would have heard of him than Elkjer. Number two, Elkjer specializes in operations people, way off base from Lufkin's line of work. And Lufkin was one of the top guys in Sajak's market niche. Sharp headhunters know who the top guys are and call them every once in a while just to see if they're happy with their jobs. They're always looking for new meat."

"You put it so delicately."

"Get dressed. We're going to see Sajak."

"Sweetstuff, it's ten-fifteen on a Saturday. She's probably still asleep."

"By the time we get there, she'll be in her office. Sajak's a Type A workaholic."

"Takes one to know one."

"She'll be there."

"I doubt it."

"Bet five dollars?"

"You're on," he said.

I picked up the phone and got Sajak's office number from information, then dialed. She picked up on the first ring. I hung up without speaking.

"Bingo. You can owe me," I said.

"Why didn't you tell her we were coming to see her?"

"Because surprising her yesterday, which was your very good idea, is what threw her off. Why not stick with a winning play?"

"I'll be ten minutes," he said, then headed for the shower. I battled with myself over how to bring up the previous night's disaster. He was graciously keeping quiet about it, giving me the chance to bring it into conversation, but finally, after he was showered and dressed, he couldn't wait any longer.

"Julie, about last night."

"What about it?"

He looked at me and smiled, and his blue eyes did their crinkling act. "I just wanted you to know that last night I was thinking about driving by your house to make sure you were home. I thought you might be out with McCracken."

"You're just saying that to make me feel better."

His eyebrows went up and down a few times in mock deviousness. "You'll never know for sure, will you?"

That was the last we ever said about it.

We reached Sajak's office building ten minutes before noon. Paoli's Porsche had stalled twice, and we finally had to pull over at a gas station so Paoli could tinker with the engine.

With no security guard in the small lobby we were able to get in with no problems. We took the elevator to the fourth floor and approached her office. I pressed the buzzer, but it made no sound.

"Are you sure she was here?" Paoli asked in a whisper.

"Of course I'm sure. She answered the phone."

"Maybe she went out for something."

"Maybe," I said as I slowly turned the door handle.

Paoli grabbed my arm. "You're going to set off an alarm or something."

I gave the door a push and it opened.

"Ms. Sajak?" I called out, but there was no answer.

"She's not here, Julie. I don't like this. Let's go get a cup of coffee and call her later and make an appointment." Paoli tugged at my arm.

"You stay here and tell me if you hear the elevator. I'm going to look around inside."

"Julie, that's breaking and entering. I can't let you do it."

I raised an eyebrow. "When did I start asking permission? Besides, the door is open. I'm not breaking into anything. An open door is almost an invitation," I said as I stepped inside the office. I turned my head toward her desk. "Holy Jesus," I said, my voice filled with fear.

"Julie?" said Paoli as he quickly stepped inside and saw what I did. Sajak was sitting in her chair, her skin bluish, her head thrown back, her eyes open and glassy. Foam and saliva ringed her gaping mouth. She looked quite dead.

TEN

FOR A FEW MOMENTS we stood frozen in place. It was the expression on her face that I remember—an expression of agony and horror, her eyes wide open as if she were looking frantically at someone, maybe in recrimination, maybe for help. This wasn't the first corpse I'd seen, but I guess it's one of those experiences that feels fresh every time. I felt nausea and tears swelling inside me.

Paoli moved quickly toward her, lifted her hand, and pressed his fingers against her wrist.

"What are you doing? The woman's dead. Can't you tell?" My voice was choked and my knees beginning to buckle. I held onto the door for support.

"I had to be sure."

"Do you see any blood?" I asked, my voice becoming hoarse.

He shook his head. "No. No blood. She could have had a heart attack, but she's got some kind of foam around her mouth."

"A seizure?"

"Maybe." He paused. "Or poisoned."

Poisoned. The idea of it grabbed hold of me, and the questions it aroused subdued my fear, at least temporarily. I tentatively walked toward Sajak's body. A caramel-colored liquid was spilled over the papers on her desk, a Styrofoam cup lying in the resulting mess. The white foam inside the cup and sprinkle of dark powder around its rim told me she had been drinking a cappuccino. I saw Paoli looking at the cup, too, and knew we had come to the same horrible conclusion.

But if the coffee had been poisoned, who put it there? The coffee had to have come from some local coffeehouse, because I didn't see a cappuccino machine in Sajak's office. Downtown San Francisco had cappuccino stands on every corner, but they all put their name and logo on their cups. Sajak's cup was plain white Styrofoam.

For some strange reason the sight of that empty cup filled me with sadness, and I felt a connection to her. Sajak had died alone in her office, working on a Saturday. She and I were probably a lot alike, I thought. I imagined her worrying that she worked too much, that she had gained a few pounds, that she had chosen the wrong boyfriend, that she never had children. Children. Why did I assume she didn't have any children? I had the sickening thought that maybe Sajak did have children, and that those children would never see their mother again. I looked around her desk and on the walls for photos of kids but didn't find any, and that provided a small, short-lived sense of relief.

The wastebasket by Sajak's desk was empty except for a single plastic lid with dried milk foam on the underside. That proved that the coffee had come from a commercial establishment.

"I'll call the police," Paoli said, his voice shaky as he reached for the phone.

"Don't. Not yet. I want to look around first."

He looked at me, startled. "What for?"

"We came here because we thought Sajak knew something she wasn't telling us. I still want to find out what it was."

"Julie, there's a dead person in this room. We've got to call the police."

I knew he was right, and my urge to get the hell out of there was as strong as his, but the difference between me and Paoli is that in a crisis his emotions take over, while mine take a backseat to iron-willed determination. In spite of the fact that my knees were shaking and I could feel bile rising in my throat, I wanted more information. If Sajak had been murdered there could be a connection to Lufkin, and if I didn't look around her office while I had the chance I might never know what the connection was. Sajak had been a professional, and if she had been in my situation she would have done the same thing. In my heart I knew she would approve.

"We're going to call the police, but we're being paid a lot of money to find Arnie Lufkin and there could be something in here that could help us." I glanced around the office and my eyes rested on a low cabinet. "I'll start with her files."

"Julie, no. It's not right."

"Why?"

"One, you're disturbing the scene of a crime. Two, it's just not right to paw through a dead person's things."

"She's not going to mind, Paoli. It won't take long, and I won't disturb anything."

While he watched, face agog, I walked over to the file cabinet and reached to open it but stopped, hands hovering in air. Fingerprints. No need to broadcast this to the police. I looked in vain around the room for something to wrap around my hands but found nothing. Finally I took off my tennis shoe, then my sock, and pulled the sock over my right hand. I opened the file drawer with one finger of my socked hand and with my other hand carefully flipped through the files using only my index fingernail.

"What are you looking for?" Paoli asked, his voice sounding thin. I knew from experience that stumbling across the recently deceased made my partner feel faint, and I looked at him to make sure he was still standing. He was. I returned my eyes to the task at hand.

"Not sure. A name I can connect with, maybe. Finding a file with Arnie Lufkin's name on it would be nice." I heard a soft thud and saw that Paoli had now sunk to a sitting position on the floor, his face turning the color of Lorraine Sajak's. "Are you okay?"

"Fine. Dandy. Doing swell. Just hurry up and get this over with before I puke." Paoli's eyes were closed, his hands pressed against his head, making his hairs stand up between his fingers.

I tried to hurry, going directly to the *L*'s and not finding a file on Lufkin. But past the *L*'s I came across something interesting. I pulled a file out of the drawer. "Paoli, I've got something."

"I'm so pleased for you," he said with a moan.

"It's Annette Parker's file."

"So?"

"So, I'm not sure what it means, but it could mean something." I didn't think I should take the file with me but instead flipped through it to see if anything looked important. There was the personnel placement contract Annette had signed with D-Quest and her résumé. I put the file back in the drawer and closed it.

"Are we through obstructing justice now, Julie? Can I call the police?"

"In a minute. I want to look in her desk first. I need you to roll her chair back so I can pull out the drawer."

His eyes widened. "Forget it," he said with surprising vigor.

"It will only take a minute."

"The time factor is not my concern here." He was sitting erect now, his annoyance bringing a little color back to his face. "Touching anything could disturb fingerprints."

"We can move her without touching her chair. We can just push on her shoulders."

Paoli grimaced. "You're on your own."

"You're stronger than me. You can move her more easily."

"Why do I always have to be the one to touch the dead person?"

"Don't be silly. You talk like we do this all the time."

"Considering the short time we've known each other, I think we're stumbling across dead people at an alarming rate."

"We'll do it together. Now get up, sweetheart. You get on that side and I'll get on the other side, and we'll just move her back a little so I can pull out the drawer."

"Is it occurring to you that this is a violation of the law?" he said as he stood.

"You already touched her when you checked her pulse. This isn't a problem. We tell the police we touched her a couple of times when we were checking to see if she was dead. It's perfectly logical." I moved to the left side of what remained of Lorraine Sajak. It was creepy getting so close to her and I fought off another wave of nausea, but I couldn't lose this feeling that Sajak had some connection with Lufkin that she had tried to conceal. If that were true, there had to be something in her office that proved the connection.

I grabbed Sajak's shoulder with my socked hand to demonstrate how easily the task could be handled. Paoli watched me, then walked over and put his hand on her other shoulder.

"We roll her back on the count of three. One... two... three," I said.

When we rolled her back a few inches, Sajak slumped to the right, her head falling against Paoli's stomach. He yelled and jumped backward. Poor Lorraine was now leaning precariously to the right.

"See what you've done?" he said through clenched teeth.

"Keep your voice down. Just push her back into an upright position."

Paoli shivered and slowly pushed Sajak back up while I looked at the drawer. Without moving anything, I scanned its contents. It was mostly paper clips, pencils, a few scattered business cards, and lipsticks, but then tucked in the

back I saw a folded letter. The paper was pale blue stationery folded in half. I knew I shouldn't touch it, so instead I
pulled the drawer toward me a few more inches and the paper unfolded enough so I could read some of what was on
the inside. It was hand-written in black ink.

"Dear Bitch," the letter started. "You think you've got
him, but you're wrong. He was just using you to get what
he wants. You're…" The rest was below the fold, and I had
to twist my head and shoulders to the left to read it. "…too
old, you hag. Leave him alone. I mean it." The letter was
signed "Miranda."

I closed the drawer.

"What were you looking at?" Paoli asked.

"A letter. It was from Miranda Owens, and it was mildly
threatening." I stopped talking and considered my next
move. "Maybe I should go through the files in the credenza."

"No, Julie, you're through. Finito. That's it. We're
pushing her back up to the desk, and I'm calling the police.
This is nonnegotiable."

I figured it was time to acquiesce. We pushed Sajak back
up to the desk. I gave her an appraising look. "Is that the
position she was in when we walked in? Seems to me she was
slumped a little more to the left."

Paoli shot a warning look at me. "I don't care if she was
slumped naked between her knees. We're not touching her
anymore."

"Sorry I mentioned it."

As I looked at the body of Lorraine Sajak I remembered
how well coiffed and perfectly made up she had looked the
first time I saw her, and it occurred to me that she would
have hated strangers viewing her like this, with her attractive face so distorted. I wanted to straighten up her makeup
a bit, wipe off her chin, and gently push her mouth closed,
but I knew I couldn't. *I'll help find who did this to you*, I

told her silently, turned my face away, then turned back. *And you weren't old,* I added.

"We'll tell the police that the body moved when I checked her pulse," Paoli said. "They'll go for that."

"Good. That sounds plausible. So, let's call the police." I reached for the phone.

"No!" Paoli said, my hand in midair. "Don't touch the phone. I'll use the pay phone in the lobby."

I followed Paoli to the lobby and waited while he dialed 911 and gave them the address. He hung up the phone with more force than was necessary and stared at the receiver.

"Are you angry with me?" I asked him.

"No, Julie. Finding dead people just makes me irritable, that's all. I'm funny that way," he said. There was no trace of humor in his voice. "I'm going back up. We'll wait in the hall."

I followed him back upstairs to the hallway, where we sat on the floor. Paoli was looking pale again. He went to the men's room.

I wasn't feeling that great myself. After he came back, we sat there about ten minutes, and during that time my mind churned over the facts in front of me, including whether or not Miranda Owens could have sufficient motive to murder Lorraine Sajak and how poison could have gotten into that Styrofoam cup. Then the police arrived—three of them, all uniformed men, one of them carrying a small suitcase. The paramedics were right behind.

I gave Paoli a nudge. "It took them long enough. Some response time. What did they do, stop to give out a few parking tickets on the way?" I whispered as the tallest of the three approached us.

"Did one of you place the call?" he asked.

"Me," Paoli said.

"Okay, both of you wait here."

They all went into Sajak's office. From my vantage point in the hallway I couldn't see what they were doing and could only hear snatches of their conversations. When there had been a murder at my ICI offices in Santa Clara six months before, the local police had virtually bubbled with excitement, but these guys were very matter-of-fact and business-like.

My nature doesn't allow me to do a lot of idle waiting. I stuck my head into the room. One of them had picked up the Styrofoam cup with tweezers and was placing it in a plastic bag.

"Poison, right?" I said.

"Back in the hall, please," the tall one said.

"Don't forget to look at her computer's hard disk. Her correspondence and business records will be there. Could prove useful," I told him.

He gave me a look. "We've done this before. Get back in the hall."

A few minutes later we were joined by more police, and soon there was bustling activity in Sajak's office. I wondered how long it would take them to find Miranda's letter. I could have given them a head start on it but knew I should keep my mouth shut.

An officer with a pen and notepad in his hands came up to Paoli and me. He looked like Ernest Borgnine, only not as good-looking.

"My name's Boskin. Tell me what happened here," he said with the tone of a guy who didn't like working Saturdays.

I let Paoli do the honors. He told Boskin just about everything except for the fact that I had looked through Sajak's file cabinet and desk drawer.

Boskin nodded and scribbled in his notebook. "Why were you here to see Miss Sajak? Did you have an appointment?"

Paoli hesitated before answering, and I saw Boskin's eyes flicker with interest.

"No, we didn't have an appointment," I said, jumping into the conversation, and Paoli suddenly looked worried.

"How did you know she would be here? It's Saturday morning, not exactly normal working hours."

"We met her yesterday and she seemed like a Type A."

His eyebrows moved upward. "What does her blood type have to do with it?"

"Not her blood type. I mean an A-type personality. The kind of person who works all the time. I assumed she would be working on a Saturday."

Boskin eyed me with skepticism, and suddenly I was very conscious of my T-shirt and blue jeans. During the week I wore my tailored suits like armor, and those serious clothes gave me instant credibility. Now I realized that in my blue jeans I looked like anybody on the street, the type of person who could perhaps be guilty of a crime. I wanted to tell him how many suits I owned, then flash him my résumé.

"Okay, she was an A-type personality. So you figured she would be working on Saturday. Why did you want to see her?"

Paoli never missed a chance to hand somebody one of our business cards. Boskin studied it. "So what is this? The computer fraud part I get, but what does that have to do with the woman in there?"

I rattled on about Lorna Donatello, her search for Arnie Lufkin, and how the recession had forced us into looking for him. I explained about how I had thought Sajak might know something about Lufkin. Boskin's eyes never left mine while I spoke, and it seemed to me he was looking at me with less than total confidence. I chose that moment to unload my theory on him.

"I think I can help speed up the process here, because I've given this some thought already." Boskin didn't react. "I think she was poisoned. The poison was put in a cappuccino that had to come from some coffee place around here. I think she was busy working, and somebody she knows well called to say he or she was coming to visit her. How do we know she knew this person well? Two reasons." I held up a thumb. "One, she asks this person to stop on the way and get her a cappuccino."

"Or maybe this person knew she liked cappuccinos, knew she would take one if it was offered to her," Paoli said helpfully.

I nodded and continued. "Now, it occurred to me that almost all of the cappuccino places around here imprint their cups with logos, but Sajak's cup was not imprinted. I think our killer bought the cappuccino, then poured it into the unmarked Styrofoam cup so it couldn't be traced."

It was at this point that I noticed Boskin's eyes growing warier. I should have stopped, but I was on a roll.

"Two, she turned off her door security system so this person could come in without her having to buzz him in. Yesterday we had to ring the bell outside the door and then she buzzed us, but today it must have been turned off because we were able to walk right in. This means she was familiar with whoever murdered her. Are you with me?"

"I don't know that anybody murdered her," Boskin said. "Who said anybody murdered her? Powell!" he yelled over his shoulder. A blond officer stepped into the hallway.

"Yeah?"

"Take these two to the station. Now."

"Why do you want us at the station?" Paoli asked, flustered.

I pushed my five-foot-three frame forcefully in front of Boskin. "Are you arresting us?"

"No," he said. "Not yet."

ELEVEN

DURING OUR NEEDLESSLY ceremonious squad car ride to the
station, I tried to explain to our two escorting officers the
numerous reasons why the San Francisco Police Department would maximize their productivity by releasing Paoli
and me and focusing their efforts on finding Lorraine Sajak's murderer.

After quickly outlining a few short-term objectives from
them, I was in the middle of verbally creating a task list
when one of the officers suggested, too forcefully I thought,
that I sit back, fasten my seat belt, and keep my mouth shut.
One look at Paoli's face told me that he agreed with the man
wholeheartedly. Annoyed and insulted, I crossed my arms
and decided to hell with them; let them figure it out on their
own.

After arriving at the station, Paoli and I were escorted to
different rooms. I assumed this separation was imposed on
us because they suspected us of murdering Lorraine Sajak
and didn't want to give us the opportunity to cook up cor-
roborating alibis. It also occurred to me that I should consider calling a lawyer, but I only knew corporate lawyers,
and corporate lawyers were notoriously inept at anything
that fell outside the world of contracts. Besides, calling a
lawyer would imply guilt on our part. We had done nothing wrong and had nothing to hide. I decided to rely on my
own resources, at least for the time being.

We spent three hours in the station—two and a half hours
waiting and a half hour being interviewed by Boskin. During the first hour I sat on a hard chair that made my behind
go numb, with my brain not far behind. They could at least

leave magazines to read like in a doctor's office, but then I suppose it would be tough to find reading material suitable for the criminal element. I made a mental note to suggest a subscription to *Guns and Ammo*.

I hate waiting. I stuck my head out the door every ten minutes and informed whoever was passing by that I didn't like wasting time, but no one cared. Once I saw Paoli wandering around asking people for the *Chronicle*'s sports section. The next time I poked my head out he had made friends with one of the policemen at the front desk, and the two of them were yukking it up like frat boys. Paoli has that kind of winning personality. I preferred to sit alone, stew, and chide myself for being stuck sitting on my tush when I could be doing something productive, maybe something that would help find Lorraine Sajak's murderer. While I sat there the sickening thought occurred to me that maybe Paoli and I were indirectly responsible for Sajak's death. Was she killed so she wouldn't be able to talk to Paoli and me? The horrible thought of my possible guilt in the situation kept rolling around my head.

I had to get my mind off Sajak. I asked to use a phone and checked my voice mail. My mother had called twice. She expected a call from me on Saturdays. I got my phone credit card from my purse and dialed her number in Sacramento.

We chatted for a few minutes about life in general, her newest bridge partner, and the rising cost of flank steak before we got down to what really mattered to her.

"Is there any talk of marriage between you and Victor?" she asked.

"We've only known each other six months, Mother. It's too soon to be talking marriage."

"Your father talked about marriage on our second date."

I had heard this story a thousand times. At that moment a young man strongly desiring his freedom was being dragged, kicking and screaming, into the station by two policemen.

"What's that yelling?" my mother asked.

I tried to think of excuses but opted, in error, for the truth.

"I'm at a police station."

My mother erupted like Vesuvius. "Were you mugged? What happened? Are you all right? Are you all right? God, this country's going right down the toilet. It's those Democrats. Baby, tell me what happened."

Closing my eyes, I could see my mother, her bleached and coiffed head bobbing, the plump body quivering, her naturally pink skin turning the color of a potted geranium, as she imagined the horrors of life swallowing her progeny whole. I loved my mother very much, but her anxiety-inducing protectiveness could make me crazy.

"I'm fine. I wasn't mugged or anything."

"Then what are you doing there?"

I took a long breath. "I'm being questioned."

"Questioned? Questioned?" She liked to repeat things. "About what?"

"About a possible murder."

Silence on the phone. An ominous silence, deep and cavernous, the kind you could spelunk through. Then she spoke.

"Maybe this is the sort of thing that keeps Victor from talking marriage. Have you considered that?"

"Mom, he's here with me. He's being questioned, too."

That stumped her, but only for a moment. "Stressful situations make people bond. It makes for a strong relationship."

IT WAS ALMOST 2:00 p.m. by the time we left the station. Boskin was suspicious of our involvement in Sajak's murder, but it was the undependability of the Porsche that saved us. After a barrage of questions and finally a call to the gas station where Paoli had repaired the Porsche on the way to San Francisco that morning, Boskin proved to his satisfaction that we couldn't have been in San Francisco anywhere near the time of Sajak's murder. Boskin never mentioned Miranda Owens, but he did confirm for us that Sajak's coffee had been poisoned. The medical examiner thought the poison to be potassium cyanide, the kind sold by any of a hundred chemical companies. They would know for sure later that day.

After Boskin's questioning, they took fingerprints and hair samples from us, and then Paoli and I were free to go, although Boskin said he would want to talk to us again later. The fact that we weren't being held as murder suspects had failed to lift Paoli's increasingly dark mood.

"We're supposed to be investigating computers," he muttered as we walked out the police station doors and onto the street. "Why couldn't we just stick with computers? Computers don't kill; they don't die violent deaths; they don't froth at the mouth or bleed on the floor. I like computers."

"May I remind you that taking on the Lufkin job was your idea?"

"Oh, great, so now it's my fault?"

It had been a rough day, and I wasn't in the mood for complaining. "I thought you said that you left NSA because you were looking for excitement. So this is excitement, isn't it?" I said with irritation as I scanned the street for a cab.

"Finding dead people and spending three hours in a police station is not my idea of excitement. That Boskin guy seems very suspicious of us, you know. He could still think we're involved with her murder."

"Well, we're not. But I have a feeling who is."

There were no cabs in sight. I started walking, but Paoli grabbed my arm and pulled me to a stop. "Who?"

I turned. "Arnie Lufkin. It's got to be him."

"How can you say that? Especially when you found a threatening letter from Miranda Owens in Sajak's desk."

"I still think it was Lufkin. Miranda didn't seem like a killer to me." Paoli rolled his eyes; then started walking and I followed him. "Okay, I know there's not a lot of evidence to support it right now, but I just have this feeling Lufkin is at least involved. Ox told us he was dangerous."

"You're right on that one, and that's why we're backing off this case. Sure, I like money as much as the next person. In fact, I like money *more* than the next person, but not enough to risk our necks." Paoli was walking fast now, and I was having trouble keeping up.

"We can't back off. We made a commitment to Lorna. We've already spent the money she gave us," I said, getting out of breath.

"So we'll give her an IOU and pay her back at a monthly rate. There was nothing in the contract that committed us to getting involved with murders. If you want, I'll break the news to her," he said, his arms waving. Paoli was half-Polish and half-Italian, but it was the Italian side that usually dominated.

"No." I said the word loudly.

Paoli stopped. We stumbled into each other. He grabbed me to keep me from falling onto the sidewalk, and he was still holding onto me as I looked up at him. For a second I thought he was going to kiss me, but he didn't.

"I know what you're thinking, but we can't quit now," I said. "If the situation is dangerous, then that's just one more reason for us to keep working on it. We've got to find out what's going on. People could get hurt if we don't."

"Julie, *we* could get hurt. You and me. I'm not interested in that."

"Nothing's going to happen to us. We'll watch our backs. But we can't run away from a situation just because there's a little risk involved."

Paoli scowled and let go of me, and we walked in silence.
A few minutes later we waved down a cab that took us to
Sajak's building, where the Porsche was parked, and to top
things off, we got a parking ticket. After a three-minute
discussion over which of us really had the keys, we got in the
car and headed for home.

Sensing our distress, the Porsche, which had already
provided us with an alibi for Sajak's murder, was addition-
ally kind and brought us to Paoli's place without incident.
I was liking this car more and more. And somehow without
speaking Paoli and I managed to call a truce. I think we were
just too tired to disagree anymore. We collapsed on his futon, too beat to go out to anything even resembling dinner
or a movie, so we had pizza delivered and spent most of the
evening playing Strip Scrabble, the strip part being my idea.
He was already down to his underwear and one sock before
I even had to take off my blouse. He lost his Fruit of the
Looms on my use of *exodus* with double points on *x,* and on
that note we called it a night.

We spent Sunday outlining possibilities about how Lufkin could break into Anco's software from outside the
company. Assuming Lufkin had been familiar with the security software, there were several ways Lufkin could have
done it. Paoli would have Lufkin's actual point of entry
mapped out in a couple of days, and he estimated that
plugging the holes in the software would take another week,
if he had at least four to five hours a day to work on it. Both
of us had written security software at our old jobs, so that
Anco puzzle wasn't that tough, but the puzzle regarding
Lufkin's whereabouts still represented a challenge I couldn't
resist. I was more than happy to let Paoli handle the technical end of things while I focused my efforts on Lufkin.

On Monday morning Paoli went to Anco to keep working on the software, and I drove to Comtech to meet Eldon. Normally Paoli and I would have squabbled over who
got the more interesting job at Anco, but he volunteered

happily for the Anco work. I knew he wanted to keep me away from Andrew McCracken. Paoli's only proviso was that I take the camera and get pictures of everyone, so I snapped the beeper/camera onto the waistband of my skirt and headed off.

After picking up the pastries Eldon had demanded, I pulled the Toyota into a parking space in front of Comtech and found Wayne Hansen pacing the sidewalk, bobbing up and down like one of those dashboard animals with a spring in its neck. Max leaned casually against Hansen's red Ferrari, her arms crossed, watching Hansen's gyrations with a look of disinterest. I couldn't help but notice that the nose of the beautiful Ferrari was smashed.

Max looked chic in what I guessed was a Chanel suit, her savoir faire in sharp contrast to Hansen's rumpled looks. Since she and Hansen had announced their engagement, Max had been striving to improve his wardrobe, but with little success. That day Hansen was wearing long pants, which was considered formal wear for him, but the pants were wrinkled and his Comtech sweatshirt had ink stains on the front.

"Hi. What are you guys doing here?"

"What am I doing here? I own this company, that's what I'm doing here!" Hansen said. He seemed more hyper than usual. I looked at Max.

"Wayne wanted to see the VR programs you gave Eldon, and on the way here we had a little accident." Max pointed to the Ferrari.

Hansen's eyes barely brushed over the collection of scrapes and dents, as if a longer look would prove too painful. "I let her drive, and she smashed the car into a post at McDonald's."

"Wayne is going through a Breakfast Burrito phase. We used the drive-through and I didn't see the post. It could happen to anybody."

"You did it *on purpose.*" Hansen said the last two words slowly and with emphasis.

Max's lips curled downward in disgust. "That's absurd."

"It's the prenuptial, isn't it? You're still angry about that, aren't you?"

"Now that I think of it, smashing your car is an excellent way of expressing my displeasure."

"Displeasure?" Hansen yelled. He pointed to his car. "This is what you call displeasure? So what happens if you get really ticked off? You burn my house down?" Hansen was shaking and bouncing now like a poodle on caffeine. Max maintained her composure. My hand casually slipped down to the camera, and I caught the moment on celluloid. I was starting to appreciate the hidden-camera concept.

"I guess you should avoid finding out, shouldn't you?" she replied.

That's what I like about Max. Her attitude about life was simple, the rules less complex than for those of us hell-bent on self-analysis. Why did she agree to marry Wayne Hansen? Wayne was three years her junior, a wiry, neurotic junk food addict who was constantly dusted with Ding Dong crumbs, but Wayne had a bank account bigger than the GNP of some South American countries. He was also the brainchild and main stockholder behind Comtech, one of the fastest-growing high-tech companies in Silicon Valley.

Hansen was intent on telling his side of the story. "It wasn't my idea. It was my lawyer's; I swear," Hansen pleaded, but Max's face remained unforgiving. "God, I'm starved," he said, displaying his usual reaction to stress. Max opened her handbag, took out a Snickers, and casually tossed it to him like a zookeeper tossing a banana to a chimp. He caught it, barely getting the wrapper off before jamming half of the candy bar into his mouth.

"We'll talk about this prenuptial thing later, Wayne. Jules doesn't want to hear about our little domestic arguments, do you, Jules? We're here to help with important investigative work. Now, who's this guy you're looking for? Wayne asked me, but I couldn't remember the name."

"Arnie Lufkin," I said.

Hansen's eyes had been fixed upon Max, but when he heard Lufkin's name they darted over to me. I couldn't miss the reaction flash across his face. "You know him?" I asked.

Hansen looked uncomfortable. "I've heard of him. That's all."

"So who is this guy? Should I know him?" asked Max.

"You would if you read newspapers. Lufkin's the programmer who stole a half-million from Anco. He's taken an unauthorized vacation, and a lot of people want him back for trial. Paoli and I are looking for him."

The perplexed look on Hansen's face remained. I wanted to get to the bottom of it but decided to wait until Max wasn't around. He would relax more if it were just the two of us.

"That's why I need to take a look at the VR programs. They're Lufkin's. Do we have the equipment set up?"

Hansen's face turned back to its normal expression of childish arrogance. He took the remaining bit of his Snickers and nodded. "Yeah. Eldon's got it all ready," he said, his mouth full of chocolate.

"Shall we go in? I'm on a tight schedule."

Eldon was waiting for us in the reception area, and he and Hansen walked several feet ahead of Max and me as we followed them through a maze of hallways. They whispered to each other, and I wondered what they were saying.

"As I told you, the programs are exceptional," Eldon said to me when he and Hansen were apparently finished with their private conversation. "Whoever created them has come up with a way to digitize photographic 3-D images. When I started out I was using a joystick, but then I realized the sophistication of what I was dealing with. The programs take a data suit and data glove.''

"Where did you get them?" I asked.

"We borrowed them from Anco."

I tried not to show my alarm. "Did you tell them why?"

Eldon shook his head. "Didn't have to. I got them through a friend. His name's Martinez. I said we were experimenting with some stuff. I have to have the stuff back tomorrow. Here we are."

We entered a large room empty of furniture except a long table and a couple of metal chairs. Near the table sat three computers, each about the size of a small air-conditioning unit. A tangle of black and yellow cables led from the computers to a pile of black nylon sitting on the table. There was also a strange-looking helmet and gloves.

"I've played with the programs. The images are the sharpest I've seen."

"Tell me about them," I said.

"Whoever did them must have been experimenting with digitized photography, but you'll understand after you experience them," Eldon said. "Here; put this on."

He handed me the pile of black nylon. Unfolding it, I discovered it was a one-piece jumpsuit with Velcro closures and cables attached that connected to the computer. I took the suit and looked at it, then at him.

"Of course we'll leave the room," he said.

I smiled with gratitude. Eldon and Hansen walked out, leaving me with Max.

I took off my jacket, skirt, blouse, and shoes, keeping a wary eye on the door. Some of these programmer types stay cooped up so much with their computers they don't get to see women too often. Max helped me into the suit. It was about five sizes too large, but we used the Velcro straps to cinch it at the chest and waist. I rolled up the pants legs and the sleeves, being careful not to tangle the cabling.

Max called the guys back in. They had serious looks on their faces.

"You've got the suit on. Good, now the gloves." Eldon helped me put on the black nylon gloves with wires running from the fingers back to the computer. "These are sensors," he said. "They'll give you the sensation of touch. And this—" He handed me the helmet. It had large, bizarre-looking goggles attached. "This is your head-mounted display. The helmet has stereoscopic lenses inside. Each lens is attached via cable to a different computer. That's how you get a 3-D effect. You've also got a motion sensor in the helmet that will let you look in any direction. Every time you move your head, the computer will recalculate where you are in the program. Look here for a minute." He picked up a flat plastic contraption about an inch thick and about eight inches wide and held it up to my face. "Look into the holes here. This measures the distance between your pupils. I have to feed that data into the computer before we start."

With that accomplished, I pulled the helmet over my head. It was heavy and I could only see blackness through the goggles. Something foamlike encased my ears.

"Does this have sound?" I asked. Something clicked in the headphone and I could hear Eldon's voice through the speaker.

"Naturally. I'll help you with the cables. Max, you can help, too. This may take two people."

I couldn't see and couldn't hear well, and the cables attaching me to the computers hindered my movement. It was an experience that might start a claustrophobic person screaming, and it was making me feel apprehensive.

"What are you saying? Did you say it takes two people? Why?" I asked. I tried to turn and felt my foot tangle on the cables. I felt a hand on my arm.

"It's me," I heard Max say.

"What the hell's going on here?" I asked her.

I heard Eldon through my earphone, his voice deepened into a mock baritone.

"Welcome to Cyberspace."

TWELVE

SUDDENLY THE BLACK VOID surrounding me burst into a kaleidoscope of shapes and colors so intense, so electric, I gasped in astonishment. It was like being in a dark movie theater, a theater with every light off, so black you can't see your hand in front of you. Then, in one split second, the movie flashes on and you're almost blinded with brilliant colors. Only you're *inside* the movie. In the blink of an eye you've been thrust into a new world, surrounded by a fictional landscape that doesn't look like the reality you're used to but seems just as real, perhaps even more.

It took a few moments for my senses to adjust. Like a space traveler who had just taken her first steps off the mother ship and onto a strange planet, I didn't move at first but instead let my eyes gaze in wonderment at my new landscape.

I was inside a room. Aware of space and depth, I guessed that the walls, a vivid blue, were about eight feet away. I saw a table in front of me, and on top of the table was a vase of flowers. I moved my head slowly to the left and the landscape changed, accommodating to my movement. Now I saw a window, a bed and a dresser. A bedroom. I was in a bedroom. The simple act of recognition sent my skin tingling. Yes, this could be addicting, I thought. The stimulation of my senses reminded me of what it was like to be a child, when simple experience still had the freshness that activated the senses and the mind.

I became aware of traffic noise. I turned my head to the right. There was another window with a street scene outside. I saw cars and pedestrians pass by.

"Julie, can you hear me?"

The sound of Eldon's voice in my earphone startled me. I was in the middle of a dream, and his voice came from nowhere. I nodded.

"This one is a very simple program, but we can use it to get you acclimated. Try walking, but take baby steps. The program accelerates movement. My guess is that it's about four to one. Okay, go ahead. Take a step," Eldon said.

Eldon's voice came at me like Command Central. I took two steps and seemed to fly forward, zooming across the floor. The 3-D effect of the program was so real that I thrust my hand in front of me to keep from smashing into the blue wall, but instead of hitting the wall, my hand just slipped through it. I must have yelled, because I quickly felt a pressure on my arm that must have been Max. I could hear Eldon's chuckling in the earphone.

"See what I mean? Keep moving around, but go slow. Touch some things. You'll like the effect."

I moved forward with slow geisha steps toward the window. The traffic noise became slightly louder. I reached my hand out toward the wall, and this time when I reached it my fingers stopped, unable to go farther. The effect was stunning. I couldn't actually feel the wall, not in the way that the sense of touch allows you to feel, but because the program wouldn't allow my hand to go through this part of the wall, the experience simulated touch.

My respect for Lufkin had skyrocketed. I wanted to know him and explore his brain, and I suddenly realized why you could become obsessed with VR. To be able to create this virtual world for yourself would make you feel like a god. You create it, you control it and own it, and under the right circumstances, you could impose it on others, and experientially it was like some fantastic drug.

"You're impressed, aren't you?" Eldon said.

"Can you see what I'm seeing?" I asked him.

"To some extent, but not the way you see it. I'm tracking you on my screen so I can tell where you are in the program. See the vase on the table?"

"Yes. It's to the left."

"Pick it up."

I walked over to the table, now feeling more comfortable with movement. My hand reached for the vase, my fingers wrapped around its circumference, and I lifted it.

"I can't believe I'm doing this," I said. "It's incredible."

"Okay, now drop the vase."

"Drop it?"

"Right on the floor."

I opened my fingers. The vase fell from my hands and shattered on the floor, complete with sound effects and splintered glass. I watched the broken pieces of the vase as they erupted from the floor. The speed of movement was a little slow and the sound slightly hollow, which only contributed to the dreamlike effect.

"Okay, Julie. Ready for the second program? It's more interesting."

"I'm ready," I said, eager to see the program that could be more interesting than this one.

"Excellent. Max is going to pull you back to the starting point."

I could feel her hand on my arm, and I moved backward. My goggles went black.

"All set? This one is much kinkier," Eldon said.

"In my book, kinky is a good thing," I heard Max say. She must have grabbed Eldon's microphone.

"Ready for takeoff," I told him.

New shapes and colors washed over me. I was standing in front of a white door. It seemed obvious that I was to open it. I reached for the door handle, pulled it open, and saw a flight of stairs. I headed up the stairs, my hand grasping the handrail, eerily feeling that I was actually reaching step after step. After the first flight I saw another door, but when I reached for the handle I realized the software wouldn't allow me to open it.

I continued up the next flight of stairs, came upon another door, and again was unable to open it. Continuing up the steps, I reached for the handle of the next door and turned it. The door opened. I passed through the doorway and found myself in a hall. Looking to the right and the left, I saw several doors and didn't know which way to go, until I saw to my right that one of the doors was open about an inch. I headed for it. When I reached the door I pushed it open. Now in front of me was an office. There were bookshelves, an antique desk, a window that looked out over buildings. There were pictures on the wall, although I couldn't distinguish the pictures' subjects. They were more like a blur of color.

A woman sat at an antique desk, her back to me. Her hair was blond, shoulder-length. She sensed my presence and turned to me. When I saw her face my stomach rose to my chest. It was the face of Lorraine Sajak.

Now I recognized the room—antique desk, a large mirror in the corner, art on the walls. It was Sajak's office. She rose from her chair and moved in slow motion toward me. Even though I was conscious of the fact that she wasn't real, I felt frightened. It was like she had come back from the dead.

She walked closer toward me, the program making her movements slow and stiff. My pulse quickened. She reached for my left hand. I looked down and saw a cup of coffee held in my fingers. Why hadn't I noticed that before? I tried to drop it, to throw the cup on the floor, but it wouldn't leave my hand. The program wouldn't allow it. Like in a nightmare, the scene around me veered out of my control. Sajak's hand wrapped around the coffee. It was poison, I told myself. I now understood the surroundings and the moment. I was there to murder her. I jerked my hand back.

"No!" I cried.

"Are you okay?" I heard Eldon's voice in my ear. Sajak kept moving closer to me. I knew Lufkin had never intended anyone to see this program, because in it he had created his murder. He had practiced going up the side stairs so he wouldn't be seen. Over and over again he had seen his victim's trusting face and built up his nerve. And now I was him, experiencing the murder the way he had experienced it.

Sajak's face was inches from mine. Her eyes closed. She moved forward, and I knew she was going to kiss me. I jumped to my left to avoid her, and with the accelerated motion I zoomed headfirst right through the wall. Suddenly I was cloaked in a blackness that felt like death. I cried out.

"Julie, please, relax. You simply moved too fast and fell out of the program. It's called falling out of reality. I love that term. Max is going to pull you back in."

Was that it? Had I just fallen out of the program? It felt like I had been hurled from one hell into another, blacker version. I was trembling as I felt Max's hands on my shoulder. I heard her voice, and the sound of it calmed me.

"Turn the damn thing off, Eldon. Are you all right?" she asked.

I could feel the helmet and goggles being pulled off my head.

"What was it, Jules? What scared you?" Max asked.

I couldn't tell her. Not then. "Nothing. It just startled me, that's all."

I could see on her face that she wasn't buying it.

"There's one more program, if you want to see it. It's not finished, though, so there's not much there," Eldon said.

"I think she's had enough," Max replied.

"No, I'm fine," I told her, although I wasn't, but it would be foolish to stop, since the equipment had to go back the next day. "I want to see the last program." I pulled the hel-

met and goggles back on and took a fortifying breath.
"Let's go."

At first blackness, then a new world popped up around
me. No vivid colors this time, everything was in variations
of gray. I moved my head from left to right. This one didn't
have the clarity of the ones before. I saw curving shapes, like
an outdoor landscape, but Lufkin obviously hadn't finished his work. I moved slowly forward to a curving line in
front of me. It seemed to drop off into nothing, and there
was nowhere else for me to go.

I took off the goggles. "This one isn't finished."

"What did it look like?" Max asked.

"I'm not even sure. Just a lot of gray," I said as I removed the data glove and stepped away from the equipment. "Where's Hansen?"

"He went off to play with his buddies. Do you have time
for coffee?"

I didn't really, but my hands were still quivering. A conversation with Max would give me time to pull myself together.

"Sure. Where to?"

"There's a place next door. You change and I'll go tell
Wayne." Max left, with Eldon following close behind.

While I struggled with the data suit and got back into my
clothes, the image of Lorraine Sajak stuck in my mind. I
now knew that Lufkin had killed her, and I thought I knew
why. She and Lufkin had been lovers. Sajak must have
known where he was. Maybe she had even helped him hide.

Max returned in a few minutes, and we walked to a sandwich shop next door. She ordered a coffee, but I had juice.
My experience with Lorraine Sajak had put me off coffee
for a while. A can of Folger's would never seem quite the
same to me.

We sat down at a table near the window and quickly
caught each other up on our work and our love lives, in that

order. After a few more minutes of Max detailing Hansen's sexual performances, she grew serious.

"There's something I need to tell you," she said.

"What's that?"

"I just wanted you to know that Wayne knows some things about Lufkin he's not telling you."

"Like what? What does he know?"

"Don't bite my head off. I'm the one trying to help you. I'm not sure what he knows. It's just that when I went to tell him we were going for coffee I heard him talking about Lufkin to Eldon. I stood outside and listened a minute, but I didn't get much. I just thought you should know."

"Thanks," I said, standing to leave. "I'm going to confront him about it. I don't want to cause trouble between you two, but this is important."

"Go easy on him, Jules. Remember, he's just eccentric. He doesn't trust anybody." She saw my expression and added, "And don't kill him. I'm not in his will yet." She smiled at me.

"I promise to leave him breathing."

We walked back to Comtech and found Hansen in the same small office talking to Eldon.

"I want to talk to you," I told him.

He looked at me without concern. "In a minute. I'm busy."

"Now." I put more force behind my voice.

Hansen's expression turned into a combination of caution and curiosity. He and I had worked on joint projects before, and we knew each other pretty well.

"Okay, okay. I'll be back in a minute," he said to Eldon, then followed Max and me out into the hall. "What is it?"

I closed in on him. "Why didn't you tell me you knew Arnie Lufkin? You know I'm doing work for a client. Why did you keep information from me?"

"I don't know what Max told you, but I didn't keep anything from you. I don't know him. I mean not personally. I've just heard of him, like a lot of people."

"That's not what I heard you say to Eldon," Max said. Wayne glared at her. "I can't lie to a friend, Wayne."

Wayne sighed with exasperation. "Look; I don't even know what the guy looks like. It's by reputation mostly. Arnie Lufkin is a legend; at least he is in VR circles. We all knew what he was doing. And he would leave a lot of information on the Net."

I was familiar with the Net. It was a nationwide network used by businesses as well as serious programmer types. Frequently used for looking up software and programming information, the Net was a vehicle for exchanging messages, leaving information on an electronic bulletin board, accessing all kinds of weird data, some of it pretty kinky. I had heard stories about a pornography group that exchanged information solely through the Net.

"What kind of information did he leave?" I asked.

Hansen looked uncomfortable. "VR stuff, mostly. But he was famous for Hacker's Highlights."

"Is that what I think it is?"

Hansen smiled. "Yeah. Lufkin left tips about how to break into different networks. The guy was ruthless. He put out a message the other day about how to break into that public PC network that gives out stock quotes."

Now I knew how Lufkin had broken into my office computer, and how generous of him to pass the details on to others. But it was something else Hansen had said that stuck in my brain.

"You said you saw the message with Lufkin's name on it the other day? It would be pretty stupid to make hacking information public and use your own name."

Hansen looked at me like I was unbelievably stupid. "It didn't have his actual name on it. He uses a code name—you know, handle. A lot of people do."

"What is it?"

"Spider. He called himself Spider."

I remembered the poem on my personal computer. "Why that particular handle?" I asked him.

"Probably because people sometimes refer to the Net as the Web, because it's actually a web of different networks."

"And a spider is all-powerful in the web."

"I suppose."

"How did he spell it?"

Hansen thought a second. "S-p-y-d-e-r," he said.

Like the poem, I thought. *"Peek through the keyhole, Spyder in your eye. If you see one near you try to get away. If he does come closer, you won't forget the day."*

"Jules, are you cold?" Max asked. But it wasn't the temperature that was making me shiver.

THIRTEEN

REALITY IS ILLUSORY. I had suspected this since I was fourteen and Joanie Jaworski first showed me the transformational wonders of lipstick and mascara, but it took Arnie Lufkin's VR programs to bring the point home. But it was not illusory that Lorraine Sajak was now dead and lying in a cold grave. I had witnessed her last moments through the eyes of Arnie Lufkin, and the experience left me chilled and frightened and more determined than ever to find the son of a bitch. I wanted Lufkin to pay for what he had done.

As Paoli requested, I stopped by Bobby and Randall's office to say hello, and at the same time captured their disinterested expressions with my camera. After getting a shot of Eldon, I headed off, leaving Max and Hansen bickering over whether loyalty to a girlfriend should supersede one's loyalty to one's fiancé. That was one argument I wished to stay out of.

I arrived at Anco about eleven-thirty, and as soon as I walked in I called Detective Boskin to give him the news about Lufkin's VR program, but Boskin was out fighting crime, so I left a message for him, giving him the number at the office, since I didn't have a phone at Anco. I was curious about the letter from Miranda Owens I had seen in Sajak's desk. I knew the police must have found it. In fact, they had probably already questioned Miranda. I wanted to chat with Boskin about it but still didn't want him to know that I had been rummaging around Sajak's desk. Instead I decided to take a chance and see if I could pry some information directly from the source.

I walked over to the M-Two building, took the elevator to the third floor, and wandered through the cubicle maze like a rat looking for some cheese. I found it near the back. Miranda was sitting in front of her computer, leaning over her desk, one hand pressed against her forehead.

"Miranda?" I said, but she didn't move. Then I noticed the headphones. I reached over and moved one earphone away from her head. She jumped, startled. Her eyes looked glazed at first, but when my presence registered her eyes flashed with an emotion I couldn't identify. What I could identify was the dark circles under those eyes and the weary pallor of someone who hadn't gotten much sleep. Her hair was stringier than it had been a few days before, and her clothes looked like she had slept in them. In general, Miranda looked like hell.

"Do you know about Lorraine Sajak?" I asked in the most nurturing voice I could manage. The girl looked like she would break in the slightest breeze.

"Get the hell away from me," she said, her voice angry, but her eyes full of need.

"Have the police talked to you?"

She nodded.

"Listen; I'm not here to cause you any problems. I just want to talk to you. It might feel good to talk to someone."

Miranda's lower lip began to quiver, her eyes filled with tears. She looked like a little kid to me, and my heart went out to her.

"Come on; let's get some air," I said. "We'll go get a Coke."

At first she didn't move, but then she slowly stood up, and together we took the elevator downstairs and walked through the lobby and outside. One of the nice things about San Francisco is the parks, and even in the middle of the Financial District they've carved out little park areas between some of the buildings. We walked two blocks to one, and on the way I bought us two hot pretzels and a couple of

Cokes from a cart vendor. Sunlight reflected off the pavement, and the air was fresh and cool. I noticed Miranda shivering, so I took off my jacket and put it over her shoulders. She was bringing out the mother in me. I kind of liked it.

"Did the police talk to you about Sajak?" I asked once we were settled on some steps next to a raised bed of pink petunias. I took a bite of pretzel. It was warm and mushy, just the way I like them. Miranda didn't touch hers, although she drank a little of the Coke.

"I was there at the station until midnight. It was awful. I thought they were going to arrest me, but they didn't."

"What did they say to you?"

Her hand jerked, knocking over the Coke, and she didn't move to set it upright. Instead she just watched the brown, fizzling liquid run down the steps and onto the sidewalk. I offered her mine, but she shook her head.

"They think I killed her; I'm sure they do. They showed me a letter I'd written her and said they found strands of my hair in her office. But I didn't kill her. I swear I didn't. My dad's a lawyer back in Virginia, but I don't want to call him. I mean I haven't talked to him in a year and a half. He'll be so pissed."

"Did you write the letter?"

She looked down at the ground. I repeated the question.

"Yeah, I wrote it, but I wrote it four months ago. It was stupid. I was really jealous about her seeing Arnie. I mean I had introduced them, and they end up sleeping together."

"You introduced Arnie to Lorraine Sajak?"

"Yeah. Lorraine got me my job at Anco. Once Arnie was out on bail he wanted to make some money doing consulting, only nobody would hire him because of the embezzling charge. I thought maybe Lorraine could help."

"How did you find out they were sleeping together?"

"The bastard told me. He laughed at me, and I went sort of crazy, you know, like screaming and yelling and everything. A few days later I wrote Lorraine the letter. But that was it. I never spoke to her after that. I told the cops all of this. I don't know how my hair got in her office. Do you believe me?''

"Yes, I do. Someone could have planted the hairs. They could have taken them from your hairbrush and just dropped them on Sajak's floor."

"Could you tell the cops that? I'm afraid they're gonna arrest me. I don't know what I'd do if that happened."

"The first thing you need to do is call your dad. I'll talk to the police. There's a lot of evidence pointing to someone else."

Miranda was quiet a second. "You mean Arnie?"

"Maybe."

"I don't believe he could do anything like that."

"Sometimes it's hard to know people, Miranda. What they seem like on the outside isn't always what they really are."

She sniffed back some tears, grabbed my Coke, and took a big sip. "Arnie treated me like dirt. First he starts sleeping with Lorraine; then he moves in with that Donatello person. And I still love him. Is that stupid?"

I wanted to say, "Yes," but didn't. "Love is an irrational process," I told her instead.

"I guess you're right." She looked down at the hand on which she wore his ring. "I know he loved me. At least he did for a while. He told me that I entered spaces inside him that no woman ever had before."

Lufkin had said the same words to Lorna, but I didn't tell Miranda. If Lufkin let any more women in those spaces he was going to have to install a turnstile at the door. Miranda finished my Coke; then I took her back to her desk and left her with my promise to talk to Boskin. She promised to call her father.

I walked back to the other building, stopped at the first free phone and called Lorna, and got her machine. My message was brief: "We need to talk. I've found out some things about Arnie." I wanted to warn her, to tell her that he was a sick and dangerous man, but it hit me that I was the one who should be worried. I was the one Lufkin had threatened.

To be honest, I was plenty worried, but I pushed that distasteful thought from my mind and stopped by Monique's desk to see if she had gotten the audit files I had asked for. A note sat on her empty chair that said: "Back in Five Minutes." Gallagher's office was also disappointingly empty. Impatient to know if she had found the file, I snooped around Monique's desk, and bingo, underneath a legal tablet I found a red file folder with the word "Audit" typed neatly on a white label with last year's date underneath. My finer nature told me not to disturb something that didn't belong to me, but I picked it up anyway and scanned its contents. It looked like what I needed.

I considered taking the file folder with me but decided it would be too cheeky. I planned to run some questions about the audit past Gallagher later that day anyway, so it would be easy to pick it up then.

Noticing a large black leather-bound calendar on Monique's desk, I flipped it open to the day's date to check when Gallagher would be available. She was free from two-thirty until three but was booked with staff meetings the rest of the day. I saw the words "Division Meeting M5!!" written in bold blue lettering in the 7:00 p.m. slot, so I penciled my name in for two-thirty.

The next few minutes I spent searching out the local coffeepot and helping myself to some inky black stuff that I discarded after one sip. When I finally reached the Pit, I found a yellow note from Paoli stuck on the terminal: "Call Monique at X2781. Got new office. Can't tell you how to get there. Couldn't find it myself. All my love to Andy."

Cute. I called the number and found Monique back at her desk. Her voice sounded thick as she told me that Mc-

Cracken had moved Paoli and me to a vacant office on the third floor. Within a few minutes she came down from the fifth and escorted me over to our new space—a moderately large office with a wall-to-wall window that faced some tall buildings, buildings so close I could look in the windows and see people at their desks. Paoli was busy at a new terminal.

"Here you go. Enjoy," Monique said, then noisily blew her nose into a Kleenex.

"Still clogged?" Paoli stopped his work to direct the question at her. "Did you try the herb tea and schnapps?"

"I couldn't find any schnapps at the drugstore." There was another nose blow. "I don't even think it's a cold anymore. Feels worse than that. I get this once a year, every year." She blew her nose one more time. "Gotta go. Call me if you need anything."

As Monique walked away I could still hear her blowing her nose halfway down the hallway. Large offices are breeding grounds for germs, and colds and flu spread through them as fast as the latest rumor.

"So how did it go?" Paoli asked. I closed the door and told him about Lufkin's VR software, my run-in with Hansen, and my chat with Miranda. Paoli was parked in a chair in front of his workstation, but I was too antsy to sit still, so I walked around the office while I talked.

"They were lovers. Sajak kissed me. Kissed Lufkin, I mean. She was another one of his conquests, and what more useful conquest than a headhunter who specializes in your field of work? Especially when you need a job."

Paoli shook his head. "But what good did it do him? You said Hansen told you that Lufkin was a legend. He couldn't risk working anywhere. He'd be recognized."

"Okay, he was a legend, but it wasn't like he was a rock star with his picture plastered everywhere. It was Lufkin's work, not his face, that made him well known. People knew his name or the code name Spyder on a computer screen, but most people never saw him. Hansen had never even laid eyes on him, and Hansen knows everybody.''

While I spoke Paoli opened a box of paper clips and began tossing them one by one into a pencil holder sitting on his desk.

"Okay, I'll buy that," he said as he continued a series of rim shots. "So Sajak helped him find a job where he could continue his VR work. Still, there would be a big risk that someone would know his face."

A paper clip bounced off the edge of the desk and hit me. I caught it against my hip, then tossed it straight into the pencil holder. A lucky shot, but Paoli looked impressed.

"What choice did he have? He has a lot of money stashed away, but he can't risk tapping into it. The guy needs money just like the rest of us. So he's careful about what job he takes. He keeps to himself. Maybe he wears glasses or a wig or something. Lorna said herself that she never knew where he was during the day while they were living together. And somebody could be hiding him."

"Why would he kill Sajak?" Paoli asked.

"Easy. He had planned it as an option months ago. She was the only one who knew where he was, because she helped get him there. He knew he might have to get rid of her, and that's why he wrote the VR program. He wanted to set it up in advance, to practice the murder so it would go perfectly."

Out of paper clips, Paoli leaned back in his chair, his hands behind his head. "But if he planned it months ago, why wait until now to kill her?"

I stopped in front of my partner and bent down, my hands braced on the arms of his chair, and looked him in the eye. "I think she started blackmailing him. It makes sense. What if Sajak really did help him hide? She would also know that Lufkin had money stashed somewhere, and I think she was the type of person who considered money very important." Having put across my point, I straightened up and leaned against a small table.

"But what was the point of blackmailing him? You said Lufkin couldn't get at his money."

"Maybe she didn't know he couldn't get at it. He might have bragged about all the money he had stashed, and maybe she didn't believe him when he said he couldn't touch it. That's why he killed her. She was putting pressure on him, he couldn't get at his money to pay her off, so he was forced to get her out of the picture. But I'm still curious about the ring."

"What ring?"

"I don't remember seeing Lufkin's ring on Sajak's finger. Remember, he gave the gold ring with the black etchings to Lorna and to Miranda. At first I thought the etching was a sunburst, but now I think it's a symbol for a spider. It was his way of making these women think he was committed to them. But Sajak wasn't wearing one."

"Once you start blackmailing somebody, it usually means you're not going steady anymore."

"But they kissed in the VR program."

Paoli shrugged. "He had to have written it a couple of months ago at least. At that time they were probably still on kissing terms."

"Good point."

Paoli leaned his chair back on two legs and put his hands behind his head. One of these days he was going to tip over backward and crack his thick skull. I started to tell him so but stopped myself. The man was an adult. He could crack his skull if he wanted to, although personally, I was against it.

"This is frustrating," he said. "We can make a lot of assumptions about who did what, but until we find Lufkin it's all conjecture. I don't think we're any closer now than we were a few days ago."

He exhaled with exasperation and seemed lost in thought. I walked over to the window and gazed out, my thoughts beginning to meander. Between two of the skyscrapers I could see the bay and a bit of the Bay Bridge. I knew I should call McCracken to thank him for the new office, but I didn't want to make the call in front of Paoli and cause any undue testosterone poisoning. I was considering my options on this important matter when I heard Paoli let out a yell. I jumped, certain he had finally fallen over backward, but Paoli looked intact.

"What is it?"

"All this time you and I have been combing through Anco's programs looking for a hack into Anco's security software. What if the hack isn't there? What if it was never there?"

"What are you talking about, Paoli? Of course it's there."

He stood up and walked over to me. "Maybe, and then maybe not."

"You're starting to sound funny."

"I'm starting to think like Lufkin."

I patted his hand. "They have medication for things like this."

"Very funny. Now, listen, I was thinking about Monique's cold and how she gets it every year."

"I know what you're going to say, but I scanned the software for standard viruses and came up with zip."

"A guy like Lufkin would never resort to a simple virus—too unimaginative. Now, speaking as one genius for another, if I were going to break into a general ledger program I would invent programming statements that were present in the software only when I needed them. Once the statements had done their dirty work, I would want them to disappear. That way they're undetectable. The only way I could think of to achieve that would be some sort of cyclical virus."

"You mean a virus that pops up once a month or something?"

"Exactly. The programming statements infected the general ledger code once a quarter or once a month, or whatever, but disappeared afterward."

I made certain no one was looking in the doorway, then kissed him. "You've got brains, Paoli."

"True. The only problem is if the statements only pop up at certain times it's going to be hard to find them."

"Maybe not. I've already found places in the code that could be weaknesses. We'll just go through the archived backup tapes, and if you're right, it'll show up in those."

Paoli called Chambers and got access to the archived tapes going back a full year. At two-thirty we had barely gotten started, but I still wanted that audit file, so I took a break and went by Gallagher's office. Monique was sitting at the front office desk, nose red and brow furrowed as she glared at her PC.

"Hi, Monique." She looked up at me. "I'm here for the audit file. Remember, I asked for it on Friday."

"Oh, I'm sorry, Julie. I thought I had it, but when Ms. Gallagher saw it she said it wasn't the right one."

That puzzled me. I had seen the contents of the file myself, although I wasn't anxious to tell Monique that. But I had seen the audit review, and it had the right date on it.

"Are you sure?"

"Yes, she told me a little while ago. She said she would find the right file for me, that it might be misfiled in one of her cabinets, although if it is, it isn't my fault. She's been so flustered lately she doesn't know up from down."

I couldn't figure it out. The audit file I saw earlier had to be the right one.

"Can I see Arlene for a few minutes?"

"Let me tell her you're here." Monique pushed a button on her phone and announced me. "She says go right in."

I opened the door to Gallagher's office and found her sitting in front of her terminal, her red glasses sitting on the tip of her nose as she studied rows of numbers. She waved me to a chair.

"Go ahead and sit down. I'm just finishing up my mail."

While she typed, I sat in one of the chairs in front of her desk and glanced around her office, looking at the photographs she had placed around the room. There were over a dozen of them. Studying them, I realized they were all pictures of someone else's family. Maybe a sister and her children or maybe a brother-in-law and his family. But the family wasn't Gallagher's, because the children were always photographed with some other adult.

I assumed Gallagher was single. She didn't wear a wedding ring. Though she could have been divorced and have children from the marriage, looking around the room I decided that wasn't the case. That was sad, I thought, to have a life in which all your pictures are of someone else's family, and it crossed my mind that Gallagher might be very lonely. I wondered if I would end up like her. Would I spend my life committed to a career? Would I end up with a big office and a great job but have only the sentimental mementos from a life that belonged to someone else?

It was while I was gazing at the pictures that I saw a black canvas tote bag lying on the credenza behind her, and the sight of it snapped me out of my self-analysis. The bag was stuffed with what looked like gym clothes, but I saw the red file folder stuck in the side. It was too far away for me to read the print on the label, but the words on the label were typed and looked about the same length and position as those on the audit file I had seen earlier on Monique's desk. If that audit file wasn't the right one, then why was Gallagher taking it with her? Why wouldn't she just give it back to Monique for refiling?

Finished with her mail, Gallagher turned toward me. "So, how's it going? I looked for you this morning, but you weren't around."

"I had an appointment. What did you want to talk about?"

"I just wanted an update on your progress."

"On finding Lufkin or how he broke into the system?"

"Either."

"I'm making a lot of progress on both," I said, and wondered if she knew I was bluffing. I was on the right track in finding out how he broke into Anco's software, but I didn't have a clue as to where Lufkin was hiding. "Something terrible happened over the weekend. Vic Paoli and I went to visit a headhunter on Saturday and found her dead in her office."

Gallagher's hand went to her chest. "Good Lord. Was it a heart attack?"

"No. It looks like she was poisoned."

Gallagher closed her eyes and made a face. "Awful. And how terrible for you to have to find her."

"I still feel queasy about it. Her name was Lorraine Sajak. Have you heard of her?"

"I don't think so. Did she handle accountants?"

"No, software developers."

"The only headhunters I know are the accounting kind. Anyway, I'm glad I didn't know her. That would be terrible, to have someone you know murdered."

"It was pretty terrible. I'm trying hard to get it out of my mind." Gallagher and I were quiet a moment while we each pondered our own mortality. I was the one who broke the silence. "The reason I'm here is that I need to see whatever files you have on last year's general ledger audit. McCracken told me that you kept the summary files. I asked Monique to get them for me, and she just told me you were going to look for them."

Now reach for the red file and hand it to me, I said silently, but Gallagher made no move for it. I watched her eyes to see if they would dart guiltily toward the gym bag, but her eyes remained fixed on me.

"Yes, I looked for it this morning but couldn't find it. But give me some time, and I'm sure I can come up with it. We moved some offices around last year, and it probably got misplaced."

Gallagher rolled her chair around so that she faced the tote bag. She pulled some stapled papers from underneath the tote and in the process turned the tote bag so I could no longer see its contents. It was a natural-enough gesture, yet I felt certain she did it because she knew the file I was looking for was sitting right in front of my face. She couldn't have known that I had already seen the red file folder and had scanned its contents, but turning the tote bag around could have been a gesture of nervousness, perhaps even of guilt. On the other hand, maybe it was innocent. I had to know for sure.

I opened my mouth, ready to confront her about the file but decided against it. All she would say was that the file in her bag was something other than the audit file. Then what would I do? Leap across her desk and grab it?

I stood up to leave.

"Will you let me know when you have the audit information?"

"I'll have Monique give you a call as soon as I find it. It may take a few days."

Or maybe a few lifetimes, I thanked her and left.

When I got back to the new office, Paoli was packing up to leave.

"Bored already?" I asked.

"You know how it is with brilliant minds."

I waved my hand in front of my face. "I feel a hot wind blowing."

Paoli put his packed briefcase on his desk. "I have some things to do back at the office. I want you to come with me."

"Can't. Too much to do here. I'll see you later." I was about to sit down but was stopped by his hand on my arm.

"Julie, you can't be here without me, not after the message you got on Saturday. You're coming with me."

"Ooh, caveman want woman." With two fingers I lifted his hand from my arm. "Listen, Conan, I'm perfectly safe. I was frightened on Saturday because I was the only person around, but there are hundreds of people here today. Nothing can happen."

"Julie, let's not argue. You're coming with me if I have to drag you."

I poked him in the chest with my finger. "You're not dragging me anywhere. I'm staying. Trust me, I have no desire to stick around here all alone, but I can't go with you now. I promise I'll leave when everyone else does. I have a lot of work to do." Paoli gave me a hard look. I had other plans for later in the day, and if Paoli knew what they were he would try to stop me. I decided to placate him. "Look; I'll call you when I leave, okay?"

I watched Paoli's expression as he ran through his choices. One: drag me out of there by the hair with me kicking and screaming; two: continue arguing with me, which he knew would be fruitless; or three: let me do things my way. He reluctantly opted for number three, and we said our good-byes.

I spent the next hour sifting through the Anco software, examining it from Paoli's new cyclical virus perspective. Around three-thirty I grabbed a sandwich from a vending machine and between bites called the Anco switchboard.

"Hi, got a question. Somebody left a note for me and it has something about 'M5' on it. I'm a consultant and I don't know what 'M5' means. Could you help me?"

"Sure," the male voice answered. "It's the numbering system for the Anco offices. We use it for internal mail, but people just started calling the buildings by their mail stop numbers. 'M5' is our office on Market Street."

So that was what "Division Meeting M5" had meant on Gallagher's calendar. I thanked him and hung up. Market Street was about four blocks away.

My efforts at work that afternoon were hampered by the seductive image of that black canvas tote bag. It stuck in my mind and refused to budge. The Julie Blake mental apparatus had locked onto that red file folder, and now an earthquake and a tidal wave combined would not keep me from it. At first I considered sneaking into Gallagher's office and stealing the file, but the chances of getting caught were too great, especially with Monique hovering around. I thought again about confronting Gallagher and demanding to see the file, but she would probably just throw me out of her office, and she would have every right to. I even pondered the idea of taking the problem to McCracken and having him demand to see the file, but it felt too much like tattling to the teacher.

There had to be another way, and I was certain that other way would include theft of some sort, but then Data9000 Investigations was a full-functioned organization. We couldn't let small roadblocks like theft and the violation of personal privacy get in the way of our work, could we?

Around three my phone rang. It was Detective Boskin. I told him about Lufkin's VR programs, but he had trouble understanding what I was telling him. I think he had a problem separating reality from virtual reality, but I guess that's understandable for a police officer. I pacified him by agreeing to have Lufkin's VR CDs sent to him that afternoon by courier. I also suggested he call Wayne Hansen for assistance in viewing the CDs. Hansen would hit the ceiling about it, but that would be Boskin's problem. It would have been easier to refer Boskin to someone at Anco, but I still didn't want anyone at Anco to know what was in the CDs. I was still thinking that Lufkin had an accomplice at Anco, and until I knew for sure I wanted to keep the contents of the CDs secret.

Before I hung up, I told Boskin my theory about Sajak blackmailing Lufkin. He said it made sense and that he would look into it. I also told him I thought the data on the CDs would help clear Miranda.

"Let me be the judge of that," he said, then hung up.

At fifteen after six I logged off the Anco computer, packed up my things, and positioned myself at the water-cooler around the corner from Gallagher's office where she would have to pass by to get to the elevators. If Gallagher didn't have the tote bag with her, that would mean she had left it in her office, and I would try to liberate it after Monique had left for the day. If Gallagher did have the tote bag with her, well, then I would just have to think of something else, wouldn't I?

I knew if Gallagher was going to make the division meeting at seven she would need only about fifteen minutes to get there, but I gave her extra time in case she wanted to run any errands first. It was hard looking natural while standing at the watercooler, but I managed by taking a long drink every time someone walked by.

At six-forty-two Gallagher walked toward me. I bent down and drank some water.

"Good night, Julie."

"Good night. See you tomorrow," I managed to gurgle.

I eyed her after she passed me. She was carrying her briefcase in her left hand, and the black tote hung over her right shoulder, the red file barely peeking out of the gym clothes, beckoning to me. Time to implement Plan Two, whatever that was. I followed her to the elevator and waited with her about ten seconds until the doors opened. We entered the elevator. I stood next to her and could see the red folder only six inches away from me. It would have been so easy to just slowly reach out and pull the file from the bag, but there were two other people in the elevator who would witness it. No, I had to be a lot more subtle.

When she got out I hung back a little so she could get ahead of me; then I followed her into the parking garage. I reached my car before she reached hers, so I got in, started the car, and drove out onto the street, pulling to the curb and stopping. A few minutes later I saw Gallagher pull out into the traffic driving a brown Jeep Cherokee.

Once she had passed me, I pulled away from the curb, easing out into the traffic onto Montgomery Street. I put on my Ray-Bans and Paoli's New York Yankees baseball hat that he had left in my car. I felt stupid wearing a business suit and a baseball hat, but I couldn't risk her looking into her rearview mirror and catching me following her. We were resourceful at Data9000 Investigations.

Even when not tailing someone I had trouble negotiating San Francisco traffic. At first I tried to stay a few cars behind Gallagher, but with the rush hour congestion the problem was keeping up. People kept cutting in front of me, and after a few minutes I was weaving in and out of lanes, honking punitively at those who dared to pull in my path.

After running one red light, angering a dozen motorists, and almost scaring the Bermuda shorts off a couple of tourists in a crosswalk, I saw Gallagher's Jeep disappear down the ramp of an underground parking garage. I pulled to the curb and let my car idle, giving her plenty of time to park and leave the car; then I drove down the ramp, stopped at the machine for a parking ticket, and began searching for her car.

The garage spiraled down several floors, and I located the Jeep on the second level sitting in a space located far from the elevators and five spaces away from the closest car. The woman obviously didn't like door dents. I looked around and saw Gallagher enter the elevator carrying only her briefcase, the door closing behind her. I pulled my car into a space on the other side of the elevator bank, turned off my engine, and sat there a moment pondering my next step. Okay, I had followed her into the garage and I knew the bag was locked in her car. Now was I supposed to lower myself to breaking and entering? The answer was a definite yes, but unfortunately, my knowledge of breaking and entering was minimal. That's what I got for spending my youth in the library.

I got out of the car, taking my purse with me, and walked to the Jeep. I heard the elevator doors open and I froze, but the Jeep was positioned so I couldn't see who was coming out. I quickly bent down and began fiddling with my shoe while the man from the elevator got into his car. So he wouldn't think that my hand was permanently stuck to my shoe and I required medical assistance, I stood up, walked over to the driver's side door, and acted like I was looking for my keys. He finally drove up the ramp toward the exit and I was alone.

Once my heart resumed beating, I looked inside the back window of Gallagher's car, but I couldn't see the tote bag. I had to get inside. I walked over to the driver's side window and saw a blinking red light on the console that indicated that the security system was on. Even if I knew how to break into a car, the alarm would make it impossible.

I was sorting out my limited choices when once again I heard the elevator doors open. I opened my purse to start my looking-for-the-keys routine and was feeling relatively calm until I heard Gallagher's voice as she said good-bye to someone. What was she doing here when she was supposed to be in the division meeting? I looked at my watch. She had only been gone ten minutes. I ran for the closest car and hid behind it and peered at Gallagher as she walked hurriedly to her car. Her face looked agitated as she took her key holder out of her purse and pointed it at the Jeep. The car responded with a high-pitched beep that meant the doors had unlocked.

She grabbed the door handle and jerked it open, but then she stopped, cursed loudly, slammed the door shut, and headed back for the elevators. Her briefcase. I remembered that she had carried it with her inside the building and now she didn't have it. She must have left it in the building and was going to retrieve it, but I had only heard the first beep from Gallagher's key ring when she unlocked the Jeep. I didn't hear a second beep locking it back up before she left.

This was the fun part, I thought. I recalled with new disdain all the endless meetings, the dull reports, I had endured in my old corporate job. This was a far more adventurous alternative. As soon as I heard the elevator door open and close I walked quickly to the Jeep and looked inside at the console. Thank you, God. The red light was off, so Gallagher had forgotten to relock the car. I opened the door fast and was looking for the tailgate release when I heard the elevator doors open. I shut the door and waited, but no one came off the elevator. Somebody must have punched the wrong button. After a few more seconds of fumbling for the tailgate release and not finding it, I scrambled between the two bucket seats and leaned over the backseat to look for the file. I figured I had a good three minutes before Gallagher would return. Anco's other building had separate elevator banks for the garage, so you had to change elevators in the lobby to reach the upper floors. All the large office buildings in San Francisco that I've seen have that setup. By having to wait for two sets of elevators, I figured it would take Gallagher at least five to ten minutes to go up, get her briefcase, and come back down again. That was only the first of my mistakes.

I felt nervous and excited as I dug through Gallagher's belongings. I knew what I was doing was wrong, but it was a fun kind of wrong, and it made me feel a little tingly. The problem with me was that I had spent my whole life being a good girl, a nice little Girl Scout always being polite, studying hard, and going for that extra merit badge. Now I was making up for lost time, and I liked it.

The car was a mess. The back of Gallagher's Jeep got an "F" for neatness, and the shadows thrown by the garage's fluorescent lighting didn't help my hurried search. I just didn't get it. I had seen Gallagher open the tailgate and throw the bag in the back, but now I couldn't find it in the jumble of clothes and odds and ends.

I felt my wrist catch on something. I looked down and saw the safety chain on my watch caught on the carpeting that lined the interior of the Jeep. I gave my wrist a gentle tug, but it remained caught, and I knew if I pulled too hard I would break the band. It was a gold bracelet-style watch that my father had given my mother before he died. She had passed it on to me when I turned twenty-one, and I treasured it. I didn't have much to remember him by, I had been so young when he died. I didn't always wear it, but for some reason I had decided to wear it that day. There was no way I would risk breaking that watch.

I had just crawled over the backseat of the Jeep down into the storage area so I could untangle my watch from the carpeting when I heard the elevator doors. I knew Gallagher hadn't had enough time to go back upstairs and come down again, but the fact that I had just broken into a car and someone might see me made me panic, and I couldn't think straight. All my previous bravado drained right out of me. I felt like a criminal.

Footsteps sounded on concrete, and I nestled down between the backseat and the rear door, pressing down into a raincoat, a smelly towel, and what felt like golf clubs, reassuring myself that as soon as I heard the person get in his or her car and drive off I would give up this search for the audit file and emerge into the stale air of the parking garage, which smelled like a breath of springtime compared to

Gallagher's gym shorts. Hadn't the woman heard of talcum powder?

I heard the hard tapping of a woman's high heels. I took a breath and waited for the steps to grow faint, but instead they came closer. Much closer. My mind careened with the horrible possibility. It couldn't be her. Only a minute or two had passed since she went back up the elevator. I pictured the scenario—she realizes that she's left her briefcase and takes the garage elevator to the lobby, switches elevators, goes up to her floor...

My thoughts halted as I heard the footsteps stop outside the door and my blood ceased pumping through my veins. I recognized the flaw in my thinking. I had assumed she had left her briefcase in the Anco offices, but she could have set it down in the lobby when she was waiting for the garage elevator. It would only take a minute or two for her to go up and retrieve it.

The good news was that Gallagher hadn't decided to throw her briefcase into the back of her car, revealing me curled in a fetal position inside. The bad news was that I didn't see how I could possibly get out of the car without her noticing, and before I knew it, the engine started and the car shifted into reverse with me still in the back.

My MBA program had failed to cover the managerial options available to a person in this type of situation. Somehow, lying there, the old corporate job didn't look so bad after all. When I left ICI, I had all these visions of being an entrepreneur, a successful independent businesswoman striking out on her own, forging a new business. Where had it gotten me? Hiding like a thief in the back of somebody's car, smothered in damp gym clothes with golf cleats pressing into my shoulder, going God knows where.

FOURTEEN

SO WHAT DO YOU DO when you've made a really dumb mistake and hurled yourself headfirst into a situation in which you will look like either a fool or a criminal? I, being a conservative sort of person, felt like jumping up from my hiding place and admitting to Gallagher that I knew very well I was a complete idiot, then asking her to please take me home, where I would pack a few belongings, and then I'd move to a small town in Missouri where no one would know me. Maybe join a convent. That's what I should have done. Instead I quietly curled into a fetal position and decided to keep my mouth shut and hope for the best.

I felt the Jeep pull up the ramp. The car stopped while Gallagher paid for parking, and I quietly tucked myself a little farther under her raincoat so the parking attendant wouldn't see me.

Outside, the sounds of horns and engines told me when we were out of the garage and onto the street. I felt the car turn left. Looking up through the back window, I could see the sky growing dusky. Gallagher was heading home, I told myself, and eventually she was going to stop the car, open the back to get her things, and find me. She would not be amused.

I tried to think of good excuses. I could leap out and yell, "Surprise!," and tell her I thought it was her birthday. Or I could claim I was on a scavenger hunt and was looking for an old gym sock. I could always pretend to look dazed and make her believe I was mentally ill. Or I could opt for the truth, that I was a not too successful computer fraud investigator who had mistakenly thought she was Nancy Drew.

Closing my eyes, I prayed that Gallagher would make another stop before going home and give me the chance to escape. Hastily I tried to think of things I could offer God in exchange for getting me out of this mess, but then, I had acted so stupidly I didn't deserve any help.

My mind was a jumble of predicted embarrassments and self-incriminations. I imagined Paoli's reaction when I told him about this little escapade. If I told him. With some luck this could end up being one of those humiliations I kept to myself. As that thought crossed my mind the Jeep hit a pothole, and I instantly regretted having consumed so much liquid at the Anco water fountain.

I heard beeping sounds as Gallagher dialed a number on her car phone. She left a message for somebody to fax a report to a manager named Miller; then I heard more beeps as she dialed another number.

"It's Arlene. I'll meet you in an hour," she said. "Tell me again where to turn."

My heart soared. Gallagher wasn't going home. Now all I had to do was wait an hour until she arrived at her destination. I lived almost an hour south of San Francisco, and an hour's drive in an unknown direction meant I could end up two hours from home. It would be a long, expensive cab ride, but the only thing that mattered to me at that moment was that I not be discovered by Gallagher.

For the next thirty minutes I felt the stop and go of heavy traffic that meant she was driving city streets. Then the road smoothed out, and from my vantage point I saw the top of the Golden Gate Bridge. We were heading North. Within an hour's time she could be traveling to North Marin or Sonoma, perhaps for dinner. Or maybe her destination was closer and she had errands on the way. I visualized a happy scenario in which she parked the car and walked away and I hopped out the back, called a cab, and never mentioned this event to anyone.

As soon as we crossed the bridge I felt the car swerve to the right. At first I thought she was heading for Sausalito, but then the car veered left. That confused me. I couldn't remember there being anything on the west side of Highway 101 besides the Marin Headlands, a national park area of scenic hills and cliffs. I felt the Jeep lurch as she shifted into low gear and began to ascend a hill, confirming the Marin Headlands as her destination.

I didn't get it. If we were headed where I thought we were headed, there was nothing there—no restaurants, no houses, not anything. I badly wanted to sit up a little and peek out the window, but I couldn't risk being seen in the rearview mirror. Driving on, the Jeep made its way down the winding road, then swerved left. I heard gravel crunch as we came to a stop.

I peeked at my watch. Almost eight. Gallagher had another half hour until her appointment. To my chagrin, she didn't get out of the car. Instead she rolled down the window and turned on the radio to the local classical station, keeping the sound low. Gallagher and I unwittingly shared a peaceful moment as a cold breeze washed through the car, and I heard the distant sound of wind and ocean while Vivaldi played softly in the background.

Cool and dark. That's what I remember most about those last moments I was in the Jeep with Gallagher, along with the numbing ache in my arms and legs. I didn't dare move. It was too dark to see my watch, but by my estimation it was about an hour later when another set of wheels rolled over the gravel and stopped. I could clearly hear the car wheels, although the sound seemed about thirty yards away.

She turned off the music, and I heard her door open, then slam shut. Gravel crunched under footsteps.

My desire to get the hell out of there was temporarily superseded by my curiosity over whom Gallagher was meeting. This was no ordinary rendezvous spot where you caught up on the latest gossip with a few friends. This place was dark and isolated, a place to hide. Was she meeting a secret lover? Gallagher didn't seem the type. With the cold wind this could never be a comfortable place for lovers unless, of course, they intended to use the Jeep for warmth and privacy. My whole body contorted into a grimace and I imagined Gallagher and her companion folding down the backseat to make room for lovemaking. I had to get out of there.

With the lightless ocean fog, the inside of the car was shrouded in darkness. I could tell from their voices that Gallagher and her companion were standing close to the Jeep. There was conversation, but I couldn't make out what was being said, at least not until a few minutes later when the volume rose.

"I need you to cosign," I heard Gallagher say. Her voice sounded heavy, raw. I listened closely for a reply, but there was no immediate response. The silence that followed her statement was ominous.

"I told you no. I don't take stupid risks." The voice was male.

"I can't do this anymore!" Now Gallagher sounded desperate, her voice thin and pleading. "I can't live this way. I'm afraid. I want to just tell everything and take my punishment."

"Only you can't do that alone, can you?" the man said.

I heard heavy footsteps across the gravel, the sound growing fainter. There was a pause; then I heard the more rapid steps of Gallagher following his.

I inched up to a semisitting position and peeked over the top of the rear seat. The moon was behind the clouds, but although it was dark, I could tell we were parked away from the road near the cliff side. I saw Gallagher and someone else standing next to a small car. In the blackness it was difficult to distinguish faces.

The photograph of Arnie Lufkin flashed through my mind, but I couldn't see this man well enough to make a definite identification. Gallagher and the mystery man spoke in low voices, but the sounds soon rose into an argument. Although I strained to hear, the acoustics of the rocky hillside coupled with the wind made it impossible for me to make out what they were saying.

Suddenly the voices became softer. I saw Gallagher slowly moving toward her companion. I thought they were going to embrace, but they didn't move that close together. Now I saw the man moving away from her, taking slow, deliberate steps backward as he spoke. I struggled to make out the words, but it was impossible; I only heard the cadence of the man's voice, which had now become hypnotically calm, and Gallagher kept moving toward him, maybe so she could hear what he was saying. She didn't speak. She just kept stepping toward him as if she were transfixed by the sound of his voice. It made me think of the death dance I had witnessed between the snake and the mouse at Comtech, the hypnotic swaying of the snake that held the mouse helpless until the snake made its kill.

I heard quick footsteps across the gravel, then muffled and unidentifiable human sounds. I ducked back down behind the seat, afraid and unsure of what to do. A sick feeling in my stomach traveled to my chest, and my throat felt constricted. There was something about what I had seen that was nagging at me. It wasn't the people but the landscape that reminded me of something. Then it hit me. The curving lines of the cliff side, the curve of the road behind us. It could be the scene in Lufkin's third virtual reality program, the one I had seen only that morning. I remembered moving toward the curving grayness and seeing where it suddenly dropped off. At the time I had assumed it dropped off because it was unfinished. Now I knew better.

I scrambled over the backseat of the Jeep toward the driver-side door but stopped when I heard a howling sound outside, which was followed by silence. I grabbed the door handle, jerked it open, and jumped out of the car.

"Arlene!" I cried, but there was now only one person on the cliff side. My yell startled him. He froze and looked at me, but I couldn't see his face in the fog and darkness. Whoever he was, he hadn't expected anyone to leap out of Gallagher's car. He stood there for only a moment; then he ran to his car, opened the driver-side door, got in, and slammed the door shut. I stood there as the car engine started and his headlights beamed into my face, blinding me with their white light.

I remember the sound of the wheels screaming through dirt and gravel as the car lurched toward me. To save myself, I dived to the left, falling hard on my hands and knees. The car passed me and came to a stop. The wheels spun at first, then caught traction. Now the car moved in reverse, heading again directly at me. I ran toward Gallagher's car to use it as a barrier, but the other car cut me off before I could reach the Jeep. It was like he was playing with me, wanting to toy with me before he actually crushed me beneath his wheels. The headlights were again in my face. I heard the transmission shift.

I ran for the road and the hillside just across it, the rocks and brambles cutting into my legs. The car came at me again. This time I jumped into a ditch by the road, escaping the car's fender by inches, saved only by the fact that the narrow road gave my attacker less room to maneuver.

My hands, feet, and knees stung in pain, but I pulled myself up and scrambled up the low hillside. The car stopped, unable to cross the ditch. Then the car pushed quickly into reverse, lunged forward, and squealed back down the road.

I crouched, as still as an animal, and concentrated on the sound of the car as it grew distant. I don't know how long I stayed there. Long enough to feel convinced that whoever had tried to run me over was really gone, that he wasn't waiting for me to come back out into the open. Finally, although my heart still pounded, I straightened up and slowly picked my way back to Gallagher's Jeep, my eyes always watching the road.

I made it to the cliff area and hunted for Gallagher. I called her name repeatedly, but there was no response and no sign of her. The moon had pushed in front of the clouds, bathing the cliff in a silvery light. I continued my search, but she wasn't there. I wanted to get to the base of the cliff to search for her, but the cliff was close to a straight drop down. I felt powerless and afraid.

Having no choice but to give up, I got inside the Jeep and locked the door. As I turned the ignition key, my arm hit something. I looked down and saw Gallagher's red glasses lying on the console, and a stab of pain went through me. With the phone now activated, I dialed 911. Someone answered after three rings.

"I'm at the headlands, the Marin Headlands," I said, my voice unsteady.

"You'll have to speak more slowly."

I tried to take a deep breath, but it caught somewhere in my chest. I forced myself to speak. "I'm at the cliffs at the north end of the Golden Gate Bridge. I think someone . . . someone may have fallen off the cliff."

"Ma'am, I need you to—"

I pushed the disconnect button, and the line went dead. Clasping my hands to try to stop their shaking, I felt panicky as I considered my next move. The last thing I wanted was to stick around and try to explain to the police how I had ended up on that cliff. No, I had to leave. I had to get out of there fast.

I pressed the phone receiver back into the cradle, pulled my blouse out of the waistband of my skirt, and used it to wipe my fingerprints off the phone and off the key in the ignition. I got out of the car and wiped the door handle, then walked back to the rear of the car. I opened the tailgate, grabbed my purse, and rummaged through the jumble of clothes for the tote bag. I finally found it, took the file, closed the back door of the Jeep and wiped it off as well as I could, then ran down the road. The moon was out fully now, but although the road was bathed in moonlight, I had trouble distinguishing where the road met the cliff's edge. I stuck close to the rock side as I ran, my body bumping into rocky protrusions and sharp-needled bushes. My foot caught on something, and I fell down in the gravel, my hands and knees stinging.

I don't know how long it took to stumble down that road. Maybe ten minutes, maybe longer. I wanted to make it down before the police drove up, because it would be hard to hide from them. Finally I was back at the north end of the Golden Gate Bridge. A sheriff's car with its siren blaring turned off the highway and ascended the hill behind me as I walked across the bridge along the pedestrian walkway. I stopped to look at the sheriff's car, and I prayed that Gallagher was all right. But I knew she wasn't.

The thunder of the bridge traffic beat in my brain as I continued walking, passing a few tourists who looked at me with odd expressions. I looked down and saw the dirt on my suit and a tiny stream of blood trickling down my left leg. I found a pay phone outside the Bridge Authority office at the south end of the span. I got some change from the bottom of my purse and dialed Paoli's number, praying he would be home. The phone rang over and over, but no one picked up. Slowly I placed the receiver on the cradle. I looked in my wallet and found only a ten and a couple of ones, which meant I didn't have enough money to pay for the thirty-mile cab ride home.

I thought of calling Max, but she lived close to Santa Clara, which was an hour's drive. Lorna was the obvious choice. She lived in San Francisco, and wasn't she the one who had gotten me into this in the first place? I found her business card in my purse and called her after-working-hours number. She picked up on the second ring.

"Donatello Bail Bonds," she said, her tiny voice businesslike.

"Lorna, it's Julie Blake."

"Oh, Julie, hey there. You called on my night line. I thought you were a customer."

"I need a favor, Lorna. I'm at the south end of the Golden Gate Bridge. I need you to come get me."

"What's wrong, hon? You sound stressed."

"You have to come get me," I repeated. "I think I witnessed a murder."

FIFTEEN

IT WASN'T UNTIL I collapsed on a bus stop bench that I felt
the cold fog cutting through the light suit jacket. I looked up
and watched the fog drifting like a giant ghost through the
bridge's amber towers. Wrapping my arms around myself,
I rocked back and forth on the damp wooden seat as the icy
wind sliced into the core of me. I couldn't stop shivering,
but I welcomed the cold because it numbed the pain in my
bruised and bleeding legs. The cold felt safely real, while the
things I had seen and experienced in the past hour seemed
vague and horrifying, like the first moments of half-
consciousness when you wake up from a nightmare.

I had chosen the bus stop because it was well lighted and
looked safe, and I was too consumed with my own thoughts
to notice the middle-aged man who sat down at the other
end of the bench a few feet from me. It wasn't until he called
to me that I caught sight of him. In the yellow light of the
bridge lamps he looked jaundiced. His hair was slicked back
with gel, and he wore a tweed jacket too large for him.

"Hey, honey," he said, his voice thick and raspy. "Ever
seen something like this?" I turned to him and saw him
stroking his exposed penis while he stared at me with a ridiculous leering grin.

He had picked the wrong woman. This poor flasher
thought he had chosen a timid, slightly nervous female,
when in reality he had exposed Mr. Happy to a woman filled
with pent-up rage, storming adrenaline, and a bad case of
PMS. An attacker coming after me with a car might have an
advantage, but one old lech with his family jewels hanging
out was in serious trouble. Seeing the reaction on my face,

he sensed his error and attempted a retreat of sorts, but the penis was slower going back inside his pants than it had been coming out.

It all happened so fast I had no control over it. All of a sudden I was punching him with my fists, then started striking him mindlessly with a flurry of hands, knees, and elbows, pummeling every part of him I could reach, and I reached a lot. The man yelped, more in shock than in pain I think, as he struggled to free himself from my onslaught.

"You're crazy!" he yelled as he stumbled off away from the bridge lights and into the relative safety of darkness. I ran a few yards after him, ready to give him more, but stopped when I realized the absurdity of what I was doing. Then I saw Lorna's green Camaro pull up next to the bus stop. She jumped out of the car and pumped her tiny high-heeled feet over to me.

"Holy shit, hon! What happened? You look awful!"

I looked at her and wondered which one of us actually looked worse. A complete fashion fatality, she wore a shiny purple full-body leotard that made her look like some sort of insect from another planet. Her frizzy hair, dragged against its will into a high ponytail, stood on top of her head pointing erratically skyward, as if her brain had erupted into a blond volcano.

"I'm okay," I told her, not sure that I was.

She rolled her eyes and put her hands on her hips. "Yeah, right, you're okay. You just look like you've been pulled across town with your panty hose hooked to a trailer hitch. And where's lover boy?"

"He's not home."

A scowl crossed her face. "Just like a guy. There's trouble, you need help and where is the scum?"

"Can I help, Lornie?"

I heard Ox's voice. He extracted his bulk from the Camaro and walked over to us.

Lorna turned to him and poked him in the chest with her finger. "Yeah, you can find whoever did this to her and beat the snot out of him."

"Not necessary, really. I'm fine," I said, not wishing to unleash Ox's brawn on some unwitting passerby. I was feeling some remorse about the beating I had given the flasher. I knew that men who exposed themselves were usually lonely and benign, and I could have put a stop to his antics with a simple scathing remark. Instead I had thrashed him. Although I knew he had deserved it, I still hoped I hadn't hurt anything vital.

Lorna put her hands on her hips and shook her head.

"Well, I gotta hear this. Come on; let me help you into the car. You know, I must have called you a dozen times this afternoon, but I kept getting your machine."

She wrapped both hands around my arms and steered me toward the car. Lumbering ahead of her, Ox opened the door for me, and the two of them helped me into the car with the care they would have used on an eighty-year-old with a hip transplant. Ox walked to the driver's side and squeezed into the backseat with Bronco, which was like trying to stuff a banana into a pitted olive, but he made it. Lorna had left the car running. She hopped in the driver's seat.

"Ox was unplugging my toilet, so I brought him and Bronco along for the ride," she said, wanting to make sure I knew that the two of them weren't on a date, I suppose. "Buckle up for safety, hon," she added, shaking a puny finger in my direction. "Now tell me everything. Don't leave one little thing out."

I considered the wisdom of revealing the night's events to Lorna. But she was a client, I told myself, and she was paying me for information, so I told her. She laughed out loud at the part where I hid in the back of the Jeep, but she became silent when I told her about Gallagher and about the car that nearly killed me.

"So who was the guy? Did you get a good look at him?" she asked, her voice solemn. She was afraid of the answer.

"It was dark. I couldn't see his face. He looked average height, taller than Gallagher. I can't be sure."

And the more I spoke about it, the less sure I became. How could I be certain that the scene at the cliff had been the scene I had witnessed in Lufkin's VR program? Everything on the cliff had happened so fast that my recollection of it was blurry. I noticed a throbbing in my right ankle.

Just then Ox's knees jammed into the back of my seat as he lurched forward.

"It was Lufkin. I know it was. I told ya, Lornie. Lufkin's trouble. You gotta stay away from him, Lornie. You gotta stop looking for him."

"Shut up, Ox!" she yelled, her voice edged with panic.

I heard Ox mumble, "My name's Vernon," but I don't think Lorna heard. Not that she would have cared anyway. She was hunched over the steering wheel, her fingers gripping it as if she were hanging on for dear life. She pressed down on the accelerator, and I was worried about her driving, but luckily we reached a red light and she slammed on the brakes.

"You don't know nothin', Ox. Just because it was a guy doesn't mean it was Arnie. The world's full of guys. That doesn't mean they're all Arnie, does it?" she said, directing that last question at me as the light turned green. The Camaro lunged forward with a screech. At that moment I might have said anything to slow her driving. "You didn't mention hair. Arnie's hair is real long. You couldn't miss it."

"I think I would have noticed hair that long, even in the dark," I said.

"Ha." She shoveled the word over her shoulder at Ox like it was a clump of fresh manure. He slumped back into the seat, temporarily defeated.

"He could have cut his hair, Lorna," I told her. "If he's trying to hide, he would cut it."

"Not Arnie. He was attached to his hair like he was Samson or something. He'd never cut it."

After this statement, Lorna kept her eyes on the road. We drove in silence for a while, and I knew what Lorna was thinking. She was thinking that maybe Arnie Lufkin had killed Gallagher. Arnie and Gallagher had known each other, had worked together. It was possible, and it was the possibility that was grinding into her.

"So what did you find out about Arnie today?" Lorna finally asked me, her voice sounding small and insecure. I knew she had been putting off the question.

"He's dangerous, Lorna. I feel sure he killed a woman in San Francisco, and it could have been him tonight. You need to be careful, really careful."

She didn't say anything. To my surprise, Ox didn't either. Since I was the one who had given Lorna the terrible news, I think Ox wanted to give her time to let it sink in, and I was grateful for the silence. Up to that point my thinking had been muddled by the shock of what had happened to me, but as I sat there in Lorna's car my thoughts began to take shape. I remembered the words Gallagher had spoken on the cliff. She had said she wanted to tell everything and take her punishment. Whoever had killed her had done so because he didn't want her to talk.

Lorna pulled the Camaro into the underground parking garage where I had left my car. The harshness of the fluorescent lights stung my eyes.

"I can drive you home. It's no trouble. I'm not so sure you're in a condition to drive."

"I'm okay; I promise. It's the white Toyota over there."

She pulled the Camaro next to my car. "I'll check on you tomorrow. If you need anything, just call me. Any time, morning, noon, or night."

I had my hand on the door handle but paused and looked back at her. "Lorna, I have to call the police. I wasn't thinking straight when I ran off tonight. I was scared and I wasn't sure what had happened. But I have to call the police tomorrow morning and tell them everything."

She looked at me with frightened eyes because she knew I meant Arnie, that I would have to tell the police that it could have been him on the headlands.

"You gotta do what you gotta do. It's sort of your civic duty."

"Lorna, be careful. Lock your doors." With the beginnings of tears in her eyes, she nodded. I took her hand and squeezed it, then got out of the car. I heard her tell Ox it was okay to get up in the front.

I drove down Highway 280 with my head full of questions. The road is very lonely at night. It runs parallel to Highway 101 about ten miles west, cutting through the hills. I chose that route because there's not as much traffic and, in my distracted state, I figured I'd have less chance of killing myself in a head-on collision. I was still feeling pretty rough, although I trusted my driving a lot more than I trusted Lorna's. The highway had few lights and few cars. I rolled down the window of the Toyota and let the rush of cool air pelt my face. The red file lay beside me.

Questions bounced around my head. Was Gallagher actually dead? I knew the answer. If I had been smarter, quicker, braver, I could have saved her. If I had jumped out of the Jeep as soon as they started arguing, he wouldn't have killed her. Her body wouldn't be shattered on the rocks if I had made one decision differently, initiated one action more quickly.

I told myself to stop it. I couldn't have predicted that he was going to kill her. I'm not psychic. But my brain was like a cartoon with two characters inside—the person who chided me and the one who took my side. It had always been that way with me, and maybe it is with everybody. Half my brain liked myself and the other half always found fault.

I had liked Arlene Gallagher, and whatever she had done wrong, she had wanted to come clean about it. She certainly didn't deserve to die. I thought about her red glasses with all the rhinestones and I could feel tears stinging my eyes, but I fought them back. I didn't want to allow myself the luxury of crying. Crying wasn't going to help.

The phone was ringing when I walked in the door. I knew it was Paoli before I picked it up.

"Where have you been?" he asked without bothering to say hello. "You never called. I've been going nuts. I waited for you at your house over two hours; then I got worried and started looking for you."

I calmed him down and told him the story, then had to calm him down again. He said he would be at my house in ten minutes, and I didn't discourage him. I needed him with me.

MY CLOTHES WERE TORN and filthy, my knees caked with dried blood, but I was too tired to undress and shower. Instead I collapsed onto the couch and, with my last ounce of energy, started to open the audit file.

When I awoke in the morning, the red file lying unopened beside me, it reminded me of graduate school, when I would work in the campus computer room until the wee hours, then sleep in my clothes so I could make it to my early class the next morning. Paoli had thrown a blanket over me. It fell to the floor when I sat up, and as my head cleared, the previous night's events came back to me, and along with the memories came feelings of panic and revulsion. I put my head in my hands and pressed against my forehead as if I could push out the demons, but instead of leaving they just took up residence in my ankle. I lifted my foot onto the coffee table. The good news was that it didn't feel painful enough to be a bad sprain.

Paoli heard me moving around, and he came into the living room with a mug of coffee in each hand. His shirt looked like he had slept in it, although by his face I guessed he hadn't slept much at all. Just the sight of him made me feel better.

"You were asleep by the time I got here last night, so I didn't disturb you. You look like shit."

"Thanks," I said with a smile. I did look like shit, and I didn't care.

Paoli sat on the couch beside me, set the mugs on the coffee table, and pulled me close to him. He held onto me a moment before speaking, and I savored the delicious feel of his breath on my neck.

"Last night I was mad as hell at you for not calling me and going off half-cocked after Arlene Gallagher," he said, his arms still around me. "I stormed in here like a maniac to tell you off, then I saw you asleep on the couch with your clothes torn and your legs banged up."

I pulled back enough so I could see his face. "But I'm okay. I'm fine."

As I said the words, I felt his arms release me. He picked up his coffee and leaned back into the couch, and I felt a subtle shift in his vibrations. Even after six months I didn't know all his moods. Spend almost every day and night with someone for that length of time and you get to know their emotional geography pretty well, but there's always unexplored territory. I should have pressed him right then to find out what was going on with him, but I didn't. I just didn't feel like taking in any more data. I wrapped my hands around my mug and inhaled the aroma before taking the first soul-satisfying sip.

"You think it was Lufkin?" Paoli asked.

I looked at him. The sixty-thousand-dollar question. Too bad I only had a five-buck answer.

"I can't be sure," I said. "That third VR scene I saw could have been the cliff."

Paoli leaned forward and put his coffee back on the table. "With something like this, you need to be sure, Julie."

"What if I could be?"

"Could be what?"

"Could be sure. Maybe I can be sure that it was Lufkin."

"How? You just said that you can't be certain that it was a cliff in the VR scene."

"I'm not basing this on anything factual. It's just this feeling I have, and it's getting stronger. I know it was Lufkin."

"Gee, nice scientific approach, Julie. I never knew you were psychic."

"Wait a minute. You're the one always telling me that I'm too concerned with facts and figures, that I don't use my intuition enough. Well this time I'm going with my gut, and my gut says that it was Arnie Lufkin on the cliff last night."

I hardly noticed Paoli's silence, because I was already planning the day's strategy. I took a big sip of coffee in an effort to get caffeine into my veins, then stood up, feeling a few aches from my tumbles the night before.

"I've got to get moving," I said. "I need to see the police in Marin and tell them what I know about last night; then I've got to talk to McCracken. I heard part of the conversation Gallagher had last night, and she said some things I need to get a handle on." I headed for the shower but stopped and looked around the living room. "Where's the paper? There might be a story on Gallagher."

Paoli jumped up from the couch and his hand flew into the air. "Forget the paper, goddammit! Julie, you almost got killed last night. If you think I'm going to let you go on as if nothing happened, you've got a serious screw loose. And don't give me a bunch of feminist crap about I don't 'let' you do anything. You could get killed, Julie. Do you get it? Dead. Deceased. No longer breathing."

His face pink and his jaw clenched, Paoli's fuse had finally blown, and he looked like smoke might start streaming out of his ears.

"I know it was dangerous," I said. "I know it was probably dumb, but it's over with and I'm fine, so let's just drop it and move on."

"I don't want to just drop it."

"Paoli, what's eating you?"

"I'll tell you what's eating me. We're supposed to be partners. We're supposed to be working on this case together, only you're off half the time doing things on your own. You purposely went after Gallagher yesterday without telling me."

"I was afraid you would try to stop me from getting the file."

"You're right, I would have tried to stop you, because you just happen to forget that there's a murderer out there, Julie. You figured you'd just pat me on the head, send me back to the office, and tell me all about it the next morning. What would have happened if you had been hurt up there?" I opened my mouth to answer, but I never got the chance. "Things are going to change around here, Julie."

"What are you talking about?"

"From now until the end of this case, you and I are together every minute of the day. It's for your own protection, and I can't get any work done if I'm constantly worrying about you. Besides, it'll give us some time to work out our problems."

"What problems? Things are going fine. We have some business; we're going to get a reference—"

"Yeah, sure, a reference from Mr. 'I'm A Big Executive' with the monogrammed cuffs. You love that stuff. You eat it up. Me, I'm just a rude, crude guy who wears his shirts unstarched and missed his ride up the corporate ladder."

"I've never said anything like that to you."

"You never had to, but I can see it on your face. In the back of your mind you're thinking, 'What am I doing with this lug of a guy when I have company presidents kissing my feet?'"

"You're wrong. I want you, and I want us to be partners, but we can't be attached at the hip."

"You can take it or leave it, Julie, because I'm sick and tired of you making all the rules. You agree to stay with me twenty-four hours a day until this case is over or I'm walking."

"So walk."

To my astonishment, he grabbed his jacket and headed out the door, leaving me standing there, staring after him, feeling like I wanted to punch something with my fist. I wanted to go after him and throw my arms around him, to tell him I was sorry, but something wouldn't let me. Maybe it was pride or maybe it was fear that what he had said about me was right, that what I really wanted in a man was someone starched and proper like McCracken.

When I heard the Porsche roar off, I ignored the sick feeling in the pit of my stomach and went outside, grabbed my newspapers off the lawn, and stormed back in, slamming the door behind me. I take the *Wall Street Journal*, the *San Jose Mercury News*, and the *San Francisco Chronicle*, but that day the *Chronicle* was all I was interested in. Determined to get my mind off Paoli, I threw everything but the front section on the floor, then dug into page one. I knew what I was looking for and finally found it on page four:

Woman Falls from Marin Cliff—Marin County sheriffs found the body of a woman Monday night on a rocky beach at the base of Marin Headlands cliff. Marin officials say the incident occurred around 9:30 p.m., about half an hour before their arrival on the scene. Identification of the woman is being withheld pending notification of relatives.

Reading the story brought the previous night's events back to me with renewed clarity, and I felt a wave of nausea. I had to force myself to read the rest of the story, but there wasn't much left. It went on to say that the sheriffs had been notified via an anonymous 911 call. I wondered if they could trace me but decided that the best they could do was trace the call back to Gallagher's car phone, which would lead them nowhere.

I knew it might be possible for me to stay out of the whole mess. All I had to do was keep my mouth shut and let the sheriff's department do the dirty work. Only I was terrible at keeping my mouth shut and as of late had developed a penchant for dirty work.

The Girl Scout in me told me to call the police. I checked my watch. Seven-thirty-six. Since I always believe in going straight to the top when you want something done, I decided to wait an hour before I called the sheriff's department. This brief delay would allow the upper echelon time to get into the office and get settled with their coffee and Danish or, since we were talking Marin, their espresso and croissant. It was only an excuse to put off making the call, but it worked for me.

Was Paoli right to say the things he did? My mind kept turning over the question until I thought I would go crazy. I went into the bathroom, stripped off my battered clothes, and threw them in the trash can, then took them out again, remembering that I was on a budget. My dry cleaner had an ace seamstress who could mend anything and might enjoy the challenge. Turning the water as hot as I could stand, I let the water hit my face and shoulders, and it felt like a baptism, cleansing me of at least some of my frustration.

Once out of the shower and into my white chenille robe, I felt human. I had work to do, and I couldn't let relationship problems get in the way, at least not for the next few hours. I curled up on the couch and opened Gallagher's red file.

There were two parts to it—an audit report and a separate transaction listing stapled to the back. An hour of going through the audit records didn't tell me anything new about Lufkin or how he had stolen Anco's money. I was hoping the audit would show that Gallagher had given the auditors carefully selected files in order to hide those that contained dummy accounts, but apparently the auditors had gone through every file in the general ledger program, so that blew that theory. Could I have been wrong in assuming that Gallagher had been in on Lufkin's theft? But if so, what had Gallagher been talking about when she said she wanted to tell everything and take her punishment? And why did Gallagher try to keep the audit information from me?

I moved on to the transaction listing, which was five pages of tiny print listing all the purchase orders over twenty-thousand dollars that were written during the audit period. Each line item listed the PO number, the amount, the vendor, and the name of the authorizing employee. I went through the list and hit pay dirt. Now I realized why Gallagher hadn't wanted me to see it. She had authorized a large number of purchase orders, all in the twenty-to-thirty-thousand-dollar range, most of them to companies I had never heard of—companies with names that sounded suspiciously like consultants.

I took my cellular phone from the kitchen into my bedroom, thought about calling Paoli, but instead dialed the Anco main number and asked for Andrew McCracken.

"He's in a meeting," his secretary informed me.

"This is important. Interrupt him."

"I'm sorry, but I can't interrupt him."

"Listen; he'll be very unhappy if he doesn't speak to me immediately," I said in my most authoritative voice.

McCracken was on the line within seconds, and I didn't waste any time getting to the point.

"I think I found out where all the extra money in Lufkin's bank accounts came from." There was silence on the line. "Arlene Gallagher approved a lot of large purchase orders that look like they might have gone for consulting work."

"And?" McCracken asked. He must not have read the paper yet, because it didn't sound like he knew what had happened to her.

"And I think she may have been embezzling with Lufkin."

There was a short silence. "Approving a large number of purchase orders hardly qualifies as embezzling, Julie. That's a big accusation. Do you have something to back it up?" He sounded angry and I couldn't blame him.

I opened my mouth to tell him about the previous night, to tell him that Arlene Gallagher was dead, but stopped. I should save it for the police.

"If you do some research on the list of purchase orders I have in front of me, I think you'll have all the information you need. And there's more. Last night I overheard a conversation between Gallagher and someone else. She and this other person were arguing over cosigning something. She was saying she needed this person to cosign so she could get her money. Do you have any idea what they were talking about?"

There was silence on the other end, followed by a sigh. "If she was embezzling with Lufkin, and I'm not saying she was, she and Lufkin may have parked the money in the same place but required each to cosign before either one could get the money out."

"So if they put their money in the nominee corporation you mentioned before, both of them would have to sign something before they could remove the money."

"That's right."

I paused. "What would happen if one of the people died? How would the other person ever get their money?"

"That wouldn't be a problem. You would just have to show proof of death."

"Do yourself a favor and take a closer look at Arlene's PO history. I may be wrong, but please, just check it out."

We said good-bye and hung up. Minutes later I was in my car en route to the Marin County sheriff's office. While I drove I took the opportunity to sort some things out. Here were the things I at least thought I knew: Lufkin was mad at Chambers and at Anco. He also wanted capital to start his own company. So to kill two birds with one stone he broke into the security software and started embezzling money in chunks up to five thousand, because he had signature authority for up to that amount.

So where did Gallagher fit in? Did Lufkin invite her in on the scheme because Gallagher had signature authority for much larger amounts? Then again, maybe he didn't invite her in at all. Gallagher was the controller at Anco. She could have easily figured out what Lufkin was doing and demanded that she be cut in or else threaten to expose him. That made more sense.

I had already guessed that Gallagher was lonely. Even though I hardly knew her, somehow I felt I knew a great deal about who she was inside. Looking out fifteen years, Gallagher is what I could have turned into if I hadn't quit my job at ICI, if I hadn't met Paoli. Gallagher saw herself getting older, and she felt she didn't have enough to show for the time she had put into the company. She saw an opportunity to make some real money fast. But would someone like Gallagher take that kind of risk?

Alan Shapiro had told me that when there's collusion between people like Gallagher and Lufkin, embezzlement is almost impossible to uncover. Maybe Gallagher didn't think there was much risk at all. And although Lufkin was brilliant, he probably didn't know much about banks and finances. It would take someone with Gallagher's knowledge to set up a nominee corporation.

So what happened next? I figured that things were going fine until Lufkin got caught for the money he had stolen prior to Gallagher's involvement. Lufkin didn't want to implicate Gallagher, because if he did then he also would have to reveal that there was an extra half a million stashed. Lufkin was arrogant enough to think he could escape conviction. He couldn't touch his money for a while because he knew the FBI had a trace on it, so he found Lorna, who put up his bond. At first maybe he was really attracted to her, but after a couple of months he grew tired of her. He was worried that the evidence against him was starting to look pretty bad, and he couldn't stand the thought of going to jail. So he planned his escape. He had already hooked up with Sajak, courtesy of Miranda, and it was Sajak who helped him establish a new identity and résumé along with a job where he could continue his VR work. Maybe it was a consulting job where he could work out of an apartment and stay out of sight.

It was at this point Lufkin started having women problems. Lorna was after him to get married. Then there was Sajak. At first he and Sajak were lovers, but eventually Sajak found Lufkin's potential fortune more attractive than Lufkin himself, and she started blackmailing him.

Meanwhile, Gallagher was also giving him her share of trouble. She was never a real criminal type, and she started cracking under the pressure of Lufkin's investigation. She was afraid they would find out about her. I remembered Monique saying how flustered Gallagher was. Lufkin saw her falling apart and knew he couldn't let the situation come to its logical conclusion. If she told all to the FBI, then Lufkin's chance of getting the money and making a final escape would be gone. Lufkin needed Gallagher playing ball with him, or he needed her dead. It would also be very convenient to have Sajak no longer threatening him for money.

So Lufkin got an idea. He used the computer equipment at his new job to create the VR programs so he could practice murdering his two victims. Maybe at first it was more of a game to him. If you wanted to kill someone, how would you do it, etc. He practiced Sajak's murder over and over until it seemed very real to him, and then, a month or so later when he was ready, he went through with it. The kill went smoothly—nice and clean, since he just handed her the coffee and then pretended he had to go downstairs for a newspaper or something, so he wouldn't have to witness the messy dying part.

After that success, the thought of killing Gallagher seemed easier. He preferred to practice her murder with the VR program, but by this time he couldn't find his VR CDs. Maybe he realized that Lorna had kept them. Maybe he didn't. Still, he started to panic. He knew we were looking for him, that we were in contact with Gallagher on a daily basis, and that she was starting to break down. He had to eliminate her fast. So he met her on the Marin Headlands and simply pushed her off. No murder weapon, no witnesses, and it could have been construed as a suicide—all relatively clean except for the part where I jumped out of Gallagher's car. He had to improvise on that one.

I shuddered when I crossed the Golden Gate Bridge into Marin County. Why had Gallagher gone up there to meet him? I considered the possibilities. Arnie had vanished and Gallagher couldn't get any money unless he was found. That's why she wanted Paoli and me to find him, and it was why she had been so interested that first day about who else had hired us to look for him. But I remembered distinctly that at the initial meeting she hadn't wanted us to look at the Anco software. She hadn't wanted that at all.

If that part of my theory was correct, the rest fell into place. Things were going okay for Gallagher until, without her prior knowledge, McCracken had hired us to investigate the software. That's when Gallagher really started getting cold feet.

I was so caught up in thought that it took me by surprise when I saw the exit sign for the Marin County Civic Center. Everything is chic in Marin County, and the civic center was designed by no less than Frank Lloyd Wright himself, only Wright must have created it during his Hanna Barbera period. The civic center looks like it came straight out of "The Jetsons"—a series of low cylindrical buildings made of pink stucco topped with an aqua tile roof. There's even a gold spear-shaped antennae that sticks up into the air and looks like it's there to pick up alien signals.

My biorhythms must have been off that day, because the Marin County sheriff's department found me about as annoying as Paoli had earlier. After I told the receptionist I had information regarding the woman who had fallen off the headlands cliff, she gave me a wary look, then made a call. A few minutes later two uniformed men came out and led me to a back office. The taller one was named Rawlings and was a deputy sheriff, and he did most of the talking. The shorter guy was named Hernandez. At first they both looked at me with bland expressions, but when I mentioned Gallagher's name they perked up considerably, since her name had been left out of the papers. I told them I had been up on the cliff when she went over it, and that I was pretty sure she didn't do a voluntary swan dive. That was the easy part.

"What were you doing up there, Ms. Blake?" Rawlings inevitably asked.

So I told him my story, start to finish, including my work at Anco, hiding in the back of Gallagher's Jeep, and hearing the argument and the final thud that preceded her fall from the cliff. I also told them my theory about Arnie Lufkin. I have to admit that the Marin County sheriffs listened to me with more credence than San Francisco's Finest, but then this time I wasn't just theorizing about a murder. I had been there.

I ended up having to tell my story four times, each time with new additions, to my audience. After several grueling hours they had me sign a statement and then suggested I remain in the Bay Area for the immediate future.

Hernandez asked me if I wanted to file a complaint against Lufkin or whoever had tried to use me for a speed bump, but I declined the offer, at least temporarily. When Lufkin was finally found he was going to have plenty of problems. And Lufkin would be found. I was going to make sure of it.

SIXTEEN

AT ABOUT ONE-THIRTY I walked out of the sheriff's office and into the Marin County sunshine feeling tired, hungry, and forlorn. Sometime during the sheriff's questioning it had hit me that my lover and business partner had walked out on me that morning. What if he didn't come back? Did I want him back? My head mumbled, *Maybe,* but my heart yelled out an ear-shattering, *Yes!* Paoli had flaws, of course. You could fill Candlestick Park with Paoli's flaws, but then I had a few flaws myself. Besides, he had only been gone a few hours, and I felt a hole in my heart the size of New Jersey.

If my love problems weren't enough, my previous night's brush with being road kill had left me with numerous aching body parts, including an ankle that now felt like it had hot coals inside it. I sat down on the civic center steps and inspected the damage, and I could see that it was swollen. It took all my resolve to get the energy to stand back up again. Thirty-four is that delicate age when your body starts telling you that it doesn't respond to stress the way it used to, and my body was now telling me to soak in a hot tub and start staying home nights.

It was the prospect of a delicious, hot bubble bath that gave me the energy to limp my way across the parking lot to my car. I drove to the nearest drugstore and bought an economy-sized bottle of Advil and an ACE bandage.

Afterward I checked my voice mail hoping to find a message from Paoli, but he hadn't called. I did get a message from Lorna checking on my general state of health, as well as a frantic-sounding message from Max. I wasted no time in calling her back. At first her secretary said she was in a meeting, but after I gave her my name Max was on the line in seconds.

It was a late lunch Max was after. My first reaction was to beg off and say that I was too busy, but she sounded anxious, which was unusual for her. I asked her what was wrong, but she wouldn't discuss it over the phone.

Choosing friendship over my bubble bath, I drove down Highway 101 with my thoughts focused on the two men currently dominating my life—Paoli and Arnie Lufkin. Half an hour of remorse over Paoli got me nowhere except depressed, so I switched to thinking about Lufkin's VR programs. The thought nagged at me that if I had the chance to look at them one more time I might learn something that would finally nail Lufkin for the two murders.

An hour and a half later, I was at the Fresh Choice restaurant in Palo Alto, one of Max's favorite restaurants because they list the fat and calorie content of the food. In the past I had scoffed at her obsession about dieting, but now, with my extra few pounds, I was counting calories myself.

It worried me that Max wasn't her usual glib self. We got our lunches and sat down at the table and she hadn't made a single remark regarding anyone's sex life. That alone told me something was amiss, but what confirmed it was the tiny chips I noticed on her French manicure. It looked as though she had actually chewed her nails. Something was wrong, but I didn't want to press her, even though the suspense was excruciating. We were munching spinach salads with no-oil dressing when she finally spilled her news.

"Wayne and I broke our engagement," she said after taking a large fortifying gulp of white wine and slamming the glass down on the table so hard the stem broke off. She stared at the broken glass a moment, then downed the rest of the wine before handing the stemless goblet to a passing busboy.

I stopped chewing. "You're joking," I said through a mouth impolitely filled with spinach. "What happened?"

"The prenup."

"The what?"

She looked at me like I had said something stupid. "The prenuptial agreement. I wouldn't sign it."

I swallowed. "So it's over?"

She didn't answer, but I saw the look in her eyes. I was floored. Sure, most women cried over their boyfriends, but Max was different from most women. Max was always cool and cocksure, and nothing with after-shave and a penis had ever rattled her. Until now. I tried to think of encouraging words.

"You'll get back together. Wayne worships you."

Max shook her head. "I don't know, Jules. He told me the engagement was off. He said I only wanted him for his money."

It's expected in many female friendships that in conversations like this you say whatever your best girlfriend wants to hear. You're there for comfort and support, not for blunt honesty. I don't subscribe to that theory.

"To be honest, Max, I always thought the same thing. I mean you've always treated him in such an offhanded way. You certainly never acted like you loved him."

Her eyes widened and her lovely brow furrowed, a facial expression she usually avoids because it causes wrinkles.

"Of course I love him!" she blurted. "I mean I must love him, or why would I be so upset?"

I'm ashamed to say that it crossed my mind that Max's broken engagement meant the loss of millions to her in future community property, but the pained expression on her face made me think that her despair had more emotional content.

Max took out a gold compact, flipped it open with one hand, and surveyed her face. It was seeing that mirror that ignited an idea in my head. Lufkin's poem had said:

"Looking in a mirror you may just see a foe." Maybe I finally knew what it meant. I asked Max for her phone. Without comment, she pulled it out of her purse and handed it to me. I dialed Eldon's number, but Bobby answered.

"Eldon's in a staff meeting. My keyboard's got a glitch in it so I'm in here looking for an extra one that Eldon's got stashed."

"Bobby, do you still have the VR equipment set up?"

"Yeah. We were supposed to have already returned it to Anco, but the police called and said we have to leave it for a few days. It's evidence."

"Do you still have the CDs?"

"No. The police took them."

My heart sank for a moment but then lifted as another thought struck me. I thanked Bobby for his help, and we exchanged good-byes.

"Max, I need your help," I said when I handed her the phone. She had repaired her makeup.

"Name it."

"Can you help me with a project tonight?"

"Do you ever have anything on your mind except work? How about a movie instead? It would be nice to actually see a film without the sound of Wayne crunching Almond Roca bars all through it. Although it's sort of cute, in an eccentric kind of way."

"You can see a movie anytime. Come on; help me sneak into Comtech tonight. I want to take one more look at those VR programs."

"Why?"

"Because I think I may have missed something the last time."

She looked at me, then shrugged. "All right. I guess I'm going to have lots of time to see movies by myself."

"Great. We'll have fun; I promise," I told her, not knowing at the time what those words portended.

WHEN I PICKED UP Max that night, she was wearing your basic burglar outfit—black turtleneck, black jeans, and running shoes—and she didn't hide her disappointment when I told her we wouldn't be scaling walls or breaking any windows.

"I thought you said we were going to sneak into Comtech. I expected something more exciting. I even bought new Nikes."

"Sorry, but 'sneaking' was a figure of speech. I assumed you knew that. We're going to saunter right past the guard at Comtech. We won't have to break into anything."

"But you don't have a badge, Jules. I can unlock the front doors with my card key, but the guard is sure to ask you for a badge. But don't worry. All I have to do is figure out which side door doesn't trigger an alarm; then I'll let you in."

"Here's a question, Mata Hari. How do you determine which door won't set off an alarm? What do you do? Open them all, set off a dozen alarms, until you find one that's silent? That sounds really sneaky."

"We'll figure something out."

"We don't have to." I pulled a Comtech badge from my pocket. "I still have this from when I was working on the Comtech project at ICI. All I need is for you to get us in the front door."

Max grabbed the badge and studied it. "If the guard looks at this he'll see the expiration date."

"Twenty dollars he doesn't give it more than a cursory glance."

"You're on. Since I'm not marrying a millionaire I guess I need the money." We both smiled at that one.

I pulled the Toyota into the Comtech parking lot, and we walked to the front door. Max pressed a thick, card-shaped piece of plastic against a square black card reader outside the entrance. The reader electronically scanned Max's card key, determined her to be a Comtech employee in good standing, and we heard the welcoming click of the front door opening.

A guard sat at the front desk listening to a radio talk show. After Max and I flashed our badges he pushed a log at us for our signatures. We were home free.

"So I don't get it," Max said as we walked down the hallway to the room that held the VR equipment. "You said Bobby told you that the police took the CDs."

"They did. But I'm betting that when we looked at the CDs the other day Eldon downloaded the data off the CDs and onto the workstation's hard disk."

"What makes you think he did that?"

"For faster response time. Reading a program off the internal disk drive is always faster than reading off an external device."

"Okay, so what if the programs are there? You've already seen them once. What else are you looking for?"

I smiled. "A mirror."

Max raised an eyebrow. "Excuse me?"

"The idea hit me at lunch today. One of the VR scenes was Sajak's office. Sajak had a large antique mirror on the wall. I never looked in the mirror."

"So? We all know that I never pass up a mirror, but what's the big deal with you?"

"Simple. Lufkin wrote the program with astonishing detail. He has a massive ego. What if he wrote the program so when he approached the mirror his face showed?"

"What if he did?"

"It would prove that he was Sajak's killer."

Max stopped and faced me. "Listen, Jules; I think you're getting confused about what's real and what isn't. This VR thing Lufkin wrote is just a computer program. It's not real. It's not like fingerprints on a murder weapon."

"That's where you're wrong, Max. If I can see Lufkin's face in that mirror, then the VR program is as good as a signed confession, at least as far as I'm concerned."

We continued walking. "I guess I see your point, but you may have to convince the police. Isn't this the room?" she asked, stopping in front of a door.

"They all look alike to me. Open the door and let's take a look."

Max shook the door handle. "It's locked." My heart sank. "Don't worry; I've got a passkey. Wayne gave it to me six months ago."

She took her keys from her purse, unlocked the door, and pushed it open. The room was pitch dark, but after several minutes of fumbling she found the light switch. The VR equipment sat there looking serene, the data suit, gloves, and helmet in a heap on the floor.

Normally a computer would require a password, but because these were set up on a temporary basis I doubted that anyone had gone to the trouble to set one up. I was right. I easily booted up the computers and found Lufkin's programs stored on the machine's internal drive, just where I had expected them to be. I ran the first program to make sure it worked; then I had Max help me put on the data suit and gloves. I gave Max some instructions on how to keep the program running; then I positioned myself in the center of the room and put on the helmet.

We had a few false starts. Max is not exactly a technical whiz, but after I wrote down a few instructions for her she managed to get the program going.

"Okay, Max, type in the third command I gave you. That should put me directly into Sajak's office."

I heard Max's voice through my earphone. "Give me a second. I'm having trouble reading your writing. All right. Are you there?"

"Not yet. Max, are you using any commands other than the ones I gave you?"

"Do you honestly think I know any commands other than the ones you wrote? Get real. Okay, I've got it now."

The black void burst into color, and I was in Sajak's office. I stepped past her desk, over to the wall, and looked into the gold-framed mirror. A face looked back at me that wasn't my own. It was the face of Arnie Lufkin.

That's when everything went black. It happened so suddenly I wondered if Max had kicked a power cord.

"Something's wrong here, Max," I said but received no response. "Max? Are you there, Max?" Still no response.

I reached for my helmet to pull it off, but before I could, I felt something slam into my shoulder and fell to the ground. My hands broke the fall, but I felt a stab of pain shoot through my injured ankle. A body was on top of me now. I punched and kicked wildly as something heavy hit the floor next to my head.

I felt one of my kicks hit squarely, and I heard a groan of pain. The weight on me lifted, and I scrambled to my knees. I ripped off the helmet, but the room was in pitch darkness and I couldn't see. The body came at me again and I swung high, with the helmet catching something hard.

I heard the door open, and a beam of light sliced through the darkness.

"What the hell?" a voice in the doorway said.

"Help me!" As I yelled, I heard my attacker running away from me. A door opened and he was gone.

It was at that moment that the security guard managed to find the light switch.

"Jeezus! What happened here?"

I saw Max crumpled on the floor. I dropped the helmet and ran over to her.

"Call 911!" I screamed.

The guard watched me helplessly a moment, looked frantically around the room for a phone, didn't find one, then ran out the door. I heard his footsteps down the hall.

Max was breathing, but she was out cold. I cradled her head in my lap. After a few minutes she opened her eyes.

"What happened?" she mumbled.

"Be quiet," I said, although I was thrilled to hear her speak.

The ambulance got there first, followed within minutes by the police. The paramedics examined Max and said that they thought she would be all right, but she had to go to the emergency room to be checked out. As they wheeled her out on the gurney, I walked beside her and held her hand.

"You're going to be okay," I said to her.

"Next time I'm going for the movie," she mumbled as they lifted her onto the ambulance.

SEVENTEEN

ONCE THE EMERGENCY ROOM staff had assured me for the third time that Max was okay and was only staying the night for observation, I dragged myself to a chair and spent a half hour answering a policeman's questions.

I was tired and hurting and not in the mood for an interrogation, but at least Officer Humphreys was nice. He kept his voice low and his manner gentle as he jotted down the answers to all the routine questions, punctuating his queries with an occasional, "Are you feeling all right?" I appreciated that small kindness, and Officer Humphreys's polite attitude made me self-conscious about my current state of disarray. I guess after rolling around the floor beneath some ape anybody would look rotten and smell worse, and I was no exception. Stress makes me sweat. My mother always said that women don't sweat, they glow. Well, Mom, at that moment I was glowing pretty heavily. I took a Kleenex out of my purse and wiped some of the glow dripping down my neck.

Two squad cars were searching the Comtech area for my attacker, Humphreys said, and an initial search of the building indicated that nothing appeared to have been stolen. I could have told him that but suggested that he have someone check the computer's hard disk. Whoever had attacked me hadn't want me to see Lufkin's VR program, and he could have erased it after he knocked out Max.

Humphreys asked me if I could identify the guy in a lineup if they found him, emphasis on the if. I felt embarrassed, but I had to tell him no. It was dark and I never really saw what my attacker looked like.

Officer Humphreys saw the expression on my face when he asked me if I had any idea who jumped me, and I noticed his jaw starting to twitch. I hesitated in answering, and he took the opportunity to show me the firm side of his nature. I gave him the Cliff Notes version of the whole Arnie Lufkin story as well as the likely connection to the intruder at Comtech, and Humphreys's eyes flashed to high beam. Was it my imagination or did I sense in Officer Humphreys a desire to be promoted to Detective Humphreys?

"Do you think whoever attacked you was trying to kill you?"

I didn't have to think about it. "Yes, I do. He tried to hit me in the head with something heavy."

"How do you know? It's not that I'm doubting you, but you said earlier that the room was dark."

"Whatever he was using for a weapon, I heard it hit the floor near my head. It was a heavy object. I don't think he meant to give me a love tap."

"You keep saying 'he.' You're sure it was a man?"

I paused on that one. "I'm not sure, I guess. Whoever jumped me was strong, I know that much."

Humphreys finished by saying that I would need to come to the station the following day to sign a statement. I nodded, failing to mention that it would be the third law enforcement facility I had visited in three days. If my mother knew, her perm would uncurl.

When Officer Humphreys exited, I found a pay phone, called Paoli, and told him what had happened and where I was. He managed to run through at least six major human emotions within a thirty-second time frame before saying he would come to the hospital and take me home.

With that deed done, I took a fortifying breath and phoned Wayne Hansen, breaking the news to him that his former fiancée had a concussion. When he asked how it happened I had no choice but to tell him that someone had knocked her on the head. She was going to be fine, I told him, but you wouldn't have known it by the commotion

Hansen caused on the phone. Making noises like a rabid squirrel, Hansen hurled accusations at me regarding what he perceived as my mental deficiencies, emotional instabilities, and generally negative influence on his wife-to-be. It seemed that Max's knock on the head had eliminated her prenuptial problems. I thanked Wayne for sharing and hung up on him.

By this time I was feeling pretty sorry for myself. I had been assaulted twice within a couple of days, my best friend was lying in a hospital bed with a concussion for which I felt responsible, I had just been yelled at, and my ankle was throbbing.

"You're limping," I heard someone say as I headed unevenly to the closest chair. I turned and saw a woman looking at my ankle with a concerned, nurselike expression. She was a thin black woman and wore one of those white polyester medical-looking pantsuits and white crepe-soled shoes, and to me she looked like an angel of mercy. I had this urge to throw myself into her arms and call her Mommy. I needed nurturing.

"I've twisted it a couple of times in the past few days. It hurts."

"You come with me, hon, and we'll take a look at it. My name's Betsy. The doctors are busy, but I can fix you up," she said, and bracing me with her arm, she led me through the double doors back to the emergency area. It wasn't until she had me on a table and began examining my ankle that I began to cry. I didn't notice that I was even doing it until the tears were running down my chin.

Betsy looked up at me and frowned. "You just let it all out," she said with a pat on my leg.

"If I really let it out, Betsy, you'll be mopping for a week."

She smiled. I smiled, and I indulged myself with a few minutes of tears until the doctor came in, pronounced my ankle as sprained, and suggested I get Xrays in the morning. Betsy had already told me as much and with less fanfare. She wrapped the ankle and gave me a removable cast that looked like a cloth boot and a pair of crutches. As I was hobbling out to the emergency waiting room to wait for Paoli, I heard Hansen's howl.

"This is your fault, Julie! This sort of thing follows you around! Once Maxine and I are married she's going to be seeing a lot less of you."

As he yelled he shook a puny finger at me, his whole body vibrating with anger, his lips sucked in so tight he looked as if at any moment he might spit out a guppy. To top off the whole effect, he was wearing pajama bottoms, a sweatshirt, and rubber thongs and, to the innocent bystander, appeared to be a demented vagrant. I think the hospital staff thought the same, because one of the nurses ran around a corner, and within seconds a large man in a white uniform materialized at Hansen's side, soon followed by another. One of them grabbed Hansen's arm as if he were going to physically eject him from the premises or at least inject him with some Thorazine.

"Sir, you'll have to leave if you don't quiet down," the man said.

Hansen looked at him, then at me, with astonishment. "This is outrageous! Julie, tell them who I am."

I considered telling the hospital orderlies that I had never laid eyes on Hansen before but didn't. "He's just upset. You'll calm down, won't you, Wayne?"

"If that's what it takes to get this guy's hands off me then yes."

I assured the orderly that Hansen would behave, and that I would assume responsibility for him. I have this Girl Scout aura about me that inspires unwarranted trust, and the two hospital bouncers retreated back behind the swinging doors.

"I suppose I should thank you, but I won't," Hansen said, straightening his soiled Grateful Dead sweatshirt. "This whole thing is your fault, and you know it."

"This all happened at your company, Hansen. It's your lousy security that caused this mess." Those were the words

I wanted to say, but they weren't coming out of my mouth, even though I heard them spoken. I turned and saw Paoli behind me. Somehow the fact that we had been fighting no longer seemed important to me, and I could see from the look on his face that he felt the same. His eyes locked onto my crutches; then he put his arms around me and held me close to him. It hurt my sore ribs, but I didn't care, at least not much. Neither one of us said anything. It was Hansen who broke the romantic spell.

"We have excellent security at Comtech. The best. Don't try to pass the buck here. Maxine is back there with a lump on her head the size of a baseball, and Julie's responsible."

I pulled away from Paoli and faced Hansen. "What, do you think I hit her?"

"No, don't be stupid, but you shouldn't have been skulking around my building after hours, especially with Maxine. Trouble follows you, Julie. You're bound to have noticed that. It's probably a genetic thing, imprinted on your DNA."

"Wayne, I'm sorry about Max. Believe me, if I could undo it I would, but you can't get away from the fact that somebody attacked us in your building."

"So what you're saying is that you think just anybody could break into Comtech?"

"Maybe it was someone from Comtech who attacked me. They wouldn't have to disarm any security system. All they had to do was stick around after working hours."

"I resent your assertion that someone at Comtech is a criminal," Hansen said.

"It's a possibility," I told him.

"What's a possibility is that you should stop playing cops and robbers and mind your own business for a change." Hansen sneered at me and went off into a corner of the waiting room to sulk.

"He's got a point," Paoli said.

"What do you mean?"

"I mean I tried to tell you not to go off on your own, but you insist on playing Wonder Woman."

"Listen; somebody attacked me because they figured out that I knew that the VR software could identify Lufkin as Lorraine Sajak's killer. It did, Paoli. I saw Lufkin in the program."

"You're sure?"

"It was the same face as in the photograph Lorna gave us. This likeness of him in the VR program was actually clearer than Lorna's Polaroid. I know it was him."

"Okay, someone didn't want you looking at the VR programs, but how did they know you would be there tonight?"

I had asked myself the same question.

"The only person I talked to at Comtech today was Bobby, and I only asked him if the equipment was still on the premises. I guess he could have mentioned my phone call to someone else. You wouldn't have to be a rocket scientist to figure out why I wanted to know about the equipment."

"Would Max have told anyone where you were going tonight?"

I considered it. "I didn't ask her not to tell anyone but just assumed she wouldn't. But I don't believe that whoever attacked us knew in advance we would be there. It would have been too easy to just erase the VR programs before we ever got a chance to see them. I think whoever did it saw us go into the VR room after hours, figured out what we were doing, and knew he had to stop us. He knocked out Max, typed in some commands to disable the program, then tried to turn my head into Swiss steak."

"Why didn't this person just disable the program and get out of there? Why did it have to turn violent?"

"He had to knock out Max to get at the keyboard without being seen. As for me, I think whoever it was had a grudge against me and wanted to permanently keep my nose out of the VR programs."

"And you think it was a Comtech employee?"

"I don't see how anyone else could have gotten in the building."

"How about the same way you did?"

"That still means a Comtech employee had to be involved, even if it was only to let in someone else. My guess is that it was a Comtech employee who was working late, someone familiar enough with the VR programs to know that even though the police had confiscated the actual CDs, there could still be a copy loaded on the computer's hard disk."

"So that narrows it down to Eldon, Randall, and Bobby. They're Comtech employees and they knew about Lufkin's VR programs," Paoli said.

"But Bobby and Randall didn't know about the programs. I told Eldon not to tell anyone."

Paoli looked at me with disbelief. "Julie, you honestly think Eldon could set up three computers as well as a data suit and helmet and the rest of the equipment and keep it from the people he worked with? If Lufkin's programs are as slick as you say they are, Eldon could never resist showing them to at least some of his VR people."

He was right. When I had called Comtech and asked Bobby if the equipment and programs were still there, Bobby had known immediately what I was talking about. Of course Eldon had shown the programs to him and Randall.

"Then that gives all three of them a connection to Lufkin's VR programs and the opportunity to attack Max and me."

"But the picture you took of those guys showed one of them in a wheelchair."

"That lets Randall off the hook. My attacker was definitely using both legs. So we're left with Eldon and Bobby."

"And we'll talk to them tomorrow. You're in no shape to do anything right now. It's after midnight and time for you to go home and get some rest."

As we walked to the hospital parking lot, Paoli asked me another question. "Since you risked your neck over it, you might as well tell me exactly what you saw in the program."

"I saw Lufkin's face in the mirror in Sajak's office. He was the one who killed her," I said.

"We knew that already."

"Now we're positive."

"But was it worth almost getting killed? Was it worth almost getting your best friend killed?"

He had a definite point, but it was one he didn't need to make. I was already providing plenty of self-punishment for the lump on Max's gorgeous head.

I TOOK A PAIN PILL that the doctor had given me before I went to sleep and didn't wake up until noon the next day. As I lay there immobile, my head filled with gray fog, I thought I knew what it felt like to be plankton—alive by definition, but not able to think or move or get your own coffee.

I made the effort to call out Paoli's name. Within seconds he walked in with a mug of coffee in each hand and a smile on his face.

"How are you feeling?" he asked as he handed me a mug.

"Like something a dog left on a sidewalk."

"I called the hospital. They're releasing Max."

"She's completely okay?"

"Better than okay, the way she tells it. I talked to her on the phone. She said to thank you for the knot on the head. Apparently, it's made Wayne much more appreciative of her. She's betting on a September wedding."

I called Max's house, but there was no answer. When I checked my voice mail there were two messages from McCracken demanding to know what I was doing with Gallagher the night she died. Apparently he had put two and two together. I put off calling him back.

I told Paoli I was going to Comtech to talk to Eldon, and he insisted on coming along. He didn't have to insist very hard. I was definitely in the mood for a bodyguard. But he

said he had to stop by the office on the way and pick up his
first check from Dayton Electronics so we could deposit it
and avoid a couple of bounced checks.

When Paoli and I walked in the office door around two
that day I couldn't help but notice the series of photographs pinned to a cork bulletin board hung on the wall. I
put my crutches down, because they were starting to hurt
under my arms, and hopped on my good foot to take a
closer look. The board contained photos of almost everyone involved in the case. With all that had been going on, I
had forgotten about our new Candid Camera habit.

"Why all this?" I asked.

"I worked on it yesterday. I'm using visual stimuli to help
me mentally put together the pieces of the case. I read
somewhere that a visual stimulus can excite the left brain so
it communicates better with the right brain. Naturally you'll
scoff."

"Not me," I said. "I'm the one relying on my psychic
abilities, remember?"

Paoli sat down at his desk, and I scanned the photos. Together we had photographed them all—Lorna, Ox, Gallagher, Chambers, almost everyone we had interviewed at
Anco as well as Annette Parker, and there were the pictures
I had taken of Wayne, Bobby, Eldon, and Randall at Comtech. All the photos were informal shots, since we took them
surreptitiously. My favorite was the one with Max and
Hansen arguing in front of his dented Ferrari. I saw that the
picture of McCracken had a Hitler style mustache drawn on
it, and I was not amused by a photo of me naked in the
bathtub, but was placated by the fact that Paoli had also put
up the picture I had taken of him in his underwear. For
propriety's sake I removed the personal photographs from
the board, and tore my bath photo into little pieces. The
picture of Paoli I saved for my wallet.

The pictures were lined up on the board with the photo of
Lufkin that Lorna had given us sitting above the rest. Its

placement made Lufkin seem like an orchestra leader, with everyone else playing according to his conducting.

I told Paoli about my morning's ruminations from the day before, including what McCracken had told me about cosigning on bank accounts.

"I have plausible explanations for everything except how Gallagher found Lufkin. Would Lufkin have risked letting anybody know where he was? Especially after what happened with Sajak?"

"Maybe she didn't find him. Maybe he found her."

"Why would he do that?"

"Remember, Lufkin had problems of his own. We were looking for him, and he must think we have a decent chance of finding him, otherwise he wouldn't be threatening you, right? What he needed was information. He needed to know what we were working on, what leads we had. What better way to find out than to ask Gallagher? And by the time he did, McCracken had already hired us to look into the security software, so it was too late for Gallagher to call us off."

That's one of the things I like about Paoli. He's great at seeing what's in front of his face. That may not sound like much, but me, I'm the type of person who gets so caught up analyzing details I sometimes miss the obvious. I was thinking seriously about kissing him when the phone rang.

"I'll get it," I told him, and walked to the desk and picked up the receiver. "Data9000," I said.

"Julie?" said a thick, sobbing voice.

"Who is this?"

"It's Lorna. Julie, you've got to come to my house right away."

"What's happened?"

"Somebody murdered Bronco."

PAOLI AND I STOOD on a cracked sidewalk on Sixteenth Avenue in San Francisco and stared at the house where Lorna lived. It wasn't what I had expected. It was a small, traditional wood frame house painted canary yellow with white shutters, lace curtains peeking through the windows, and pink geraniums in terra-cotta pots perched on the front steps. Warm and welcoming, it was a smaller version of the house where, as a kid, I had always imagined Beaver Cleaver lived.

It touched me that Lorna had created this quaintly traditional environment to make up for the fact that her life was anything but that. Maybe this house was her own sort of virtual reality, a place where she could simulate the tradition and stability that eluded her in real life.

The front screen flew open, resounding against the opposing wall with a thump as Lorna burst out of the house, black rivers of mascara streaming down her cheeks. She threw herself into Paoli's arms.

"He's dead," she sobbed. "Somebody murdered him."

Never in my life had I seen a human being as broken by grief as Lorna. Her small body shuddered against Paoli's as she cried; then she went limp and slumped onto the sidewalk at our feet. I dropped my crutches and knelt down to help her, and Paoli followed. He stroked her hair as he spoke to her.

"Lorna, you have to tell us what happened. Where's Bronco now?" he asked, his voice tender.

She inhaled a deep, shuddering breath, then pointed toward the house. "The backyard," she muttered through her sobs.

Paoli helped Lorna up, and the two of them walked to the gate of the chain-link fence that enclosed her backyard, with me hobbling behind on my crutches. We passed through a narrow alley by the side of the house and continued around to the back. I saw Bronco lying on the patio. Lorna's crying resumed with new vigor.

I held onto her while Paoli checked out the dog. The expression on his face confirmed Bronco's death. He looked up at me and waved me over. I told Lorna to stay put.

"Looks like he was poisoned," he said, pointing to the white froth on the dog's mouth. I had seen the same thing on the mouth of Lorraine Sajak.

"Some lousy bastard poisoned my baby!" Lorna cried, now behind us. "I shouldn't have left him home. I never should have left him," she said, choking on tears. Paoli held onto her, but her eyes were now on me. "I had to be at the courthouse a long time today. You see, I was worried about leaving him in the car that long."

I put a hand on her shoulder. "Listen, Lorna; Bronco could have gotten something out of a garbage can. It could have been an accident."

She shook her head. "No. Somebody did it." Her grief temporarily channeled into anger, she seemed steadier, and Paoli dropped his hand from her arm.

"How do you know?" he asked.

"Because they did it so they could break into the house. Somebody got inside and tore the place up. Bronco never would have let anybody in the backyard. He would have ripped their leg off."

True, Bronco was not the type of dog to let a stranger trespass. "So you think someone fed him poison?" I asked.

"There was some meat. Whoever did it must have tossed it over the fence to him. I pulled part of it out of his mouth. He loved meat." Her lips began quivering as she fought back a fresh round of tears.

"Did you call the police?"

"What are the cops gonna do? They can't do anything. Bronco's dead."

"Lorna, things are probably missing from your house. Did you notice anything gone?"

"Didn't look. I don't care about my stuff. I care about Bronco." She said the words, then doubled over, her arms wrapped around her stomach.

"What's wrong? What is it?" As Paoli said the words, he and I grabbed her again.

"I feel sick, like I'm gonna throw up."

"Lorna, listen to me; could you have gotten hold of some of the poison?" Paoli asked.

"I think maybe I got a little bit when I tried to give Bronco mouth-to-mouth."

"I'm going to call a doctor," I said.

"No, I'm okay. I don't want a doctor." Lorna straightened up a little, but I didn't want to let go of her.

Paoli headed for the house. "You take care of her. I'll go call the police," he said over his shoulder.

Just then Ox pushed his way through the gate and ran toward Lorna as fast as his lumbering body would allow. "Lornie, where is he?" Ox walked a few more feet but stopped cold when he saw Bronco's body. I watched his face twist with pain. He walked over, got down on both knees, and cupped the dog's limp head with his hands. "Bronco, what happened, boy?" he said, stroking the dog's head.

Lorna looked up and saw Ox with Bronco. She called out Ox's name, and he turned and looked at her with pained eyes; then he gently placed Bronco's head back down and went over to her. Wrapping his arms around her, he pulled her close and laid his head on top of hers. She didn't fight him.

"We'll find who did it, Lornie. I promise; we'll find him and I'll break him in two."

I moved toward Ox and touched his shoulder.

"Bring her into the house when you can," I told him. He looked at me and nodded with Lorna crying in his arms.

Walking through the back door that led into Lorna's kitchen, I found Paoli hanging up the phone. Lorna's kitchen was homey and country-styled, with pine cabinets and wooden countertops. A collection of wicker baskets hung from the ceiling.

"I just called the police. It was going to take them a while to get here, so I talked to that guy I made friends with at the station on Saturday. He's coming right over."

I nodded. "Let's look around." The kitchen hadn't been disturbed, so we passed through to the other rooms.

The rest of the house was a disaster. In the living room, chintz sofa cushions were thrown to the floor, drawers were pulled out, and the contents of a coat closet had been strewn across the salmon carpeting.

Lorna's bedroom looked terrible, with all of its contents spilled to the floor, although I suspected that Lorna's boudoir had a disconcerting effect even when neatly arranged. Carpet, bedspread, pillows and upholstery were all done in various textures and shades of a deep and shiny pink, giving the impression of seeing one's stomach lining turned inside out. A jumble of clothes and about a dozen issues of *Modern Bride* magazine lay in a heap in the middle of the room.

"You know one thing that's weird?" Paoli asked.

"At this point it would be hard to choose just one."

"The fact that whoever did this didn't seem to really take anything. Look; her jewelry is still sitting there," he said, pointing to a gold-rimmed glass box lying on an antique dresser.

"Lorna's jewelry is probably all imitation. A thief wouldn't be interested."

"But a thief would at least look through it to check it out. It doesn't look like it's been touched. And there's a CD player and some expensive speakers in the living room that were pretty small and could be carried out with no problem. This guy didn't care about either. Instead he went through her underwear drawers. It doesn't make sense. What was the guy looking for?"

I didn't have an answer for him. I sifted through the things I already knew to try and come up with some connection. If Lorna's house hadn't been tossed by a burglar, then who would have a reason to break in?

"The CDs," Paoli said. "Maybe Lufkin tried to get the CDs back."

"But the police have them."

"Julie, we should have thought of this before. Did you ever put hours of work into a program and not make a backup copy in case something happened to the original? Lufkin had to have made backup CDs for his VR program. Maybe he came here looking for them.''

He was right. A nasty thought stuck in my mind. "You think Lufkin would stoop to killing Lorna's dog?" I asked.

"He may have killed two people, Julie. What's a dog to him?"

In the back of my mind I wanted to believe, at least for her sake, that Lufkin cared for Lorna and wouldn't murder her beloved pet. Bronco was like a child to her.

"I'm trying to think this through, and there are some pieces here I don't understand. Lufkin couldn't have wanted the CDs to eliminate murder evidence. What was the point when the police already had a set?"

"So you think he was looking for something else?" I asked.

Paoli stared off into space a second, then spoke. "No, it was the CDs he was after, but for another reason."

"What are you getting at?"

"Julie, when you write a complex program you always make a backup, but there's something else you do as well."

I thought for a moment, and then it hit me. "You document it."

"Bingo," Paoli said. "You document everything. To Lufkin, his programs were like the Mona Lisa, but they were science as well as art, and he had to have compiled extensive technical notes on how he did things. He could have kept the tech notes on the CDs that contained the programs."

"But if Lufkin was after the CDs, why did he wait until now to risk breaking into her house to get them?" I asked.

"Because whoever jumped you last night was probably planning to get the VR programs as well as the tech notes off the computer, but you interrupted. Whoever it was had to knock out Max and quickly erase at least part of the program to keep you from finding out more than you should. After that he escaped and knew that you would tell the police to confiscate the computer's hard disk. That means to get the documentation he had to locate the backup CDs.''

"Wouldn't you assume I had given all the copies to the police? Why would Lufkin think Lorna still had them?''

"Because I told him I did,'' a small voice said behind me. I turned and saw Lorna in the doorway. ''He called me late last night and asked me about the CDs. He said he was missing a second set, and I told him I had them. He said he wanted them back. He said he still loved me.''

"You knew the second set was still in your house?''

"When I talked to him I wasn't sure, but I didn't let him know that. After we hung up I looked through all my CDs and found two of them that didn't have labels.''

"So he's probably got them now,'' Paoli said.

"I doubt it.'' She walked to the bathroom and came out with an economy-sized box of Tampax, reached in, and pulled out the CDs. ''I knew he'd never look in here. Guys are weird about things like that.'' She held the CDs out to me, and I took them.

"Lorna, why did you tell Arnie you had them? I told you he's dangerous,'' I said to her.

She bit her lips and her eyes closed for a second, then opened. ''Because I thought it would get him to come over and see me. I said I'd give them to him if he would just come over and talk to me, you know, tell me he was okay and that he hadn't done anything horrible. I would have given him the stupid CDs. I don't care about them. He didn't have to kill Bronco. Why did he have to kill Bronco?''

She looked to me for answers, but I was fresh out.

EIGHTEEN

IT WAS A STINKING, rotten morning. Blanketed with a thick layer of fog, the world had turned the color of spoiled milk, and everyone in Silicon Valley was in a lousy mood. There was more punitive honking during the morning commute, an increase in frowns from the people on the street, and a general feeling of crankiness in the air. Even Lydia at the Hard Drive Cafe shoved my coffee at me with a scowl.

I was faring no better. Drained and depressed, I sat at my desk chugging Maalox out of the bottle while Paoli, having come close to actual levitation from drinking three double espressos in less than an hour, sat beside me, atypically silent and edgy.

Bronco's death had taken its toll on us. We had left Lorna's house the previous day with a sick emptiness in our hearts that hadn't yet subsided. In the middle of this web of thievery and murder, Bronco alone had maintained a state of grace under life's burdens, and now he had become a victim. The images of Lorna crying and of Ox lovingly holding the dog's head in his hands stuck in my brain. They would be with me forever.

The phone rang. Paoli answered it from my desk, frowned, then handed me the receiver, holding it with two fingers like it was covered with something sticky.

I took the phone, wondering who could arouse such a reaction. "Julie Blake here."

"Hi. It's Andrew McCracken." I should have known. "You were right. Arlene had been signing fake POs for over five months."

I refrained from saying "I told you so." "Have you figured out how much she took?"

"We're still adding the numbers, but we're coming up with an amount that would more than make up the difference between what Lufkin stole previously and the amount of money he transferred around those banks."

"If it makes you feel any better, my partner thinks he'll have the holes in your security fixed by next week." At this point Paoli made an obscene gesture that good taste keeps me from describing. "After that I don't think you'll have any more problems."

"At least that's good news."

"Let me know if we can help you with anything else," I said, a comment that drew the evil eye from Paoli.

"There's one more thing."

"Yes?"

"Would you go to dinner with me tonight? There's a new Italian restaurant in North Beach I want to try. I've heard the food's spectacular."

I took a breath. I could see Paoli over at his desk trying to look like he was busy and not absorbing into his pores every word I was saying. Since we had started on the Lufkin case Paoli had been wearing suits every day, but he only owned two, and neither one fit him quite right in the shoulders. At that moment his jacket was off, his tie was loosened, and his feet were propped on his desk. I could see a yarn rendition of Bullwinkle peeking out between his pants leg and his loafer. Paoli could force his body into a suit when he had to, but the man couldn't stomach wearing executive-style socks. I never liked executive-style socks much anyway.

"I'm sorry, Andrew, but I'm involved with someone," I told him. I looked over at my loved one, who was now openly displaying his interest in my conversation. "Real involved."

There was a brief silence on the other end of the line, followed by, "If that ever changes, promise you'll call me?"

"If it ever changes. But you'll still be a reference?" I said, only half-joking.

He had the good taste to laugh. "Of course."

Andrew McCracken and I exchanged good-byes.

I put down the receiver and swiveled my chair to face Paoli. "So let's get to work," I said. He looked over at me, trying hard to maintain a bored expression. "I think we're finally closing in on Lufkin."

"How so?" he said. "By the way, you have a Maalox mustache. I find it attractive, but I wonder what Andy would think if he saw you like that." Paoli grinned at me and I grinned back.

I grabbed a Kleenex, wiped my mouth with one hand, and held up a thumb on the other. "First, we know he probably has a connection to someone at Comtech. Second, we know he used two of the VR programs to plan murders, and now with the CDs, the police have some evidence to prove it."

"You can prove it 'til the cows come home, but it's not going to matter much unless we find him."

Therein lay the problem. Settling into my chair, I began running the poem through my mind. The first lines of the poem referred to me, I felt certain. I had swooped down from the mountain of ICI and peeked through the keyhole by accepting Lorna's proposal to locate Lufkin. The reference to a "spyder," that was obviously a reference to Lufkin himself, and it seemed reasonable that the line about "what is real and what is not" referred to virtual reality. And the line about the mirror—I now understand that one. But the part about "life and death turn like a wheel" and "the one you fear may be the one you know" had me stumped. I had received the poem the day after Lorna had first visited us, before I had met most of the people involved in the case. The only ones I had known prior to the poem were Lorna and Ox. Then I thought about Eldon Gannoway and Wayne Hansen. I had known both of them prior to getting Lorna's case. Hansen I had known for years and there was nothing about him that was the least bit sinister—weird, eccentric, and erratic, but not sinister. Wayne wouldn't hurt anyone. Eldon was more of a mystery to me, and I told Paoli my thoughts. Eldon knew about the VR programs, he was someone I had known prior to accepting the Lufkin case, and he could have seen Max and me go into the VR room that night. And his motive? Perhaps he was hiding Lufkin.

I picked up the phone and dialed Comtech's main number.

"Who are you calling?" Paoli asked.

"Eldon. We need to see him right away."

"Julie, wouldn't it be better to just tell the police our suspicions about Eldon? That's their job."

"If we had some real proof, yes. But right now we're just guessing. I'm not going to turn the police on Eldon because of a guess. If we're going to run an investigation business we need to establish a reputation for discretion. Let's go see Eldon, press him about where he was last night, and go from there."

"But what if Eldon is the guy who tried to whack you last night? He could be dangerous."

"Nothing can happen if we see him in a public place. Besides, I'm going to call him and say we want to talk to his whole VR group. I'll tell him it's something about the program, and I'm sure he's not going to try and kill me in front of his coworkers. We'll also have witnesses to everything he says."

I got Eldon on the line. When I told him I wanted to meet with him, Randall, and Bobby, he started to say no, but then I told him I had some new information about Lufkin's programs, information I thought they would all want to hear. It wasn't true, but it hooked him and got Paoli and me into a meeting with all three of them.

I hung up the phone and started to say something to Paoli but was interrupted by the door opening. Lorna and Ox walked in, Lorna wearing a loose-fitting black dress with a white lace collar that looked like it belonged on a nun. I assumed it was her mourning outfit. I liked her better in her regular clothes.

"I know you're busy working and everything, but I just wanted to stop by and invite you to Bronco's funeral," she said. "It's tomorrow at three. We're burying him in the little pet cemetery in the Presidio."

"He's going to have a monument," Ox said.

Lorna looked at him and smiled. "Yeah, a monument. A big one. I'm not sure yet about the inscription. I was wondering if you guys could help me with that. You know, think up something meaningful."

"Of course we'll help. It'll take some thought," said Paoli.

"Oh, sure. I wouldn't want to just take something off the top of your heads." Lorna's eyes grazed across the bulletin board where Paoli had pinned up the photographs. She walked over to it. "What's this? Some sort of collage?"

"Just some of the people associated with your case," Paoli said casually.

I saw Lorna's eyes locked onto the bulletin board. "Lorna, do you recognized anyone?"

"Why are all these pictures grouped together?" she asked.

"They all work at Comtech," Paoli answered as he flipped through his mail. He didn't seem to notice anything odd about Lorna's manner, but I did. There was a subtle change in her voice, and the expression on her face had grown intense. Her wheels were spinning, and I wanted to know why.

"Lorna, you recognize somebody. Who is it?"

She hesitated before answering. "This one." She was pointing to the picture of Eldon.

"He's a software developer we interviewed to help us find Arnie," I said. "Where do you know him from?"

Lorna's eyes left the bulletin board and she turned toward me. "Nowhere. He's just kind of cute, that's all."

"In that case, we're meeting with him and his pals in a few minutes. Want to come?" Paoli said jokingly before he had the chance to see the jealous look on Ox's face. "Oh, sorry, Ox. Didn't mean it."

Paoli looked to me for help, but my eyes were still on Lorna.

"Lorna, if you know him, if you ever saw him with Arnie, you need to tell us." I held my breath as I waited for her response.

She turned to me, her eyes flashing, hands on hips. "What are you, my mother? I don't know the guy, okay?" She took a deep breath and regained her composure. "Sorry. I didn't need to snap at you. I'm just stressed, that's all. Come on, Ox; we've gotta go. We've got an appointment. You guys will be at the funeral tomorrow?"

If she knew something, she wasn't going to tell me. "We'll be there; I promise," I said.

"That's great. Well, I know you guys are on your way somewhere. See you tomorrow."

"Sure," I said as she and Ox headed for the door. Lorna let Ox go out in the hallway, but she stopped.

"I just want to tell you guys thanks for being good friends to me. I haven't had a lot of good friends, you know."

She looked sad as she said the words. She turned and left, shutting the door behind her.

"Why would Lorna be interested in Eldon's picture?" I asked Paoli.

He stood up and peeked through the blinds and watched Lorna and Ox walk across the parking lot to the Camaro. "Maybe she had seen Eldon with Lufkin. The two of them could easily be friends or at least acquaintances. Suddenly I'm extremely motivated for a trip to Comtech."

"I don't like the idea much, but it's conceivable that Eldon has been hiding Lufkin," I said.

"You think Eldon is the one who attacked you? Julie, if Eldon was protecting Lufkin, then why did he ever let you see the VR program in the first place? He's the one who set it up for you, remember?"

"I don't know. Maybe he didn't realize at first that the VR programs were Lufkin's. I'm sure Lufkin tried to keep them secret."

"Well, there's still some reason Lorna took such an interest in Eldon's picture. I'm going to Comtech to find out what's going on, but I want you to let me do it alone. We can't be sure it's safe."

"Don't you think I would be safer with you at Comtech in broad daylight with hundreds of people in the building than sitting here all by myself?"

He mulled it over for a few seconds, but he knew I had him. "Okay, let's go." He pointed his finger at me. "But let me do the talking. I mean it. If anyone's going to get pissed off, let them get pissed off at me. I can defend myself better."

"I think I've done a pretty good job of defending myself."

"Oh, yeah? Don't forget your crutches."

The traffic was light and it took fifteen minutes to get to Comtech. When we got to the lobby I called Eldon from the house phone. He said he would meet me in a minute and we would all go to the executive briefing room, which was located to the left of the lobby.

The seconds passed with the speed of a glacier, but then Eldon and Bobby walked out, with Randall behind them in his wheelchair. When I looked at Randall's face, for the first time I saw something familiar. If I hadn't seen the face in the mirror in Lufkin's VR program, I probably never would have made the connection. I had to get past his glasses and cropped hair, plus the fact that Randall was heavier than in Lorna's photograph, but I knew it was him. He was so clever. People don't want to stare at someone in a wheelchair. I thought back to my own reactions when I first met him. Out of embarrassment or pity, our eyes tend to graze quickly over the handicapped. But this time I looked hard at Randall, then I looked at his wheelchair. "Life and death turn like a wheel," Lufkin's poem had said.

"What happened to you?" Eldon asked when he saw my crutches, but I didn't answer. I walked up to Randall. He and I looked at each other a moment. I think he knew then that I recognized him. At first I was numbed by my own astonishment, but as the reality of what I had discovered sank in, I felt a white heat rising inside me. Part of me wanted to hurt him, to kick and claw and scratch at him like an animal, but it was my civilized exterior that controlled me.

"You bastard." I said the words slowly, my voice heavy and raw.

"Julie!" Eldon looked at me with bewilderment. "Watch your mouth, please."

I felt Paoli's hand on my arm. "What's happening here?"

"What's happening here is that Randall is a murderer," I said, my eyes never leaving Randall's.

"This is crazy," Eldon said, his face turning pink. He moved closer to me. "Julie, the man's in a wheelchair," he said.

"He can walk," I told him. "He can run; he can push people off cliffs."

Randall pressed a button on his chair and moved it backward. "Get this fucking bitch away from me. She's nuts," Randall said in a voice that was deep and angry, like the voice I had heard on the Marin Headlands. He started down the hallway.

"I'm not letting him leave," I said, moving toward Randall, but Paoli stopped me.

"Julie, I'm not getting this. Lorna picked out Eldon's photograph. I thought we were coming here to question Eldon."

I shook my head and talked fast. "It was Randall's picture she recognized. She just didn't want us to know it, and I think I know why. Go call the police and get them over here. Trust me. Do it now."

I broke Paoli's grip, moved to Randall's wheelchair as fast as I could, and shoved one of my crutches into his right wheel. The chair jolted to a stop, and Randall looked at me with hatred. Paoli had grabbed the phone at the reception desk. I think everyone watching was too stunned to move.

Randall grabbed my hand, gripping it tightly. I didn't know if that gesture was one of intimidation or, in some bizarre way, a gesture of acknowledgement. He looked at me with intelligent eyes, and if I hadn't hated him so much, I would say that, for that brief moment, he and I shared a sort of bond.

I leaned close to Randall so our conversation could be private.

" 'The one you fear may be the one you know.' What did you mean by that?'' I asked, the words coming out brittle and tense.

His grip on my hand loosened into a caress, and his touch made my skin crawl. I tried to pull my hand away, but he wouldn't allow it.

"You've disappointed me, Julie. I assumed you knew that line was meant to misdirect you. You have to determine what is real and what is not, remember? That's part of the game.'' One of his fingers lightly stroked the top of my hand. "You're a beautiful woman. Very bright. Those of us blessed with true intelligence always fear ourselves, I think. We're afraid of what we're capable of, aren't we? It's those lesser minds that go along blithely, like your boyfriend over there. Do you keep him like a pet?''

He started to say more, but his eyes moved from mine to the doorway. I remember seeing them suddenly filled with fear. He dropped my hand and stood up.

It sounded strangely benign, like firecrackers going off. The force of the first bullet pushed him backward, but it was after the second and third shots that he hit the floor.

My recollection of the precise moment is sketchy. I remember hearing the receptionist screaming, finding myself on the floor, Paoli on top of me, having leaped onto me as soon as he saw the gun. From my position on the carpet I could see Randall's face, and I knew he had left reality permanently.

"That's for Bronco."

The words, shrill and trembling, came from behind me. I looked back toward the door and saw Lorna standing about ten feet away from us, the gun quivering in her hand, its barrel still pointed at its victim. Pulling himself off me, Paoli looked at the crumpled body on the floor, then up at Lorna, his face wild with confusion.

"Why? Why kill this guy?" he asked.

"Because that's Arnie Lufkin," I told him.

NINETEEN

IT WAS HUBRIS that killed Arnie Lufkin. Hubris, plain and simple. When the police searched his apartment that day they found his bags packed. Lufkin was ready to run, but he couldn't bear to leave without his VR programs—his Mona Lisa. The police found fresh fingerprints of his all over the VR computer keyboard. Apparently, in the hours before Lorna shot him he had logged onto the VR computer at Comtech and tried desperately to reconstruct some of the files he had erased the night he had attacked Max and me. Paoli had been right. All of Lufkin's technical notes were tucked away in an innocent-looking file attached to the VR program itself. When he couldn't find the backup CDs at Lorna's, I think Lufkin realized that there might be a copy on the Comtech computer's hard disk. He was probably planning to investigate it the night Max and I showed up and beat him to it.

Lorna and I spoke on the phone twice after the police arrested her at Comtech. She had me call her lawyer; then Paoli and I stayed up half the night with Ox, who was an emotional wreck. Ox ended up sleeping on my couch, and the next morning he and I went to the jail to see Lorna, bringing her the meatball sandwich, Pepsi, and fresh panties she had asked for. Our conversation with her was constrained and brief.

For the first twenty-four hours after she killed Arnie Lufkin, Lorna seemed stunned by what she had done. Stunned but not regretful. "The bum deserved to die," she told me, but I strongly encouraged her to at least feign regret when she spoke to the police and to her lawyer. She took my advice.

I gave the police all the information I had about Lufkin, including both fact and supposition. They spent four hours quizzing Eldon and Bobby and walked away believing, as I did, that they had no idea about Randall's true identity. The real Randall had died of AIDS two years earlier in Oklahoma. By tapping into the county computer system, Lufkin had gotten Randall's Social Security number and other vital information and assumed the dead man's identity. When they asked Eldon how Randall had been hired, he said innocently that Randall had been sent to him by Lorraine Sajak.

Within twenty-four hours after the shooting, Paoli, the currently self-proclaimed Prince of Programs, sliced through Anco's security software and put an end forever to their cyclical virus. McCracken was ecstatic. Although he agreed happily to pay our invoice for close to ten thousand dollars, it didn't do much for our bottom line, since we loaned the money to Lorna for her bail, and that was fine by me. Lorna needed it more than we did, and with Anco as a reference, I knew other jobs would be coming our way. All I had to do now was figure out some new way to stall our landlord on next month's rent, and after dealing with Arnie Lufkin, how tough could that be?

It was two days later before Lorna and I had a chance to really talk. Paoli and I were in the office discussing the prioritized order of certain past-due bills when Lorna and Ox walked through the door. To my surprise, Lorna was wearing a gray suit and high-necked white blouse. She couldn't help but notice my stare. She looked pale and tired, but when she smiled at me I knew she was okay. Lorna and I were an unlikely combination, but after you've seen a woman shoot someone, after you've followed her to the police station and brought her Pepsi and fresh panties—out of your own lingerie drawer—you can't help but feel close.

"I'm due at the courthouse this afternoon to meet with the DA, and I'm trying to look, you know, responsible and serious-minded. I went to Macy's this morning and said to myself, 'Now what would Julie wear?,' and I came up with this. Do you think it will help?''

"Depends on the DA. I hear some of them lean favorably toward Spandex," Paoli said.

I put my hand over his mouth. "Don't listen to him. You look just perfect."

Ox put his arm around Lorna with a familiarity I hadn't seen before. She looked up at him and smiled. "Lornie's gonna do just fine," he said. "Her attorney says the DA likes dogs."

"Yeah, we're gonna go for a major plea bargain. My lawyer's gonna explain how Bronco was like a kid to me." Her eyes turned soft and she looked down at her sensible low-heeled pumps. "He was, you know."

I knew. I had already spoken to Lorna's lawyer. Luckily for her, the district attorney was on the board of the local SPCA and was buying into her attorney's idea that Bronco was a child substitute, and that when she shot Arnie Lufkin she was avenging the death of her child. That, combined with the fact that Lufkin was somewhat less than a model citizen, would probably get Lorna off with a relatively short prison stretch. Lorna was doing her best to be optimistic.

"If I do end up in the slammer, it'll be a gold mine of business contacts. I mean, you've got to look at the bright side."

"And they allow conjugal visits," Ox said proudly. Paoli and I exchanged a look.

Lorna's expression turned soft as she wrapped her small arms around Ox's big chest and gave him a squeeze. "Yeah, we're getting married. If I go to jail, Ox is gonna wait for me, aren't ya, babe?"

"Forever if I have to."

I hoped for their sake it wouldn't be quite that long. My intuition said it wouldn't be.

Ox and Lorna left for the courthouse, and Paoli and I watched them from our window as they walked arm in arm to the battered green Camaro.

"That's one coupling I wouldn't have predicted," Paoli said.

"Why not?"

"Because they're so different from each other."

"They're a lot alike, too."

"You've got to be joking. They're like night and day, chocolate and vanilla."

"Some people would say the same thing about us. Now how about looking at our bank balance to see if we have enough to pay the light bill?"

I sat down at my personal computer and accessed my accounting software. When it came up on the screen I noticed a file listed that didn't jibe with the rest. I opened it, and staring at me was Lufkin's poem. Lufkin's virus had placed the poem on my hard disk, and since I hadn't used my accounting software since that day, I simply hadn't noticed it. Just looking at it sent a shiver up my spine.

"Be careful for the one you fear may be the one you know," Lufkin had written, and the words had foreshadowed his own death. Lufkin had been fascinated by alternative realities. It made me wonder what reality Lufkin was residing in currently. I hit the delete key, and the poem evaporated, this time forever.

Luckily for me, I liked my own reality just fine. I had a man I loved and a business with potential. At the moment, there was only one thing I lacked that I could think of.

"What do you say we go to the Hard Drive and get a couple of doughnuts?" I said to Paoli and flashed him a grin. "My diet starts tomorrow."

First Time in Paperback

THE POISON POOL
PATRICIA HALL
A Yorkshire Mystery

CLOSED RANKS

When old Tom Carter is found bludgeoned to death, Inspector Alex Sinclair makes quick work of arresting the only suspect, Joey Macready, a young man living with his mother.

Social worker Kate Weston is convinced that Joey is innocent and persuades Sinclair to probe further. But queries are quickly stonewalled by his superiors. Worse, he's accused of accepting bribes and is suspended from the force.

Together, the two discover a dark conspiracy deep in the tightly knit Yorkshire community. Closing in on its dangerous secrets, they must challenge an invisible enemy who is implacable and desperate enough to silence them forever....

"Auspicious debut..."   —*Publishers Weekly*

Available in April at your favorite retail stores.

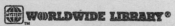

WORLDWIDE LIBRARY®

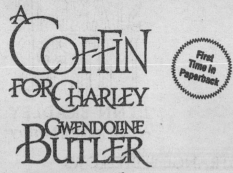

A COFFIN FOR CHARLEY

GWENDOLINE BUTLER

First Time in Paperback

An Inspector John Coffin Mystery

IT'S HOT...AND GETTING HOTTER FOR COMMANDER JOHN COFFIN

His wife, actress Stella Pinero, is being stalked. Adding to his worries, London's Second City is terrified by a cunning and inventive serial killer. Coffin has cast a wide net, but the killer is elusive...and continuing to kill.

Somehow connected is a murder that occurred twenty years before. A young girl had witnessed the crime and testified. Now the killers are free and returning home, possibly for revenge. When Coffin's niece turns up missing, he fears the worst—pushing himself and his force into London's darkest underbelly to match skill and cunning with crime's cleverest own....

"Butler excels..."   —*Publishers Weekly*

Available in May at your favorite retail stores.

 **WORLDWIDE LIBRARY®**

CHARLEY

STAND-IN FOR MURDER

First Time in Paperback

LYNN BRADLEY
A Cole January Mystery

STRANGE BEDFELLOWS

It all began when a very hung over Cole January stepped out of a warm bed and onto a stone-cold corpse—a beautiful blonde in a slinky number that would have done his male ego proud if she'd had a pulse.

She is identified as Molly Jones-Heitkamp. That is, until the real and remarkably alive Ms. Jones-Heitkamp asks January to find out who's trying to kill her. So who's the gorgeous stiff? And who's trying to frame Cole?

The answers take him to Houston's mayoralty race, as well as the dirty laundry of some prominent citizens. Cole begins to wish he'd stuck to insurance fraud, because murder was becoming bad for his health.

"Will please mystery lovers." —*Abilene Reporter-News*

Available in April at your favorite retail stores.

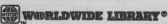 **WORLDWIDE LIBRARY®**

STANDS